Praise for
The Englisch Daughter

"Cindy Woodsmall and Erin Woodsmall are a gifted writing team! This book is perfect for those who love Amish stories that handle contemporary issues with grace and wisdom. Family drama, romance, and a touch of mystery will keep readers up late, turning the pages to learn the outcome for these special characters."

—CARRIE TURANSKY, award-winning author of *No Ocean Too Wide* and *Across the Blue*

"Cindy Woodsmall is such a gifted writer: her stories are captivating, her understanding of Amish life is spot on, and her characters never fail to come alive. Highly recommended!"

—MINDY STARNS CLARK, best-selling author of *The Amish Midwife*

"With a deft handling of a marriage in crisis, Cindy Woodsmall and Erin Woodsmall take readers on a compelling emotional journey depicting the healing power of love."

—LISA CARTER, author of *Under a Turquoise Sky*

The Englisch Daughter

New York Times and CBA Best-Selling Author

CINDY WOODSMALL
& ERIN WOODSMALL

The Englisch Daughter

A Novel

WATERBROOK

THE ENGLISCH DAUGHTER

Scripture quotations and paraphrases are taken from the following versions: King James Version; New American Standard Bible®. Copyright © 1960, 1962, 1963, 1968, 1971, 1972, 1973, 1975, 1977, 1995 by the Lockman Foundation. Used by permission. (www.Lockman.org); the Holy Bible, New International Version®, NIV®. Copyright © 1973, 1978, 1984, 2011 by Biblica Inc.® Used by permission. All rights reserved worldwide.

Trade Paperback ISBN 978-0-7352-9102-7
eBook ISBN 978-0-7352-9103-4

Published in the United States by WaterBrook, an imprint of Random House, a division of Penguin Random House LLC.

WATERBROOK® and its deer colophon are registered trademarks of Penguin Random House LLC.

Library of Congress Cataloging-in-Publication Data
Names: Woodsmall, Cindy, author. | Woodsmall, Erin, author.
Title: The englisch daughter : a novel / by Cindy Woodsmall and Erin Woodsmall.
Description: First Edition. | [Colorado Springs] : WaterBrook, 2020.
Identifiers: LCCN 2019027353 | ISBN 9780735291027 (trade paperback) | ISBN 9780735291034 (ebook)
Subjects: LCSH: Amish—Fiction. | GSAFD: Christian fiction. | Love stories.
Classification: LCC PS3623.O678 E54 2020 | DDC 813/.6—dc23
LC record available at https://lccn.loc.gov/2019027353

Printed in the United States of America
2020—First Edition

10 9 8 7 6 5 4 3 2 1

In loving memory of my
precious brother Leston.
—*Cindy*

To Lincoln:
The sweet fourth born of mine
You came at just the right time
To help us all remember the joy
To rock and hold a tiny baby boy
And just like Heidi, this story's treasure
You too are precious beyond measure
—*Erin*

One

Snuggled under her great-grandmother's quilt, Jemima woke to the sound of slow, easy movement in the room. She opened her eyes and saw silhouettes of the furniture despite the darkness of a winter night. Her husband was up. Without shifting her position to confirm that, she knew it was true.

Familiar warring emotions tugged at her. She wanted to get up with him, fix a pot of coffee, and talk the way they used to. At the same time, she wanted to hide from him, so she lay still as if she were asleep.

Shouldn't today be a great celebration for them? Exactly a year ago her husband and their oldest daughter, Laura, had been headed toward town in a horse and buggy when a car topped the hill behind them and hit them. They were grateful that God had spared Roy's and Laura's lives, but navigating that time and coming back together as a family had been difficult. In those early months of healing, she constantly gave thanks to the Almighty that Roy had survived, and when Roy and she were able to be in the same home at night, she'd held him close, whispering her gratefulness aloud. But with each passing day, he seemed to become more distant. What happened to him while she was staying with her family?

The news of the accident had reached Jemima within the hour, but her husband and daughter had already been airlifted to a hospital. By the time she arrived—thanks to the help of an *Englisch* neighbor—both were in surgery. When she finally saw her husband and daughter, they were unconscious and connected to tubes and monitors. Roy woke within forty-eight hours and Laura a day later.

His steps were quiet as he approached the bed, and she closed her eyes. The aroma of her husband, freshly showered for the day, filled her senses, and she longed to reach through the darkness for his hand. He seemed to wait at the side of the bed. Was he thinking of waking her? Was he praying for her?

It wasn't likely. Not these days.

Why was he up this early? It had to be at least two hours before sunup, although she couldn't see the clock to know for sure. He owned a horse farm but also had horses boarded elsewhere, and tending to those horses required long hours and often pulled him from home.

"What?" His whisper sounded angry. She hadn't heard his cell phone ring, but apparently he'd taken a call.

When she opened her eyes, he was going toward the bedroom door, holding the cell phone to his ear. She missed the days when Amish men had cell phones only for business and were required to turn them off before entering the house.

He paused in the doorway and turned, seeming to look straight at her. He was bathed in moonlight, but her face was hidden by a shadow, and she knew he couldn't see that her eyes were open. What was on his mind as he paused, looking into the bedroom? A moment later he closed the door behind him.

She moved her hand to his side of the bed, hoping to feel the warmth from where he'd been. It was as cold as it was empty, and her heart thudded with loneliness. What had happened to them?

The baby cried out from his crib behind her, and Jemima rose. She pulled a blanket over eight-month-old Simeon and patted his back until he fell asleep again. Her white nightgown was no match for winter in an old farmhouse, so she grabbed the knit shawl from the rocker, put it around her shoulders, and went to the window. Roy held a lit barn lantern by the metal handle as he walked toward the stables.

What were they doing? He was right there, just outside the home they'd shared for ten years, yet they seemed isolated in separate worlds.

A desire to be who they'd once been washed over her, and she knocked on the window. He continued onward. She knocked harder and then jolted back, fearing she'd woken Simeon. The baby didn't stir, but Roy stopped walking and turned around. As she hurried toward the bedroom door, the moonlight reflected off something on her pillow. He'd written her a note.

Most of their communication of late was through notes. Nothing of marital value was ever said. They were only memos of where they were going and when they'd return. Is this who they were now?

She flew down the creaking wooden steps and opened the back door. A blast of cold air rushed inside, and her husband was there, so close she gasped.

"Jem, is something wrong?" The light from the lantern revealed his green eyes and the compassion she used to see in them.

She wanted to cry out the words *everything* and *nothing* and then fall into his embrace. But his phone buzzed. He pulled it from his coat pocket, texted a quick response, and slid it back into his pocket. He needed to go, and here she stood, wordless. And thankless and spoiled as well, she supposed.

He walked back into the house, shutting the door behind him, and she retreated a few steps. His lantern was the only source of light, but it was plenty. She wanted an honest conversation. She longed for him to love her as he once had, but she couldn't voice those feelings. Following the accident, he'd given his all, and maybe he had nothing left to give. Maybe he was like a field that needed to rest before it could yield another harvest.

A small smile tugged at his lips. Did he feel obligated to respond with kindness to the delay she was causing? That's how he treated her these days—as if she were another duty on his long to-do list. But in her presence, he never stepped outside of being respectful. However, he seemed to go out of his way to be sure he was rarely in her presence.

"Did you get my note?" His voice was as quiet as the house itself.

She hadn't read it, but it was in her hands, so she nodded. "*Ya.* Can I fix you some breakfast?"

"*Denki,* but I need to go."

Did he even remember? "Today is the anniversary."

His brows knit, and he barely shook his head before she saw realization come to him. Then they both seemed lost in the memory of it.

Even after he and Laura had regained consciousness in the hospital, Jemima's hands had trembled constantly for days. She was five months pregnant with Simeon at the time, and she began having horrible headaches, blurry vision, and shortness of breath. Roy had insisted she be seen by a doctor. Her blood pressure had gone from normal to high. Her doctor said the new condition put her in the high-risk category, and he'd ordered eighteen to twenty hours of bed rest daily. How was she, a pregnant mom with an injured husband and a child in the hospital, even supposed to go home for a good night's rest, let alone take care of her other two healthy children while resting that much?

The man standing in front of her, the one she hardly recognized these days, had come up with the answer. He had ignored his doctor's orders and his own pain and stayed with Laura every night so Jemima could go home and sleep. When Jemima arrived at the hospital each day, he returned to the farm and worked. He asked their families to set aside their usual work schedules and responsibilities to take shifts at the hospital each afternoon until he arrived for the night shift.

He made no move to hug her or sit at the table with her for even a few minutes. She wanted to hit him . . . or embrace him. Above all else, she wanted to demand that he return to her. But she refused to ask one more thing of him.

His eyes held her. "It'll get better, Jem. I promise," he whispered.

She bit back tears and forced a smile and a nod. His statement meant he felt the barrier between them too, didn't it? Yet despite her asking him what was wrong several times, he'd offered no insight and no explanation. If she asked again, he'd tell her the same as always: *Nothing. Just work.*

He drew a breath. "I've made arrangements with Chris, that farmhand I've talked to several times. He's good with horses, and years ago he took a few computer classes, so he'll be able to assist with all manner of record keeping, scheduling, and bookkeeping, if need be. He should be here early next week."

She was glad to hear that Roy was putting effort into getting some relief from the workload, but why hadn't he told her this before now? "Does Abigail know?"

Roy's younger sister was an odd, beautiful creature who was their sanity most days. She had more energy than she knew what to do with, and she purposefully kept life busy in order to cope with it. She taught at a local Amish school, worked with special-needs children outside of that, and volunteered regularly at several places within the community. But for the last year, she'd given as much time as possible to the horse farm.

"I mentioned it was a possibility. She *really* wants to get back to her volunteer work and scheduled off days, so I didn't want to get her hopes up until I knew for sure he was coming."

"You just told me that he was coming, didn't you?" Had she misunderstood?

"I've tried to get him here a few times over the last several years, but it's never quite worked out. Still, I think he's coming this time."

"But you don't actually know, despite what you said just a minute ago." The disbelief in her voice said it all, and his eyes moved from her face to the floor. Why had he talked as if it was a sure thing, but when she asked one question, he wavered? It seemed that she was no longer important enough for him to take the time to explain the situation unless she pressed him.

"I said he *should* be here next week, which means *maybe*, Jem. He doesn't intend to move to our area or live on our farm, but I believe we've struck a deal where he'll work part time and it'll give us some decent relief from the workload. That's all I know. You think I'm not being honest with you about a farmhand?"

She should've stayed in bed. It hurt less to lie there in loneliness than to be chided by a man who was clearly trying to keep the farm going—the buying, training, and selling of horses. "I didn't mean . . ." She drew a weary breath. "I'm sorry."

His phone buzzed again, and he glanced at the screen. "I need to go. I doubt I'll see you again until tomorrow afternoon."

"What?"

He pointed at the note in her hand. "You didn't read it, did you?"

Embarrassment singed her cheeks as she shook her head.

He pursed his lips and gave a nod. "There's a horse auction tonight in Virginia." His words were slow and soft, seemingly filled with patience. "My sources say it's a good one with good stock. If it is, this may be the break I've been looking for. But it's five hours by car, and it won't end until late, too late to return tonight." His phone vibrated, and his face grew taut with frustration. He drew a deep breath. "I need to go."

"I forgot the horse auction was this weekend. There's a food-truck auction in town. It'll have a few trucks, and one of them will be the Smiths' truck."

He stared at her as his breathing grew shallow. "The Smiths are selling now? I thought they'd decided to keep the food truck for a few more years."

She'd had her eye on that truck for a long time. It currently sat in the perfect spot, so if they could get the truck and the license for the same spot, that would be perfect. "I guess they changed their minds, and we always said when that truck came up for auction, we'd be first in line. The auction is tomorrow at one."

"Our little ones are so young. Starting a new business now would be a lot to take on."

They'd talked about this for years, and he'd been on board, hadn't he? His sister Abigail would give up her teaching position, and she and Jemima would divvy up the work hours. The plan was to operate seven hours a day, six days a week during tourist season—May through August—and only on Saturdays in the fall and spring. They wouldn't open at all during winter.

"Really?" Jemima asked.

He grimaced. "Ya, okay." He sighed. "Whatever else happens, I *will* meet you tomorrow afternoon on the town square with money in hand for the auction."

He remained in place, studying her.

Why did he sound so reluctant? Was it simply the timing—that he needed to be in Virginia tonight for the horse auction and back here tomorrow for the food-truck auction? They'd been saving for her dream since before they'd married, and Abigail had been saving along with them for the last nine years.

Jemima's dream of having a food truck, a dream she'd had since she was a young teen, was unusual for an Amish woman but not forbidden. She wanted to serve authentic Amish foods. When Roy had asked Jemima to marry him, he had promised that her dream wouldn't be lost because of becoming his wife and the mother of his children. He would make sure of it.

But maybe she should offer to give up that dream if it would help them even a little. She would celebrate giving it up if somehow that would tear down the walls between them and bring Roy back to her. But even now as he stood in front of her, making promises, she felt powerless in their relationship. The idea of owning a business brought more than hope. It gave her a much-needed sense of being in charge of one thing in her life.

His phone buzzed multiple times in quick succession. He looked at the screen, and without saying anything else he left, taking the lantern with him.

She stood there, barefoot on the cold floor, darkness surrounding her. How had they gotten to this place? And who would they become as the years went by?

Two

Roy burned with frustration as he rode his horse bareback across the west field. Jemima was too inquisitive for her own good. If she knew half of what he held back from her, it would break her heart. She would grow to hate him, and there would be no getting free of him since divorce was forbidden.

As impossible as it seemed, he had to continue down the path he'd chosen.

He dug the horse with his heels and clicked his tongue. She picked up her speed, and soon the gray cottage came into view. *Her* cottage. Actually his *Daed* owned this cottage and had rented it to Tiffany. He glanced at her white sedan as he rode past. It looked as if it was stuffed with her belongings. Was she planning to leave? A surge of hope was met with fear, snatching his breath.

He slid off his horse and looped the reins around a shrub. Roy walked up the few cement steps. Blue paint was peeling off the door. Before he knocked, he heard a soul-piercing wail. An infant.

His infant.

The moment he'd heard his firstborn's cry, it had aroused primal feelings. Protect. Soothe. Fix. The same had been true when his daughter Carolyn and her brothers, Nevin and Simeon, were born. Protect. Soothe. Fix.

When this infant had first cried, Roy was overwhelmed with nausea and a desire to flee. What was he supposed to do in this situation?

He knocked and tried the door handle, but it was locked. Tiffany had called him less than an hour ago and then about every ten minutes since. She wanted an equal partner in the care and feeding of the baby, but he had a family. She'd known that from the start. He pounded louder, hoping she would hear him over Heidi's screams.

The door jerked open. She stood in front of him, dark smudges under her eyes and her dyed-platinum hair sticking out everywhere. "Took you long enough."

He stepped inside and closed the door. The small living room lacked any decorations and was furnished with only a well-used couch, a recliner, and a television that was at least a decade old. This house needed a lot more than just a paint job, which was partly why his Daed had offered it to her for such a pittance of rent—an amount Roy had been paying for almost a year. But it had electricity and water and was structurally sound.

"I got here as quickly as I could. What's wrong?"

Heidi continued to wail. Should he pick her up?

Tiffany laughed but without mirth. "I've been up all night. And the night before. I can't do this." She pointed to the portable bassinet in the corner of the living room. "*You* need to take it. It's yours."

It? How could a parent refer to a child so heartlessly?

He strode across the room and looked in the small crib. Heidi was red faced but looked unharmed. She'd kicked off her swaddle blanket, and it was bunched around her legs. He scooped her up and looked her over, touching her soft light-colored hair. Her footed sleeper looked clean. "Is she hungry?"

Tiffany made a dismissive sound. "I'm not a moron, Roy. I know how to feed a baby. I just gave her an entire bottle twenty minutes ago. And I changed her outfit and diaper. She won't stop crying, and I can't take one more minute of it."

Maybe it was just the lack of sleep talking. Tiffany wasn't usually this bad. If she were, he wouldn't be able to leave Heidi with her. He lifted the baby girl into the crook of his arm and looked around the room until he spotted a burp cloth. He put the cloth over his shoulder and eased the six-week-old onto it. Laura had liked this position as a baby. Carolyn had liked to be burped belly down, lying across his knees while he sat in a chair, and Nevin and Simeon did best when propped upright on his forearm. He patted up and down Heidi's back. She'd seemed to be constantly fussy the past week. Perhaps this fussy phase was due to a touch of colic. None of his other kids had been like this, but they had Jemima for a mother.

Roy patted Heidi's back while he paced the living room, the baby wailing in his ear. But her cries weren't enough to drown out his thoughts of meeting Jemima at the food-truck auction tomorrow. That had him rattled. To participate in the auction, he would have to take proof that money was set aside in an account to back any bids Jemima made. But the money was no longer there. So the new plan, the one he'd been negotiating with the bank for nearly a month, was to get a loan so he could put money back into the savings account before she realized it was missing. Yesterday the banker said they had everything they needed to conclude the process. As long as Roy went there today and signed the papers, the money would be available first thing tomorrow.

Obviously not a day too soon.

If for some reason he couldn't get the money, how would he explain the missing savings to Jemima? The knot in his stomach tightened.

Heidi continued to cry.

Come on, little one. After what felt like forever, Heidi at last let out a big burp, and her crying quieted. He walked back to the bassinet and swaddled her tightly in the blanket she'd kicked off earlier. There was a good chance he could get her to go to sleep and stay asleep now that her tummy seemed to feel better. Maybe then Tiffany could get some sleep too and wake up feeling more like herself.

After he paced about ten more circles around the nearly bare living room, Heidi was asleep in his arms. He laid her on her back in the bassinet, taking care not to jostle her. She shifted in her swaddle blanket but didn't wake. *Phew.*

Tiffany sat in the worn recliner, staring out the window into the dark, her knees pulled to her chest and her arms wrapped around her legs. It had been six weeks since Heidi was born, and Tiffany seemed to struggle more each week. She *had* to pull herself together. They'd made a mess of things, and all they could do now was muddle through.

"Look." His voice startled the baby, and she poked out her bottom lip. He waited, anxiety nipping at him.

He motioned for Tiffany to get up and then pointed to the narrow hall that led to the house's two bedrooms. They needed to talk, but he didn't want to wake Heidi.

Tiffany rolled her eyes but stood and followed him.

Her bedroom came into view, and he froze in his tracks. He didn't want to talk in there.

Ten months ago he'd come over to fix the plumbing. Jemima had been on full bed rest, so she and their children were staying with her *Mamm*, who lived an hour away. Because of the injuries he'd sustained in the accident and his need to keep working with the horses, he was taking three pain medications to help him cope. But he recalled Tiffany's friends murmuring in the background in another room as she held out an icy glass of Coke. He took it, and they talked for a minute.

She'd moved in closer, and they had kissed. He'd backed away, saying he needed to go. What little he remembered after that was murky, but this much he knew: he'd stayed.

Why? Dear God, why?

He'd never understand it, and he cringed because of how betrayed Jemima would feel if she knew. She'd *never* believe she was the only woman who mattered to him. But she was.

Three weeks later Tiffany sent a text saying she was pregnant.

Between the trauma of the accident and the haziness caused by the drugs, he had times he could barely remember. But everything about the day he received her text was burned into his brain. He'd been in the round pen, training horses, when he read the text. Horrified, he'd stood there, staring at the text, feeling as if everyone in the world could see the news even though he was on the farm alone.

Shame had filled him. His lungs burned when he tried to breathe. He longed to crawl into a hole, but there was no hiding from this or from the shame he had to carry with him night and day.

Tiffany's next text hit a minute later. She needed money to terminate the pregnancy. The temptation to fork over the cash had been powerful, but it lasted only a moment.

He went to see her and talked her into keeping the baby, assuring her that he wouldn't abandon her and the baby. Now he was chained to this woman forever.

Making it even harder to tell Jemima the truth, Roy and Tiffany had dated a few times back when he was in his *rumschpringe,* a fact about his past that had bothered Jemima when she began dating Roy. What troubled her was his seeing someone who was not Amish, as if he was more attracted to Englisch girls. But the truth was he'd felt bad for Tiffany, who had grown up with an alcoholic for a dad, while his own Daed was a pillar of his Amish community. Hadn't the Word commanded him to be kind to the less fortunate? He remembered thinking that if he befriended her, he could help steer her life to something better than what her parents had. But he'd soon realized that her issues were too deep for him to really help and that going out wasn't ministry. It was a date, intended to be fun for two people attracted to each other.

"Hello?" Tiffany's voice brought him back from his thoughts.

He shook off the weight of the past and stepped into the other bedroom. Tiffany followed him. This room was supposed to be the nursery, although there was only a wooden crib that Heidi didn't like to sleep in and a windup swing that she wouldn't stay in for more than a few moments. Bits and pieces of baby clothing were strewed about.

Tiffany leaned against the doorframe. "Are you going to lecture me about the baby? Of course *you* can get her to calm down. She'd be better off staying with you. Take her and give me some cash to start my life over. Then everyone would be happier."

Was this Tiffany's plan? Was this the reason for the packed car?

Roy shook his head. "Heidi needs her mother, and besides that, I don't have any money to give you." With the exception of the seed money to purchase horses at the auction, his accounts were drained. Tiffany didn't have health insurance, so he'd paid out of his own pocket for all the prenatal care and hospital bills and her living expenses for the last nine months.

Tiffany scraped dried formula off her shirt. "You have money. You're going to that stupid auction to buy horses, and I know that means you have cash, lots of it."

He hated having to reason with her about his life and farming business. Why couldn't she take his word for anything? "Look, Tiff, I don't mean to minimize how tough this is for you, but we both know that every baby needs its mother. We agreed to that months ago, remember? Just because it's a rough phase with Heidi, don't do something today that you'll regret later."

Tiffany folded her arms, looking childish and stubborn. "You can't decide that for me. I want out, and I need cash to do it."

"The money I have is seed money. I could give every penny of it to Jemima or you or spend it on myself, but all of us will need more money in a few months, and without fresh, retrained horses to sell, I have no income to meet anyone's needs. I'm buying more horses than usual because life is costing more than usual. The horse farm is a small business, and horses are the only product I provide to buyers. The good news is I have a buyer lined up who wants a dozen retrained horses come mid-May, so in three months I'll have at least double, hopefully closer to triple, the money I'm spending today to acquire the horses. Understand?"

She unfolded her arms, seeming interested in his words. "Triple the amount of money in three months?"

"It's not all profit, because of the cost of feed and vet bills and hired help, but ya."

She nodded, seeming to mull over his words. Perhaps now was a good time to mention how busy he'd be once the horses arrived. "I'll be focusing all my time and energy on training the horses while the hired help tends to everything else. The only way for small businesses to stay on their feet is to buy fresh products to sell at a profit. But it takes time and commitment."

Tiffany rolled her eyes. "Yeah, I get it. You're gonna be too busy to help. But I told you that I didn't want to be a mother back when something could've been done about it. You wanted me to keep it, so I did. But it's not at all working out as you said."

Roy's chest was so tight he could barely get a breath. What would happen if she disappeared, leaving the baby behind? "We talked about this. We talked about the hormone changes and the mood swings. You just need to ride it out, okay? I believe you'll bond with her yet. She's only six weeks old."

Tiffany hadn't wanted to name the baby girl when she was born. The hospital staff kept returning to their room, asking if the baby had a name yet to put on the birth certificate. Roy had pulled up a website of names on his cell phone while they sat in the hospital, and he read one after another until Tiffany heard one she was willing to use.

Tiffany's pregnancy had been a wake-up call. He now realized it was impossible for him to be alert to all that life required while strung out on pain medicine. It'd been a miserable battle, but he got off the painkillers and went back to praying daily for his family. As much as he wished he could undo that night with Tiffany, he couldn't regret Heidi's life. That would be wrong. But he'd helped create a beautiful, innocent person who would grow up in an unstable home. And all he could do was pray for her and try to make her life have as little chaos as possible.

His phone buzzed in his pocket, and he pulled it out to check who was calling. The call came from the Kurtzes' phone shanty. John would leave a message, but Roy knew the call meant he was needed there.

He put the phone away, but he had to get back to horse business. Whatever was going on, he'd already stayed here too long.

"Go rest while she's sleeping, and maybe take a shower. You'll feel more human and hopeful."

"A nap and a shower can't fix this."

"I know they can't. We'll talk again soon, but I have to go. I

promise I'll come back later today and . . ." He racked his brain to
think of anything that could help her feel better about the situation.
"I'll hire a nanny to come in for several hours every day to help until
you feel like you can handle the baby alone."

How was he going to afford that? But he couldn't deal with that
worry now. He'd just have to find a way.

Tiffany looked at the floor. "Yeah, okay. Maybe I could make it
with some good help. I can't continue living here. I just know that
your dad will drop by one day to get rent money like he used to do,
and he'll have questions about the baby once he sees her. Regardless
of what I say, he's not likely to accept my word on the matter. Besides
that, what happens if he sees you coming or going at odd hours?"

Roy couldn't imagine what it'd do to his Daed to know the
truth. It'd been awkward trying to convince him to stop coming in
person to get the rent, but he'd managed it. "I can't afford another
place for you right now, but, ya, it's probably a good idea to look into
that a little later down the road. But if we make sure he has the
money by the due date each month, he won't come by."

"You hope," Tiffany mumbled.

Anxiety pressed in again, and his chest ached. "Get some rest."

She walked toward her bedroom, and Roy hurried out of the
house. What a mess.

Three

Chris stood in the abandoned barn as his bishop turned off the portable electric floodlights that were aimed at the makeshift ring in the center. The roar of the crowd was gone, as was the bookies' money. Chris had logged too much time in the gym with a trainer for this to be the outcome. Since he hadn't actually lost the fight, did that mean another one would have to be arranged fairly soon? Even in his state of disbelief, he realized the answer rather quickly. He'd made a deal with people his brother owed money to, and there was no backing out of it.

This old barn was way off the beaten path. Who had gone to his home and informed his Daed? Then in turn his Daed had gone straight to the ministers, and all of them came here and broke up the fight. Those who'd wagered on it had taken their money and disappeared.

The bishop walked over to him, carrying a lantern. "You need to join the Amish faith or get out. It's that easy: come in or get out. You're influencing the young men to fight and disobey not only their parents but also the founding principles of our life of nonviolence. You make a sport out of it!"

Chris rubbed his nose with the back of his hand. He had no defense. He'd known when he agreed to fight that if he was caught, he would be without an excuse or a reason he could share. His parents didn't know about Dan's secret. It was deeper and darker than they could bear.

Was the bishop right? Should he either join the faith or leave altogether? The topic wasn't that cut and dried, not by a long shot.

When Chris didn't say anything, the bishop shook his head and cleared his throat. "We understood when you stopped instruction years ago because of what happened with your fiancée. We gave you grace for that, and I even stood up for your right to take that time. I was sure you would come back, finish instruction, and join the church. But you didn't. And now you're fighting and betting. I've seen this type of thing before—young men hiding behind our Amish ways to make moonshine or gamble or run drugs. I will not tolerate this. Am I clear?"

Chris simply nodded. If he told the truth, his brother would be excommunicated, and if Chris didn't finish the fight, his brother's gambling debt could cost him far more than what he currently owed. The bishop passed the lantern to Chris's Daed, and then he and the other ministers left the barn.

He never should have agreed to fight in this abandoned barn, but the Englisch bookies wanted it here. They'd promoted his distinction as an Amish fighter, and they said that it had to be held in an Amish barn. So Chris thought this out-of-the-way, abandoned barn would make them happy without the ministers or church members finding out.

His Daed picked up Chris's hat from the dirt floor and brushed the brim of it against his pant leg. Dust flew from it, scattering into the darkness just beyond the reach of the lantern. Chris's greatest fear was that his brother, along with his wife and children, would be like that dust—brushed off and dispersed into darkness. His brother was attending Gamblers Anonymous and staying clean. He just needed a way to pay off a debt to his Englisch bookie.

Chris took his hat from his Daed. "I can't stay in these parts." Now that the ministers knew about tonight, if Chris stayed, they'd be like detectives trying to unravel a mystery, and their findings would eventually land squarely on his brother's doorstep. But if Chris left, the ministers would have no cause to keep digging into tonight's events. They would assume that the fighting and gambling began and ended with Chris and he'd moved on.

But there would be a rematch. It just couldn't happen under his bishop's jurisdiction.

Who would've thought that the worst thing wasn't losing everything that had been riding on his winning tonight's fight? The worst thing was that his parents were hurt, and the ministers now knew too much.

Daed fidgeted with his long, bushy beard. "Do you have somewhere to go?"

"Ya." But it would mean leaving the well-paying job he currently had for something that barely paid. Although he'd had compassion for the fix Roy Graber was in and Chris had agreed to work on the man's horse farm part time until Roy found someone else, Chris had hoped to avoid leaving his good-paying job. Still, it would be a windfall for Roy Graber, and maybe the man needed that.

"I never expected something like this of you." His Daed's voice cracked. "Your Mamm and I knew you had some worldly thinking from your teen years, but all this time later we believed you'd grow into a good and godly man, especially since you were going through instruction to get married."

"*That* ending has nothing to do with the reason I'm here now." It didn't, right?

His Daed drew a ragged breath, and the confusion in his eyes haunted Chris. "By the time you were born, the sixth son, we were tired, maybe too tired, to teach you the way you should go."

He hated this for his parents. "You were *gut* parents."

They were so very good, and he hurt for the pain this would cause them. In all his scheming and efforts on Dan's behalf, he'd never imagined this would be the outcome. But Dan had a wife and young children to protect. He was clean now. No more gambling. But he couldn't get free of those he owed money to until he paid off the debt.

Chris's left eye ached, and he knew it was swelling. His opponent had popped him a good one when the bishop called Chris's name, pulling all his concentration from the fight.

"Your Mamm sent your clothes." His Daed pointed at two brown grocery bags near the entrance of the barn, each one apparently full.

His Daed's words meant two things: Mamm didn't want to see him, and he was no longer welcome to enter their home.

Chris hugged his Daed, and his Daed held him tight. Should Chris tell him the truth? Would that lighten their disappointment or make it worse? "I'm sorry, Daed."

His Daed sighed and backed away. He gestured toward Chris's scraggly beard. "I guess this means no one will hassle you to stay clean shaven." Daed smiled, but Chris saw the tears in his eyes.

Chris rubbed the stubble on his chin, playing along as his Daed both complained and joked with him. Chris wasn't leaving the Amish, although it did seem the bishop had a point: get in or get out. Still, he was going to a new Amish community, and he would have to shave before the next Amish church meeting in that district. But with church Sundays held every other week, he grew plenty of stubble in the fourteen days between meetings. If Graber's district held church services on different Sundays than Chris's, he might have an extra week before needing to shave.

He and his Daed walked out of the old barn. His Daed got in the buggy and tapped the reins against the horse's back. Chris wouldn't go to Roy's tonight. He needed time to think. He pulled out his cell phone and opened the Uber app.

Abigail rode horseback across her brother's land, taking in a glorious Saturday morning as Pippi trotted. If this wasn't every teacher's dream, it should be—to be in a saddle, riding freely for at least an hour on the weekend. Despite having on riding pants under her cape dress and wearing her thickest winter coat, she shivered as cold air rustled her dress and the strings of her prayer *Kapp*. But spring would arrive next month.

Frost glazed the grass under the sun of a February morning, and sunlight sparkled off the patches of remaining snow. Any morning in any season when she was astride her beloved Pippi, smelling the leather saddle and the aroma of the horse, was a good one.

The fence line of the east pasture came into view. Her Daed used to own all this property, but Roy had purchased the horse farm and accompanying property years ago. Roy and she had four other siblings, but none of them lived in the state. They were all married with children and living near their respective in-laws.

Roy's prized stallions, Lucky and Thunder, were majestic as the sun glistened off their well-groomed coats. Several other horses—colts, yearlings, mares, and geldings—were grazing quietly in a separate pasture from the stallions. Most had their heads down, but something about the way Lady Belle's head drooped indicated she still wasn't feeling well. Abigail had first noticed cold symptoms a couple of days ago. Had the old girl eaten anything recently? Maybe she should check her temperature again.

Movement deeper in the field and along the edge of the woods caught her attention, and excitement ran through her.

Jonas Fisher. Her cousin appeared to be out enjoying this beautiful morning. Was he off work today? Maybe he was running an errand. She would check Lady Belle's temperature in an hour when her free time was over. Right now she wanted to race her cousin, and she urged Pippi toward the edge of the wood. Pippi gained speed.

Her cousin was quite the rider, and it'd been months since they'd raced. Her desire to challenge him pumped through her veins as Pippi went faster and faster.

"I'm coming for you, Fisher!" she screamed with all she had.

He glanced back at her, and despite her blurred vision from riding a galloping horse, she saw his horse pick up its pace. She leaned in, urging Pippi onward, and soon she passed him, laughing. They rode for several minutes, and then she no longer heard hooves behind her. She slowed Pippi and turned around, to stare into the bewildered, handsome face of a complete stranger.

Abigail blinked. "You're not my cousin."

The man didn't seem amused, but he nodded with a hint of a polite smile. His horse stayed put, and she squeezed her heels into Pippi, and her horse walked toward him.

He wasn't clean shaven, nor did he actually have a beard. So was he married or not? He looked to be about her age—late twenties—and most men had a thick beard from several years of marriage by then.

Her curiosity was piqued. Once beside him, she tugged on the reins, stopping Pippi. "I hope I didn't startle you."

She'd given her horse a full head of steam as she'd come up behind him. What she'd thought was their racing for a few minutes could well have been his horse panicking because of the thunderous hooves from behind. The horse was one of theirs that boarded at the Kurtz farm, so the man had borrowed it or leased it, but she wouldn't mention that right now. He seemed rather addled.

His golden-brown eyes stayed focused on her. His horse pranced about, and he tugged the reins one way and then the other until the animal grew still. But he said nothing, just stared. He seemed rugged enough, especially with a puffy, bruised eye, broad shoulders, and a beard that even had a mustache to it. But the bruise on his face indicated he'd recently taken quite a hit. Maybe her stunt had been too much for him in his state. She'd need to get closer to see if his pupils were dilated.

"Are you okay?" She dismounted. *"Kumm."* She dropped the reins to Pippi, knowing the horse would stay put. Abigail motioned for him to get down. "Let's walk for a minute."

He drew a breath and chuckled. "I'm fine." He patted the horse.

Still, she would feel better if he would walk with her so she was sure he was thinking clearly and could find his way back home. "Please."

He nodded and dismounted. His stare was intense as she moved in close, studying his pupils. They appeared normal. Maybe they should walk to the creek, give the horses a drink, and watch water ripple past them. Watching any natural body of water was comforting, restorative to the soul in a way nothing else was. She took Pippi by one rein, and he did the same with his horse. They walked slowly.

"You're new to our neck of the woods."

"Here on business, ya."

She didn't recognize him, so wherever he lived, it had to be more than a day's ride by horse in any direction. Her uncle was the bishop, and she knew every Amish person under his church responsibility.

This man wasn't a talker, at least not right now. "I'm Abigail."

He fidgeted with the leather rein. "Chris."

She stopped at the creek's embankment. He held out his hand to her and motioned for her to go first. With Pippi's rein in one hand, she took his hand and stepped two feet lower. The rich, sandy soil easily shifted under her feet, and he held tight to her hand as she tried to find steady footing.

A loud boom ricocheted, making the air tremble. Chris clutched her hand tighter as Pippi reared. He tried to grab her reins and help Abigail hold on to her, but he missed, and Pippi pulled free of Abigail's grasp. Whinnying, both horses took off. What was happening? The blur of events seemed to be occurring in slow motion. Another explosion thundered, sounding closer than the first.

Gunfire!

She tightened her hand around his and pulled him down the embankment. They landed on their backs and ducked their heads under the earthen rampart so that they came nearly face to face with thin, scraggly roots. A third shot fired, and Chris rolled on top of her, wrapping her head with his arms.

"I appreciate the gesture, but please get off." She pushed him, but he didn't budge. They had thick coats on, and he wasn't trying to be inappropriate, but he wasn't being helpful at all. "Seriously? Move, please!" She shoved at him, and he rolled off her. She cupped her hands around her mouth. "Hello! People are here! Hello! Stop shooting!" Her breathing was labored as she waited. "Hello!" She elbowed

Chris. "Join me. Yell 'Stop shooting' on three." She counted and they both cupped their hands and yelled, "Stop shooting!" several times.

They lowered their hands, listening. Probably a hunter, and maybe he'd heard them, but she wasn't moving from the safety of this embankment. She leaned her head back against the dirt, gasping for air. "You okay?"

"Ya." He grimaced as he bent his right leg at the knee back and forth with great care.

"You sure?" She pointed at his leg.

"I'm fine, just sore. Landed hard."

"Welcome to Mirth, Pennsylvania."

He panted as he fell back against the soil. "So far there's been nothing cheerful about it."

"You just described half of everyday living here, but the other half tries to make up for it."

Neither of them spoke for nearly a minute.

He brushed his palms against his black coat, wiping muck from his hands. "I wanted some time to think, so I rode out this way."

She had so many questions. Where was he from? Why did he have one of their horses from the Kurtz farm? How had he managed to meander into her riding area without knowing the lay of the land? But she wouldn't ask, not yet anyway.

He rested his hands on his chest. "The woods were so quiet, and I was praying while feeling uneasy."

"Uneasy? Did you see someone, maybe a person with a gun?"

"No. Definitely not." His brows barely wrinkled into a frown. "A better word would be *haunted*, I guess."

"Haunted?" He considered that a better word? Seemed like a weird one.

"Ever had a plan that seemed good, but while it helped someone you love, it hurt others?"

She couldn't think of a time that had happened, but he didn't sound as if he expected a real answer.

Still lying on his back on the slope of the embankment, he stared at the barren treetops or maybe at the sky beyond them. "Anyway, the next thing I knew I heard a voice rumble across the land, 'I'm coming for you, Fisher.'" He looked at his filthy palms, saying nothing for several moments. "I'm Chris Fisher, by the way."

"Oh." She stifled a laugh. "Sorry about that." It would be startling to be in prayer over something troubling and from nowhere hear someone scream your name and say what she had.

"Not your fault. Then when you stopped your horse and turned, I couldn't believe my eyes." He held up his index finger. "No, I'm not elaborating."

She didn't know what that meant. Was it a compliment or an insult? Had he been unsure if she was real or an apparition? Did she remind him of someone he'd rather forget? "I do have that effect on people. It's the coppery color of my hair and freckles. Perhaps you were unsure if I was a woman or a large penny on horseback."

"Uh, *nee*. That wasn't it at all. And then"—he cupped his hands to his mouth and blew warm air into them—"about the time I got my head wrapped around the situation, we were shot at."

"You're in a place that is filled with Amish who have the same last name as you, and the gunfire wasn't aimed at us. Just hunters."

He shrugged. "The words of someone with a clean conscience."

"True." She'd like to know what was really haunting him, but since her interest was only idle curiosity, she wouldn't ask. "So, Chris Fisher, what kind of business brings you to Mirth?"

"Horses."

Her brother had told her a few days ago that he was trying to work out an affordable deal for a skilled horseman to help on the farm.

"Clearly I'm off to a great start, ya?" He laughed. "Within the first hour of being in Mirth, I've lost two horses: yours and mine."

"Unless someone stops her, Pippi will go straight home, and your horse will probably follow her lead."

He chuckled. "Is it your nature to be sensible in the face of danger?"

"Um, maybe."

As a recovery coach, her bishop uncle gave rooms in his home to Amish who were in recovery or to at-risk teens who were abusing alcohol. Like every other woman in this district and the neighboring ones, she regularly volunteered hours there to help with laundry, cleaning, and meals. With the exception of this past year after Roy was injured, she helped out more at the recovery center than other women did, and she did so for two reasons: she liked her uncle, and being single she could get away from home more easily than most women. But because of her time helping in the men's recovery home, hearing their stories, and seeing the damage their issues caused their wives, she'd formed an Amish type of Al-Anon to help the spouses understand the addicts in their lives and all the problems that came with addiction. She attended as time allowed, but the women didn't need her, which was good, since it'd been difficult to get to the meetings the last few months.

The men at Endless Grace often saw everyday problems as if they were the wages of sin coming to harm them, but she didn't think that way. Life was filled with mystery and coincidences and God's love reaching toward His children.

"Is your husband a jealous man, Abigail?"

He assumed she was married. Amish women her age—the very elderly age of twenty-seven—were married. All of them except her.

When she didn't respond, he leaned on one elbow, looking at her. "You chased me, insisted I walk with you, and then there was gunfire."

"Ah, I see. No husband. No boyfriend."

His eyes hinted at disbelief. "It seems as if that should not be true."

"Ya, well, I find men annoying. Present company included, because although I don't know you yet, I know that given time—"

His laughter startled two crows in a nearby tree, and she couldn't help but smile. She'd said that to a few men who'd wanted to date her, and they found her attitude ungodly and in need of correction. It was pleasant that this man didn't mind what she'd said, which was partly in jest but also had plenty of truth to it.

She stared at the swaying treetops, feeling the cold, damp earth creeping through her winter coat. "But I see what you're aiming for, and I'll admit it's been so long since I've had a boyfriend that if my Daed saw us riding or walking just now, he'd throw a celebration."

Chris grinned. "Perhaps that's what we heard—a great-sounding horn of celebration."

"Or, you know, hunters. They tend to shoot guns, and it is quail, pheasant, and cottontail rabbit season for a few more weeks."

"I see how it is. You lead me to deduce one thing and then turn it around." He grinned. "A robust rider. Practical. Brave. And beautiful."

Beautiful? "I take it you're not married despite the facial hair."

He rubbed his hand over his stubble. "Just lazy, I suppose."

"I daresay that few men would be caught in your position, unshaven and resting near a creek while in town on business, and admit it's because they're lazy. Kudos to you for that."

"Denki." He lay back. "How long do you think we need to stay on this dank, smelly soil?"

"I have no idea why a hunter is carelessly shooting his gun, but I'm not taking any chances by jumping to my feet before I'm sure it's safe. You, however, are free to follow whatever inner leading you wish, Chris Fisher."

His brows furrowed as he studied her. "Wow. Did you just encourage me to go first, knowing I might get shot?"

"No. I laid out the truth plainly and said you were free to do whatever you deem is right for you." She didn't waste time or energy trying to convince men of anything. Whether they had hearts of gold or of stone, men did whatever they made up their minds to do. End of story.

Was that a horse snorting?

Chris wiped a smudge of dirt on his face, which only made a bigger splotch. "But—"

"Sh." She rolled over and eased her head above the embankment. A man had Pippi by the reins and was taking small, slow steps as he searched the horizon. He had a hunting gun strapped to his back. "Kumm." She patted Chris's shoulder and stood. "Lester!"

Chris climbed the embankment and offered his hand. Abigail accepted it, and with a quick hoist, her feet were back on solid ground.

"What were—" Chris's booming voice was aimed at Lester.

She grabbed his arm. "Don't."

He faced her. "I most certainly will."

She did her best to subdue her eye roll. *Men.* "He's mentally challenged and a sweetheart. If you go off on him, he'll cry for weeks, which will break my heart." She lifted a brow. "I am asking nicely. Please."

He looked from her to Lester and nodded.

"Lester." Abigail hurried to him, but her ankle ached for some reason. "You broke the rules." She tugged on her muddy coat. "Look."

"Are you h-h-hurt?"

"A little, ya."

"I'm sorry. I'm so sorry." His eyes were wide. "Don't tell. Please don't tell."

"Give me the gun."

He pulled the strap off his shoulder and gave her the gun. "I was in my backyard when I saw a deer running." He pointed a shaky hand along the creek line.

She wouldn't point out that it wasn't deer-hunting season. The news of that would distract him from the truly important information.

"But that's due east, and you can't shoot in that direction. Remember?"

"But I saw a buck—a big one."

"Lester, there are homes with children, and you have friends, like me, who are due east from your property." She unloaded the rifle and passed it to Chris. "Look at me."

He stopped fidgeting and gazed into her eyes.

"It's the law."

"No police! No police!" He looked at her dirt-smeared legs. "I coulda killed you."

Finally he understood.

"Ya. Then who would make you caramel popcorn balls every fall?"

"I sorry, Abigail. So sorry." He started sobbing and pulled a handkerchief from his pocket.

She held him until he calmed. "You need to go on home. I'll come by later this evening, and we will talk to your Daed together."

"He's gonna be mad."

"Ya. That can't be helped. But I'll stay until he calms down. What happened to the markers? Are they missing, or did you ignore them?"

"I moved them so this way wouldn't be east no more."

If the situation weren't so serious, Abigail would've found his response humorous. Instead, she put her hands on her hips.

His shoulders drooped. "It don't work that way, do it?"

"No." She put her hands on his arms and turned him in the direction of his home. "Go on home. It'll be okay."

"I won't hunt no more, not ever. I don't like killing no how. It's just all so pretty, and I wanted to shoot it."

"What do you mean?" Abigail asked.

"Shoot it. Bam. Bam."

Chris put the gun strap over his head and shoulder. "Like a picture?"

Lester put his hands around his eyes and clicked his tongue. "Shoot it. Shoot it."

Abigail sighed. Most days, Lester understood about hunting and where the limits were, but today was not one of them. "We'll talk about this later. Go on home."

"You come see me tonight. Bring caramel popcorn balls." He hurried off across the field.

Her legs seemed to turn to gelatin, and she longed to melt onto the wet brown February grass, but she stayed on her feet, patting Pippi. "His Daed needs to lock up his hunting rifles and ammunition."

"And buy Lester a good camera."

"You think?"

"I do. The word *shoot* is connected in his head to a gun, but the fact that he finds it beautiful and wants to shoot it sounds to me like he needs a camera."

She closed her eyes, trying to center herself. Now that the danger was over, she felt woozy. If she had the strength to get on her horse and ride to the farm, she would. But her body trembled.

"In the words of someone I met in these very woods earlier today, let's walk." Chris motioned.

He was right. She needed to walk and breathe deeply and gather herself. They strolled in silence until she felt less shaky.

"What a morning, huh?" he said.

"Ya."

"I'm glad you didn't let me yell at Lester." He gestured south. His horse was grazing a few hundred feet ahead, and they quietly moved in that direction.

"Trust me, I understand the temptation. But it would break his heart and make no difference in the long run." She'd have to look for other solutions, like Lester's Daed locking up the guns and maybe giving him a camera. "Where are you from?"

"Scarsdale, a little town on the other side of the Cumberland Narrows."

"You're about a hundred miles from home."

"Ya, and will be for at least a week, maybe a month." He shrugged. "Any chance you know where the Graber Horse Farm is?"

He sounded rather displeased to be here, and she wondered if he'd left a girl at home in order to come to the farm.

"Ya, I—"

He held up his hand for her to stop walking, a silent request to keep either of them from startling his horse. She didn't budge, and he eased over until he had his horse by the reins.

The idea of seeing Chris regularly held some appeal, which completely caught her by surprise. She often felt guilty that men so easily grated on her nerves, but most did. Her Daed said it was because from the time she was old enough to wash dishes and do laundry, she'd seen men at her uncle's recovery home, mostly alcoholics and at-risk alcohol abusers. The men were emotional wrecks with guilt for all they'd put their loved ones through, and it spilled out in every conversation. If that wasn't it, her time spent attending the meetings with the men's spouses and listening to their painful stories as they cried was certainly enough to taint her attitude toward men.

Chris took a canteen from its holder on his horse, opened it, and held it out to her. She took a long drink, grateful for the water.

"I asked and then stopped you from answering," he said. "Any idea where the Graber Horse Farm is?"

"Ya." She held out her hand to him. "Abigail Graber, sister of Roy Graber."

The nonchalant look in his eyes turned into interest. "Nice to meet you." He shook her hand. "So I take it you have no idea where the horse farm is."

"Why would you say that? I'm confused."

He smiled, revealing perfectly white, straight teeth. Was every physical feature about him perfect? He leaned in. "This is where you deny knowing where the farm is."

"*Ach,* I see. Sorry." She patted her horse. "No, I have no clue where Graber Horse Farm is."

"Gut. Then we shall ride together in search of it." He gestured at her horse. "Do you need a hand?"

Did she need help? Was he serious? The horse farm used to be her Daed's. She'd spent half of her childhood on a horse. "I'm fine, denki. Do you need a hand?"

His laughter stirred her. "Touché."

They mounted the horses.

Abigail settled into the saddle. "How are you on a Graber horse, one kept on the Kurtz farm, and yet you have no idea where our farm is?"

"Your brother filled me in concerning the Kurtz farm, and I knew each of those horses would have to be ridden sometime this week. Since I needed some quiet time on a horse before I showed up at the Graber place, I had an Uber drop me off there. John Kurtz showed me around, and I saddled a Graber horse and went for a ride. Problem?"

"No." She liked how much he'd made himself at home. It said he was confident with horses *and* new situations. "I was just curious."

He looked toward the skyline, first east, then north, then west. "I've researched the area a little online. It says there is a ridge with a beautiful overlook of the valley, and there is supposed to be a cave with a pool somewhere. Is that true?"

"It's true." Her sudden desire to show him the cave surprised her. "The cave you mentioned, or one similar to it, is only about two miles from here." She pointed at the mountain in the distance.

"Care to ride with me?"

"Sort of, but I have chores I need to do."

"On the horse farm?"

She nodded.

"Your brother wasn't expecting me to arrive today, so we can tackle them together in no time." He propped his forearm on the horn of the saddle and leaned in. "You game?" he whispered.

An odd feeling came over her. She knew nothing about this man except that he seemed comfortable in his own skin and with women. Was she being naive, taken in by his newness in a community where the few single men were as stale as last month's homemade bread? What if she went off gallivanting with him and he had a girlfriend?

He pulled his phone out of his pocket. "Should I order pizza while you decide?"

She laughed. He was entertaining.

"Are we spelunking or not?"

She wanted to go, but . . .

He studied her. "I sense reluctance."

"You do."

"What is it you need to know? That I'm single? I assure you I am. That I'm trustworthy?" He held out his hand and tilted it back and forth, indicating so-so. "Eh." He shrugged.

She laughed.

"But I did willingly become a shield for you against flying bullets."

"This is true."

He smiled. "Let's go to the farm. The cave can wait." He looked around. "We need to head east, right?"

"Nee. Let's go spelunking." She tugged the reins and turned Pippi in the opposite direction. "This way."

Four

Jemima hurried about the bedroom, changing into her best dress for the food-truck auction. Why was it so difficult to get out the door on time? A loud thud echoed down the hall, and she didn't need to hunt for the source to know what had happened. Laura's cane had fallen.

Jemima slung the strap of the diaper bag across her shoulder and left the bedroom. Once in the open space of the kitchen and living room, she leaned over the rail of the playpen and picked up Simeon. "Okay, *kumm mol, Liewi. Loss uns geh.*" Although Laura understood English well, Carolyn knew only a few words. Jemima grabbed two folded quilts off the couch and motioned for her three older children—eight-year-old Laura, five-year-old Carolyn, and three-year-old Nevin—to follow her.

As soon as she said, "Come on, dears. Let's go," they headed for the back door to put on their coats. On a normal day they might balk or dawdle, but today they'd been promised hot chocolate and a treat from the bakery. She set the quilts on the table, put on her coat, and put one on Simeon as the older girls helped Nevin get his on.

Despite how alone she felt, hope and excitement stirred inside her at the prospect of getting a food truck. Maybe the emptiness between Roy and her would let up once she had the distraction of her own business. One of the three food trucks that would go on the block today had real promise, and if they bought it, today would be the start of a new chapter in her life.

The cane thudded to the floor again, a constant reminder that Laura needed assistance to get around.

Jemima scurried to the back door. "Ready?" She picked up Laura's cane and handed it to her. When Jemima opened the door, February's cold air rushed inside as her small brood went out.

With Simeon on Jemima's hip, Laura using a cane and Jemima verbally guiding Carolyn and Nevin, the Graber family moved like molasses as they left the house. Jemima locked the door while the three older children made their way down the ramp that led to the driveway. Thank goodness Laura no longer needed a wheelchair, but the ramp still made it easier for her to go in and out of the house.

"Mamm, *guck*." Carolyn pointed.

Jemima looked, and relief washed over her as she saw their horse and carriage coming toward them. There wasn't anyone in the driver's seat, but soon she saw an unfamiliar man leading the horse with Abigail beside him. "I got a text from my brother, reminding me to hitch the horse to the rig for you and bring it to the house."

Every time Jemima's patience with her husband wore too thin, he did something that renewed her faith in him. "Denki."

"*Gern gschehne.*" Abigail gestured at the man. "Jemima, this is

Chris Fisher, the new farmhand. Chris, this is Jemima." She pointed as she continued. "And Laura, Carolyn, Nevin, and Simeon."

Hope seemed to fill a big hole inside Jemima. Farm help had actually arrived, and his presence here could take a lot off her husband. "It's so nice to meet you."

"Same to you. Abigail's been showing me the ropes in your husband's absence."

Jemima held his gaze while cradling her chin and stroking it as if she had a beard.

Chris followed suit. "Just lazy, not married."

"Gut." Jemima immediately regretted her enthusiasm. "I mean, it's my understanding you'll be staying with us on the nights you'll be in Mirth, at least until you find a place, and your room only has a twin bed."

"A twin is just fine."

When he turned away to check something on the rigging, Jemima opened her eyes wide and nodded toward him, wanting to know if Abigail saw any possible dating potential in him.

Abigail smiled and shrugged. That response seemed promising. She tended to size up men's likability factor really fast, often without sharing so much as a cup of coffee with them.

Abigail lifted Nevin and put him in the forward-facing car seat. Once all the children were strapped in properly, Abigail closed the passenger door and went around to Jemima's side.

Jemima closed her door and unsnapped the pliable plastic window. "Since there is help here today, any chance you can go with me? You've been saving dollar for dollar with us for nine years."

"I'd love to, but I actually forgot about the auction, so I got a late start on chores. With a new string of horses arriving Monday, I need to walk the fence line with Chris so we can mend as needed. Since tomorrow is the Sabbath, we really only have today to get ready."

"True," Jemima said.

The tasks of buying, tending, training, and selling racehorses to be workhorses were as endless as the piles of dishes from cooking three meals a day for her family.

Abigail pushed against the carriage door, making sure it was properly shut. "I trust you to buy the right truck. You know that."

"Uh"—Chris looked baffled—"Amish women are buying a truck?"

"Ya." Abigail shrugged. "It's a food truck, which is perfectly acceptable, because anything that couples women with kitchens is looked on with favor."

"Abigail," Jemima chided, "that's not a polite thing to say."

Abigail turned to Chris. "Take note that she didn't deny it's true."

If Chris's expression meant anything, he found Abigail's sense of humor entertaining.

"Abigail Louise Graber, you tell him something honest, please."

Abigail tapped her forehead as if thinking deeply. "Oh. My uncle is the bishop, and I'm his favorite niece, possibly more favored than his own daughters, so when I asked if I could have a truck, he asked what kind and if he could chip in."

Jemima sighed. "I didn't mean for you to tell him something that honest."

"You're hard to please. You know that?"

Jemima laughed. "I'm gone." She snapped the supple thick plastic window back in place, and the horse trotted out of the driveway. Although town was only five miles away, going by horse and carriage, with the horse pulling a family and contending with hills, would make the journey about forty minutes. She shifted her thoughts from Abigail and Chris to other things.

She and Abigail had been very patient about getting the right truck for what they wanted. Finally, after ten years of hoping and saving, she felt confident that she'd win the bid on the best truck: the Smiths' truck. Jemima's life would change a lot once they had a truck. Was Abigail ready for the changes to her own life?

Abigail had loved teaching for almost a decade now. Would she discover that fixing food for tourists wasn't as satisfying as investing in young people's lives? It was important to Abigail to feel fulfilled in her day job, and she said it was fulfilling and fun to cook. Although they'd not done so together in the last week or so, Abigail and Jemima had a great time preparing meals together, whether for the family or neighbors or community functions. But in all these years, Abigail never considered working on the farm full time, although Roy had asked her twice if she'd like to. The endless hours spent outdoors in all kinds of weather didn't appeal to her, nor did constantly mucking out stalls or sowing, harvesting, and hauling hay. Oh, and Abigail had no interest in her brother being her boss.

Jemima chuckled. Abigail got points for knowing when too much of a good thing would be bad for her.

The food truck would operate full time only during tourist season and on weekends in the spring and fall, but they would likely make more money during that time than Abigail made during a year of teaching. What did Abigail intend to do with her extra time once she wasn't teaching nine months of the year? She said she wouldn't stop her work with special-needs children outside the classroom, and Jemima knew she'd do a decent amount of volunteer work—at the school, at her uncle's recovery home, and on the farm—but would that be enough for someone as energetic as Abigail?

For herself, Jemima looked forward to living out a long-held dream and bringing money into the household budget. But just as important would be her ability to teach a trade to her daughters. Learning to cook was one thing; being able to run a business with that skill was completely different.

How many conversations had Roy and she had while courting and throughout their marriage about her acquiring a food truck and building a business? Careers for newlywed women and the ones with young children were frowned upon, but Roy and she had been careful to pay their dues and step lightly so that no one frowned on this plan even though she still had little ones.

Forty-five minutes after leaving home, Jemima parked the rig, got the children their hot chocolate and treats, and set them up on a quilt near the auction block. Where was Roy? While watching for him, she saw other bidders arriving. The minutes on the digital clock in front of the town bank kept changing until only ten minutes were left before the bidding would begin. But there was still no sign of her husband. She should've thought to borrow Abigail's cell. At least that way she could call him. But when her husband gave his word about where he'd be and when, he always kept it.

She searched the sidewalks.

Warm hands rested on her shoulders. "Hey." Roy kissed her cheek.

Her anxiety eased, and she turned. "Goodness. You're finally here. Is everything okay?"

He nodded, but his eyes told a different story. "We need to talk," he whispered.

How many times this past year had she seen that look of concern? "What's going on?"

He turned to the children. "Laura, you and Carolyn watch your brothers. No one leaves the quilt. Ya?"

Laura nodded, and the girls returned to whatever patty-cake game they were playing with their brothers.

"Kumm." Roy put his arm around her shoulders and led her a few feet away.

She stopped cold. "I'm good right here. What's going on?"

Roy's lips moved as he talked, but his words made little sense, and his promises to make this up to her seemed like a foreign language spoken by a stranger. Everything around her seemed to be happening in slow motion.

She stared into his eyes. "I . . . I don't understand."

"I'm so sorry, Jem."

"All of our savings is gone? How?"

Before he could answer, an electronic popping crackled through the air. A man holding a microphone spoke. "Testing. Testing. Okay, it's working. The auction will begin in five minutes. If you haven't . . ."

His voice faded, drowned out by the noise inside Jemima's head.

Her blood pounded. She paced while fisting her hands and then opening them wide over and over. "How is this possible?" She stopped abruptly, studying his face. "How, Roy?"

"I haven't handled much of anything right since the accident. That's how. It's my fault, every bit of it."

"Are you saying all forty thousand was used for medical bills?" she screeched, and the moment the words left her mouth, she regretted it.

He didn't answer.

He carried a lot of guilt for the accident even though it wasn't his fault. The road had signs for Englisch drivers, warning that they shared the road with slower-moving horse-drawn carriages. The driver who hit her husband and oldest child had passed such a warning sign a hundred feet before running into them. Still, her husband's guilt persisted. Now she stood here adding to it.

Thoughts of how much he'd changed this past year tugged at her compassion. Laura had remained in the hospital for a month after the accident, and Roy stayed with her every night and continued to work seven days a week—doing as little farm work as possible on Sundays. When Laura was released, Roy took Jemima and all three children to her Mamm's place, which was an hour from the horse farm. He stayed home and muddled through his pain and trauma without any aid from his wife, trying to keep as much stress off her as possible. When money and time allowed, he hired a driver and visited Jemima at her Mamm's, sometimes for only a few hours, sometimes for a night or two.

Her husband had put everyone ahead of himself, and they'd survived. Her blood pressure had returned to normal. Simeon was born healthy, and it seemed to her as if Roy might keel over from relief. He sat in the rocker beside her bed, and whenever Simeon wasn't nursing, Roy held him, unable to take his eyes off their healthy son.

She wiped the cold sweat off her forehead. She was sweating in February? "Why are you just now telling me about this?" She knew she sounded accusing, but she couldn't find any other tone.

Again her husband's eyes didn't meet hers, but that didn't hide the embarrassment etched on his face. "I thought I had everything worked out with the bank."

Something didn't add up. It just didn't. They'd had a lot of bills from the accident, and she hadn't kept up with them. She'd left them unopened and put them in the stack of mail for Roy to take care of. But their family was one of the few Amish who had medical insurance. And the man who ran into Roy and Laura had insurance. So why had Roy needed to empty their earmarked savings?

"Look, I know you're disappointed about how busy I've been lately and about our finances, but I'll make it up to you, Jem. I promise."

Her heart clenched. Her husband and daughter had survived. None of them were the same, but they were together.

Her anger drained. "You're doing your best. I know that." Tears choked her, and she hugged him.

Roy held her tight as if trying to save her—or maybe him— from drowning.

Five

Geh langsam and schtamdhaft. Langsam and schtamdhaft." Chris encouraged the last of the twelve horses to go slow and steady as he guided the animal to back down the ramp of the trailer. The driver of the truck and horse trailer shut the doors and lifted the ramp. He waved and then left as Chris led the horse to a pasture and closed the livestock gate. Roy was in a nearby corral, trying to calm a new horse. The new horses were placed in separate corrals in groups of three. If the farm had more corrals, they wouldn't have put any of the horses together until they settled down and acclimated. As it was, even in groups of three, the horses had to be monitored closely for the next few days. Roy and Chris needed to be ready to single out the domineering ones so they wouldn't bite or kick other horses. Roy had put his prized stallions, Lucky and Thunder, in the stables before the new string arrived, aiming to keep them calm during this transition. If they got flighty or combative, people and horses could be injured. Based on the way Roy looked after Lucky and Thunder, Chris was sure they were more valuable to this farm than all the new horses combined.

Chris climbed the split-rail fence and took in the sight: thoroughbred, standardbred, and American saddlebred stallions, geldings, and mares, but no colts or fillies.

The string of horses that were here before the new arrivals were in a nearby pasture, some running back and forth at the fence line, others jerking their heads in frustrated excitement and maybe in a desire to get at and run off the new horses or at least set the hierarchy straight.

A thoroughbred stallion reared up, punching his hooves uncomfortably close to a smaller stallion. Chris hopped off the fence and yelled long and loud to get the thoroughbred's attention. Then he calmed his voice and talked softly as he approached. This one needed to be isolated for a spell.

It would take days, maybe weeks, to establish trust and get the horses in a routine so that Roy and he could begin training them. How had Roy intended to handle all this on his own? Maybe he'd had a backup plan Chris didn't know about. It wasn't as if they'd talked much since Roy and Jemima returned empty handed from the food-truck auction.

"Roy?" Abigail sounded agitated again, but he couldn't see her. Apparently school had let out for the day.

He'd been snared two days ago when he first saw Abigail. Music seemed to ring in his ears, and a voice inside him whispered words he couldn't quite make out.

It had felt like a spiritual experience, as if God Himself was behind him, shoving until Chris landed here. Their outing to the cave had been beyond great, and the fun continued as they spent most of

Saturday working side by side. Ya, he'd been caught in rare but full-on attraction.

Then around five o'clock Saturday evening, Roy had come out of the house, looking for her. They walked away to somewhere more private, but as Chris continued feeding the horses and giving them fresh water, he heard her yelling, "You did what? Why would you do that? Who does that?" Those were familiar browbeating phrases that Chris hated. At that point, he couldn't resist moving a few steps so he could see her, and she had her finger in Roy's face, telling him he needed to get help—another phrase Chris had heard and hated with all that was in him. In his experience the person screaming those words was the one who needed help. She'd stormed off and returned to the stables, barely speaking to Chris as she slung objects and mumbled the word *men* a lot.

That was familiar behavior, too familiar, and he would never again allow that kind of woman in his life. Besides that, his life was too odd and messy for even a good-tempered woman to deal with.

Why would the only woman he'd been attracted to since being engaged seven years ago also have fits of rage? That said something about him, didn't it? But he'd spotted the red flags in less than a day this time. Still, his attraction to her was disturbing. Why had it felt so right, so very God inspired, when he saw her? Maybe he'd been lonely and hadn't realized it. All the whys aside, he needed to take some steps back and not give off any more vibes of being interested in her.

Abigail came around the corner. "Roy?" Her voice was louder this time.

"He was in paddock six last I saw him."

She smiled. "You're in six."

"Oh, then he's in one."

"Who's on first?"

Her mood was definitely lighter now than it had been since Saturday evening. And he knew the comedic routine she was referring to, but he resisted the urge to banter with her. "Paddock one," he repeated.

She paused, tilting her head slightly. "Everything okay?"

He hadn't expected her to be so direct, but he probably should have. "Maybe we moved a little too fast."

"Too fast?" Her expression hid nothing as inquisitiveness mixed with disbelief. "We've not had a date or a kiss."

"It's me, I think."

She studied him, clearly waiting for him to give a reasonable explanation. If she wanted him to be blunt, he had no problem with that.

"Look, I'm not comfortable with any woman who loses her temper like you did with Roy on Saturday."

She blinked, obviously disappointed. "But maybe I was in the right and he deserved it."

"Maybe so. Still . . ." He shrugged.

She stood firm, staring at him as if she might argue back, but then she sighed. "Okay." She elongated the word. "Not a problem. Denki for your honesty." She started to walk off and then paused. "Listen, the standardbred five-year-old bay, Houdini, seems to be acting strange. His hind legs seem a little wobbly and he looks lethargic, although I only caught a glimpse of him, so I could be completely wrong. Have you noticed anything unusual?"

That was it? She was as willing to let go of him as he was of her?

"Nee, but our hands have been full with the new string."

"Ya. Denki." She walked off and disappeared behind the array of horses and corrals.

Maybe he'd been wrong about her. *Stop.* He wouldn't second-guess himself. People who were endearing at first and yet given to fits of rage knew how to control themselves when it suited them. He knew that.

The next few hours passed quickly as they walked among the horses, feeding them from their hands, talking to and grooming them, giving those who would allow it a sense of safety. That was the first step in building trust.

As the horses settled, it was easier to see Roy and Abigail as they worked. Abigail had taken Houdini to the stables a couple of hours ago, and then she tended to the established herd. As she worked with ease despite the horses' skittish and surly moods, she didn't seem unreasonable or cantankerous. But that's how those with hidden rage hooked unsuspecting people. They seemed normal but then flew into fits of rage and lied for no sound reasons. It seemed rather rare for women to fit that mold, but apparently he was good at finding them and being instantly attracted to them.

Chris and Roy each had a horse by the harness in adjoining corrals, soothing them. Chris had received a few texts today from his brothers, but Roy's phone seemed to be blowing up with texts.

Abigail came out of the stable. "Houdini needs to be seen."

"What?" Roy's eyes grew large, as if he was about to panic.

"His fever is 102.5, and I've called the vet, but he's fifty miles out with several other farms to go to. He said he might be able to get here today, but it's more likely he won't arrive until around noon tomorrow."

Roy left the corral and confronted his sister. "You called the vet?"

"I'm sure it's fine." Chris slowly went toward them, hoping for Roy's sake to de-escalate any impending argument, since Roy had seemed to come out on the short end of Saturday's discussion. Chris remembered all too well similar scenes with his fiancée. "It's probably a cold. Maybe a flu at the worst."

"Ya, and I'm hoping for that." Abigail tightened the black wool scarf around her neck and dusted her leather-gloved hands against each other. "But we can't take any chances. We need to isolate him and disinfect his stall and everything in it just to be on the safe side."

What she was hinting at was every horse owner's worse nightmare: the dreaded EHV-1. There were a lot of types of EHV, but type one was deadly, and it spread like wildfire through direct and indirect contact.

"Houdini has a fever and is lethargic. All we need to do is keep an eye on him for a few days," Chris said. "You checked Lady Belle's fever half a dozen times on Saturday, and she clearly has only a cold."

Abigail angled her head. "Could you drop the accusatory tone, please? It's not as if I'm making up symptoms just to create work. Houdini is dribbling urine, and he seems to be struggling with his balance."

"The phrase 'seems to be struggling' is key here. We watch and wait," Chris said.

She stepped closer, her brown eyes boring into him. "Your statement didn't sound like a suggestion, Chris. Look, you and I are frustrated with each other right now, but let's not allow that to spill over into this. This is about the horses, and my opinion counts." She turned to Roy. "We can't take any chances. Once the vet does the test, it could take as long as three days to get the results. If it's EHV-1, we've got to put distance between all the horses and start disinfecting everything, including our hands every few minutes."

"You know the chance that you're wrong is really high." Chris couldn't see jumping through hoops just because she *felt* something needed to be done. Hadn't he done that enough in the past to last a lifetime?

"That's true, but worst-case scenario, we work our fingers to the bone round the clock for a few days for no good reason. However, if I'm right, we will have done everything possible to keep the virus from wiping out the entire string days before we receive confirmation of a diagnosis."

Heat ran through Chris, but was he angry with Abigail or with his ex-fiancée? "There's no time for all that."

"We'll be better at making time now than we'll be at replacing a string of horses weeks down the road."

"Okay. Enough." Roy held a hand out, palm up, to each of them. "We'll split the difference. Lucky and Thunder are already isolated. I disinfected everything of theirs earlier today. Quarantine Houdini.

Go ahead and separate Pippi for your peace of mind, Abigail. But we don't take the time to do anything else special for the older string until the vet gives us his opinion. If he believes it may be EHV-1, we'll do as you want before getting the test results. Until then, we keep working with the new string."

Six

Jemima's body felt too heavy for her to remain standing, and her heart physically ached. Fog had taken over her mind, but she was in the kitchen, fulfilling her duties. She lifted the lid from the large pot and stirred the chicken tortilla soup. The aromas of the chicken and vegetables simmering with the cumin, garlic, and chili powder helped her feel grounded, as if doing a chore brought an ounce of normalcy to her world regardless of what was going on inside her. Earlier today while Laura was at school and the boys were down for their naps, Carolyn helped wash the vegetables and add spices. Somehow the familiar routine put salve on Jemima's raw emotions.

She'd been sorting through her thoughts and feelings for two days. Maybe if yesterday hadn't been a between-Sunday for Mirth Amish with no church service, the preachers would've shared a helpful insight and she would've gotten her thoughts and attitude in the right place. What nagged at her the most was a sense of betrayal she couldn't shake. Had Roy's act of emptying the account without telling her been disloyal? It'd been a hard hit. That was for sure. Why had he kept it a secret from her?

As bad as that was, it only added to the deeper concern. No matter where her thoughts and emotions dragged her, she couldn't shake this one thing: Roy wasn't himself. He hadn't been for quite a while.

She checked the time. Almost seven. What? She looked outside, and blackness greeted her. She'd had no idea it was that late. Anytime horses arrived on the farm, it was a day of monumental tasks: calming them, cleaning them, fitting the ones that needed new shoes. Roy, Chris, and Abigail had to be swamped. Maybe she should take dinner out to them instead of waiting here in the house.

Behind the darkness, she saw lanterns shining from inside the stables. When Abigail arrived at the farm after school, she usually came inside to eat and chat before starting to work. But she hadn't today. All three workers should've been in for supper an hour ago. What was keeping them?

Jemima had fed the children two hours ago. She'd then bathed Simeon and Nevin, who managed to wear as much of their dinner as they had eaten. Laura was currently doing her homework while Carolyn and her brothers played.

The baby giggled, and Jemima turned in that direction. In the play area of the kitchen, Carolyn was on the floor, making silly faces at Simeon. Nevin was nearby, playing with an array of toy marine life.

Jemima grabbed the large round thermos from a cabinet. Within a few minutes, she'd ladled into it enough soup to share and packed it in a picnic bag, along with a few mugs, some tortillas to dip into the broth, spoons, napkins, bottles of water, and a couple of apples.

"Carolyn." When her little girl looked up, Jemima spoke Pennsylvania Dutch, telling her they were going to take mugs and soup out to her Daed, Abigail, and Chris.

"Gut." Carolyn clapped her hands and jumped to her feet.

Earlier, she and her brothers had seen the horses arrive while Laura was at school. They'd watched from the window for quite a while before growing restless and moving on to other things. *"Kann Ich helfe?"*

Jemima appreciated her daughter's desire to help, but she'd told her, "Not today." The workers were too distracted when they received new horses, and the horses were flighty. It wasn't a good time for a five-year-old to do anything but observe from a safe distance.

But now Carolyn ran to the back door and grabbed her and her brothers' coats. *"Bischt geh,* Laura?"

"Nee." Laura looked up from her homework, catching her Mamm's eye, and smiled as if to say, *Aren't those little ones the cutest?* It was sweet of Carolyn to ask Laura if she was going.

Jemima nodded and grinned. Her heart felt a little lighter as Carolyn helped her brothers get their coats on. Their family could do this. Roy and she could get the finances under control and buy a food truck. It would be a while, but the dream wasn't dead, only postponed.

A desire to pray for Roy washed over her, but anger stared it down. She wasn't ready to pray for him, not yet. Why hadn't he told her about using the money? *Why?* Maybe Abigail was right after all: men did whatever they made up their minds to do. But Jemima couldn't afford to look at her marriage with cynicism. Roy was struggling with something, and she needed to respect his right to work through it on his own.

When the honeymoon was over—and for them it had lasted about two years—marriage seemed to be a constant war between gratefulness and resentment, between contentment and restlessness, between what was too real and what wasn't real enough.

A lot of women criticized Abigail for being too picky and finding reasons to push away every interested man, and there had been many of them. But on days when Jemima was painfully honest with herself about what marriage was and wasn't, she secretly cheered for Abigail. However, being single wasn't for Jemima, even on those days when she felt as if she were crossing a stretch of desert in search of an oasis. She loved Roy and their children with all her heart.

She strapped Simeon and Nevin in the little red wagon that she frequently used to transport the littlest ones and other things across the farm. She placed the packed supper on the other end of the wagon.

Jemima put her coat on and grabbed a flashlight. "Kumm, Carolyn." She turned on the flashlight and passed it to Carolyn. *"Loss uns geh see Daed un Aenti Abi?"* There really wasn't any reason for Jemima to ask Carolyn if she wanted to go see her dad and Aunt Abi. Of course Carolyn wanted to go see them.

"Un guck beim wege da gauls!"

Jemima nodded, agreeing that they would look at all the horses.

Carolyn bounced out the door, and Jemima followed her, pulling the wagon.

Why was the veterinarian's car here? Jemima had seen the small SUV many times over the years. Ed provided good medical care to their herd, but she couldn't think of another time when he'd come the same day as the new arrivals.

The wagon wheels crunched the gravel and then the brown grass on their way to the stables, and Carolyn went ahead of them, having a great time making the flashlight beam go wherever she wanted. After a few minutes they reached the stable, and Jemima slid the door open to let in herself, Carolyn, and the wagon with the boys and food. She shut the door behind her, but the group of adults didn't seem to notice them. Abigail was standing next to the vet, listening, her thumb curved around her chin. Jemima had seen her make this face before. Something was wrong. Roy was next to his sister, and Chris stood apart from the group but was still in the conversation.

Roy reached into a stall and rubbed Thunder's forehead. "How much contact has Houdini had with Lucky and Thunder this past week?"

Abigail shrugged. "I'm not sure. They spent one afternoon in the same pasture, but that's all, I think."

Roy looked into Lucky's stall, probably searching for signs of illness.

Abigail spotted her niece and waved. "Hey, *mei lieb.*"

Carolyn's face lit up, as it always did when Abigail called her "my love."

"*Hallo,* Aenti Abi! Hallo, Daed!" Carolyn held up a mug and blurted out in Pennsylvania Dutch about the tortilla soup and helping to make it. Abigail smiled and responded warmly, despite whatever was troubling her. Jemima continued to pull the wagon and moved in closer.

Roy looked up from his phone, quickly slid it into his pocket, and came to embrace Jemima. "We have something of a pickle going on." He turned to his young daughter and pointed across the barn. "Carolyn, can you go sit on that bale of hay and keep an eye on the horses in those stalls over there?"

Jemima reached into the picnic bag, handed an apple to Carolyn, and told her that when she was finished eating it, she could feed bits to some of the horses as a treat.

Carolyn's eyes lit up at the mention of feeding the horses a treat. She took it and the flashlight and went across the barn to sit on the hay bale her Daed had pointed out.

The vet tucked items into his bag. "As I said, I don't have the right equipment to test for EHV-1, so I'll send off these blood and nasal secretion samples to be tested. I might get the results back in two days, but it could take as much as three."

"Your advice?" Abigail asked.

"I agree with you. If it was my string, I'd treat this situation as if we already knew it was EHV-1."

"EHV-1?" Jemima's heart moved to her throat. "I've heard of it, of course, but would you tell me more?"

Ed gave her a sympathetic half smile. "It's in the family of herpes viruses, though it can't be passed to humans. A large percentage of horses have it but are asymptomatic, meaning without symptoms. Sometimes stress causes it. Has Houdini been sick lately?"

"Not that I know of." Roy pulled his phone from his pocket and gave a quick look at the screen. "He was leased out last week to an Englisch family who's leased many horses over the years. They have one horse, so I'll call them a little later to give a heads-up and see what the week was like for Houdini."

"Stress may not have been the cause. It's a very contagious disease. Maybe their horse has it. Either way, it can result in neurological symptoms. See how he's holding this back leg?" Houdini was standing on three legs, but the other leg was wobbly.

Jemima turned to her husband and his sister. "What does this mean for the herd?"

Abigail drew a deep breath. "Hopefully nothing more than two tons of work. But the timing couldn't be worse."

"Ya." Roy shook his head, looking anxious. "The new horses are under stress from the move. The older horses are under stress because of the arrival of the new horses. Both situations make them more susceptible to catching the virus. If they catch this strand that's causing the hind-limb weakness, they could develop the same symptoms, or way worse, and then have to be euthanized."

"Euthanized?" Jemima couldn't believe it. She knew such an illness existed but never imagined it might happen to their horses.

Ed snapped his bag closed. "We see breakouts of this virus at racetracks. Roy is right. You could lose a decent percentage of your new herd if the virus runs rampant."

Abigail took down a couple of ranch ropes hanging on the wall and looped them over her head and shoulder. "We need to separate the horses as quickly as we can." She grabbed several harnesses.

Ed held up his phone, showing the screen. "The Doppler radar shows the temps dropping more than they already have. The cold snap—*colder* snap—will hit in a few hours, and it's supposed to start sleeting around three in the morning. Cold weather can cause stress too. Plus, treating a virus like this should take place in as warm and comfortable a setting as you can get."

Abigail rubbed her forehead. "We don't have enough stable space to put a disinfected empty stall on each side of every occupied stall."

Roy seemed distracted. How was that possible? The lives of the horses and the family's livelihood were at stake and he looked bored with all of it. He looked at his phone again.

Chris stepped closer. "When I was out riding on Saturday, I saw an old poultry barn about a mile from here."

"Ya." Abigail looked pleased. "It belongs to our *Grossdaadi,* and it hasn't been used in forever. All we need is wood to put up temporary stalls."

"Is there a sawmill nearby where we could get wood this time of evening?" Chris asked.

Roy looked up from his phone before he shoved it back into his pocket. "Not this late, but we should have the supplies over in—"

The phone buzzed several times, as if someone was calling, and he seemed to lose his train of thought. He looked at his phone again.

"Roy?" Jemima said.

"Uh, ya." He shoved his phone back into his pocket. "Abigail, you know where the whole Graber family stores leftover wood from their projects."

"Ach," Abigail gasped. "That's right. I haven't thought of that in a really long time. Everyone still does that?"

"Ya." Roy pulled out his phone and glanced at it again.

"Okay." Ed slung his bag over his shoulder. "You guys have a plan. The quicker you act, the better. I'm going to send these samples off to the lab. Good luck to you all." He gave a quick wave and left.

Roy gestured at the food Jemima had brought. "We better wash up and eat while we have time. We may not get another break until daylight. Should we—"

His phone rang again, and he walked away. "What?" He used the same tone as he had that early morning three days ago. He stormed out of the barn.

Jemima gestured to Roy's exit with her head, silently asking Abigail if she knew what was going on.

Abigail shrugged and turned to Chris. "The horses still outside need to be caught and tethered at fence posts a good distance apart."

"What can I do?" Jemima asked. She would have to get the children in bed quickly and get Laura to keep watch until they fell asleep, but she needed to help in some way.

"We'll need some sort of food and water containers for every horse," Abigail said, "just big and strong enough that we can keep them comfortable for the next twelve hours. We'll also need enough blankets to cover them."

Chris grabbed ropes and harnesses. "Every container that's not coming from your kitchen, even if it's been in storage in a barn, needs to be disinfected, just to be on the safe side."

"Ya, no problem," Jemima said. "But what—"

"Sorry." Roy hurried back into the barn, his face drained of color. "I *have* to go. I'm so sorry."

"What?" Jemima's knees threatened to give way. "This is *your* horse farm, and it's in crisis!"

Roy pointed to his sister. "She can do anything I can. And Chris is all the help she needs. I'm sorry. I'll be back as quick as I can." He grabbed a bridle off the wall and opened the stall to his horse.

Jemima looked at Abigail and gestured at the children. "Watch them for a sec?" The boys were still in the wagon next to the adults, and Carolyn hadn't moved from her perch on the bale of hay as she continued to sing to herself.

"Ya." Abigail patted Simeon's head.

Jemima went to her husband. "Roy?"

He turned to face her, wearing a grimace as if he was in pain, but didn't slow down as he put the bridle on his horse and led it out of the stall and out of the stable.

She followed, the cold wind biting through her coat. As he put his foot in a stirrup, she said, "Wait!"

Roy lowered his leg and faced her, and in the silvery glow of the moon, she saw unbearable stress on his face.

"It'll be fine. I promise. But I have to go."

"Who called you? What's going on?"

"There's no time to explain, but I'll tell you everything later. I promise. Right now I need you to trust me and let me go."

He had made a lot of promises of late and kept very few.

Holding on to one rein, he took a few steps closer and kissed her on the forehead. "Okay?"

She nodded.

He rode off, his retreating figure soon blending with the nighttime shadows. Was one or more of their boarded horses sick too? That had to be it, but why didn't he just tell her that?

Seven

Roy nudged his horse to go faster as he rode toward Tiffany's, each gallop of Amigo's hooves jolting him further into his grim reality. The wind blew his hat off, but he couldn't stop to retrieve it. How on earth was this his life? It was all wrong.

How could a night he barely recalled bring this much grief?

The trees whooshed by as he turned the corner to Tiffany's long gravel driveway. Good grief, he was such a fool. A fool to think Tiffany could be a decent mother, a fool not to tell Jemima what was going on as soon as she recovered from giving birth to Simeon, a fool to have entered Tiffany's house without a family member with him. He was choking on all the lies and regrets that had grown wild like weeds, and he had no way to get rid of them or even pare them back. He couldn't stay outside the barn today for even five minutes and tell Jemima what was happening because he had no time.

Tiffany's last text had read, If you want to have a say in where Heidi will be for the rest of her life, I need cash now. We both know the Amish stash their money at home more often than in banks. If you don't have any, your Daed does. Get it. In twenty minutes I'm gone. Alone.

Would innocent little Heidi pay the price for his and Tiffany's mistakes? He couldn't let that happen. He urged his horse faster until he arrived at the rental house.

He dismounted in one motion and wrapped the reins loosely around a shrub near Tiffany's house. Amigo was a good horse and wouldn't go anywhere without Roy. Tiffany's car was parked in the driveway. He glanced in the sedan's window. Despite the darkness, he saw that the removable infant car seat was gone, but the base was still buckled in. *Please, God, let Heidi be okay.*

With a few giant strides, he bounded to the front door and banged on it with his fist. "Tiffany, are you here?" He looked through the window next to the front door. No sign of anyone. He could see Heidi's bassinet but couldn't hear her. He pounded on the door again. "Tiffany!"

He could hear stomping, and then the door was yanked open. "I told you I couldn't do this! I asked you to bring me money and take her. Did you at least bring it today?"

What did that mean? He hit the door with his fist. "*Where* is the baby? Where is Heidi?" Who was he becoming? He couldn't recall ever raising his voice this way to another person. When she didn't answer immediately, he pushed past her and ran through the house. His heart thudded as if he'd sprinted here.

As he looked in Tiffany's bedroom and hurried to check the tub in the bathroom, memories and shame flooded him. The night he'd come here to fix the plumbing, Tiffany and her friends had been drinking pretty heavily. He remembered the cold drink in his hand, the ice clinking against the glass. He recalled some flowery scent that clung to Tiffany as she leaned in and kissed him on the lips.

He tried to shake the memories. The bathroom was empty, but as he left it, he saw the bed, Tiffany's bed. His gut twisted at the thoughts of that night, but everything had gone blank after the kiss until the next morning when he woke with his pants missing.

Would it matter to Jemima that he had no recollection of wanting Tiffany, no memory of their night together? He swallowed the fresh shame and remorse and thundered into Heidi's room.

There was no sign of her other than the clothes and baby items strewed about the small rental house.

When he came back to the living room, he saw Tiffany standing by the door with her arms crossed. "She's safe. I'm not a monster."

That's what she told herself—she wasn't a monster. Not long ago he would have agreed with her assessment. He'd convinced himself that she was struggling under the confines of their unfair, unwanted relationship, overwrought with changing hormones, and pushed to the brink from lack of sleep. But maybe reality was trying to get the truth through to him. Maybe she was a monster. Whatever was the most accurate description, he wanted to shake some sense into her. "Where is Heidi?" He punched each word.

"I'll tell you when you bring me the money I need to start my life over. I know you have it, with your beautiful horse farm that your father just *gave* you, and your herd of new thoroughbreds."

He took a deep breath to try to avoid completely losing his temper. "I've given you all the money I have. I paid for Heidi's birth and medical bills. I bought you a car. I've paid Daed his rent on this place for the past nine months while you've lived here for free. I bought all the baby items, diapers, and formula. There *is* no more money."

"Fine. I'm gone." Tiffany grabbed her coat, went out the front door, and ran to her car.

The door slammed behind him as he followed her across the dark lawn and hopped into the passenger's side. He wouldn't let her leave town until Heidi was in his arms. "You're going to take me to Heidi *now*."

"Get out, Roy." Tiffany started the car. Amigo shuffled his hooves a little but didn't run.

Roy closed the car door and buckled the seat belt. "I won't. Just drive me to wherever she is. Then you can leave me there and be gone. You can keep the car and anything else you want. I don't care. I just want to know where Heidi is."

Tiffany rolled her eyes. "You want to go for a ride? Let's go for a ride." She put the car in reverse and jammed her foot on the pedal, whipping it around, the gravel flying. The car lights moved across the yard, giving only glimpses of scenery. Amigo reared, but his reins didn't pull free of the shrub. Roy couldn't worry about him now. Tiffany put the car in drive and sped down the driveway. Was she trying to scare him? She pulled onto the main road, and the car's tires squealed as they got traction on the asphalt.

He wanted to yell at her and rail against how awful she was being, but that wouldn't get him closer to Heidi. Instead he closed his eyes and prayed, *God, forgive me. Protect Heidi until I can find her.*

"Tiffany, I need you to tell me where Heidi is. She's a baby. She's helpless and innocent. Please. *Please.*"

Tiffany said nothing.

Roy studied her face, trying to gauge what she could possibly be thinking. "I've been good to you. I'm sorry about that night I was on meds and you'd been drinking. But I've tried to step up the best I could. I understand if you need to leave, but please tell me where Heidi is."

She accelerated through a curve in the road, lights illuminating the way. "Ugh, fine! You're being so ridiculous about this. She's with Amber, okay? I dropped her off this morning."

Amber? Roy first saw her the night of the incident, and he'd seen her a few times since. Even if she wasn't drunk or high, she didn't seem capable of taking care of others. "Where does she live? Take me to her place. I'll get Heidi, and you can go."

"So you don't trust my judgment? Sheesh, Roy, maybe you should come up with some money and I'll take you straight to your daughter." Tiffany's front right tire ran off the side of the road, and the car jolted.

"Be careful." Buggies also used this road. Roy had a flash of the helplessness he felt the day of the accident with Laura in the rig.

Tiffany yanked the steering wheel, overcorrecting and crossing the double yellow lines before straightening the car again. "Please. You don't drive. Don't you dare try to give me driving lessons." As if to push her point further, she drove in the center of the road, the car straddling the double yellow lines.

"What are you doing?"

"You're used to being in control, aren't you? With your perfect little family and the horse farm your heart always desired. Well, welcome to my life: an out-of-control nightmare."

Control. Was that what he was trying to hold on to by not telling the truth to Jemima? But now the situation had spiraled beyond anything he'd ever imagined. Dealing with this situation was like trying to grasp the fallen reins on a bucking unbroken stallion.

As they drove over a hill, a horse and buggy came into view. Time shifted into slow motion, just as it had the day of the accident. He covered his face with his hands so the passerby couldn't see he was Amish.

Tiffany accelerated. "It's dark. How are they going to see you? You're an idiot, Roy. I can't believe I ever put my future in your hands."

Covering himself had been a silly move, but his guilt was so thick that he felt as if it was obvious to everyone all the time.

"Yeah, you're right. I've been an idiot. I never should've let you move onto our property. Never should've had anything to do with you at all."

"So now you're saying that our daughter is a mistake? I thought she was *so* important to you. Are we finally hitting a bit of truth, Roy?" Tiffany steered the car around a sharp bend.

"Of course she's important!"

Tiffany looked over at him, taking her eyes off the road. "But her mother is disposable, huh?"

As the car drifted to the middle of the road, Roy pointed and yelled, "Watch where you're going!"

"I know how to drive!" Tiffany yanked the steering wheel back to the right, but the guardrail had ended. All four tires left the road as the car went down an embankment.

Roy felt weightless as the car skidded off the road and began careening sideways down the steep slope, ripping through shrubs and trees as if they were toothpicks. His body was like a rag doll, but his seat belt held him in place.

Time stood still, but the car kept going. This was it. He was going to die in this car with Tiffany. A surreal acceptance and peace took over his mind. *Jemima, I'm so sorry. I love you.*

The world went black.

Eight

Abigail's hands ached as she pounded another nail into plywood, securing a temporary wall to the final stall. Because her phone battery had died, she didn't know what time it was. All she knew for sure was that exhaustion had set in a couple of hours ago and there was no rest in sight. But she and Chris had turned her grandfather's former commercial-size poultry barn into a makeshift stable with stalls the proper distance apart so any infected horse wouldn't share the virus with its neighbor.

Despite the conversation they'd had about twelve hours ago, Chris had been dutiful and polite. She'd kept her emotions reeled in, refusing to wish that the two of them could be warmer and friendlier, and avoiding saying anything that might make him leave the farm.

The clattering of rigging echoed through the old barn, and Abigail caught a glimpse of Pippi shaking her head. She was at the far end of the barn, hitched to a work cart that Chris and Abigail had used to move wood from her grandfather's storage shed to here.

Chris walked into the barn, carrying two five-gallon buckets of fresh water. They'd built most of the stalls together, and then he'd gone to a nearby well to get water while she finished securing this wall.

He set the full buckets on the dirt floor and picked up two empty ones. "You about done?" His tone was kind enough, but it held little warmth, little friendliness. That was annoying. Where was Roy anyway? This was *his* livelihood, not hers or Chris's!

"Close to being done." She forced a chuckle, trying to keep things light between them. The last thing Graber Horse Farm needed was for Chris to walk away. "Why? Did you need a hand carrying the water?"

She chided herself for asking him that. The importance of keeping a lid on her naturally spicy attitude couldn't be overstated. Despite being thin, Chris was physically strong, and that was a necessary asset right now. It was imperative to get the animals inside before the sleet began.

"I'm gut, denki."

Was that a smile tugging at his lips? Should she tell him what Roy had done with her money and why she'd come unglued with him? Her instincts said no. Chris hadn't asked why she'd lost her temper. He saw it happen and decided she wasn't worthy to pursue, which said a lot about him, none of it good.

As he left the barn, she smacked the stubborn nail with the hammer over and over again. Her Daed and uncles would be here lending a hand if she told them what was going on. But the family had provided so much help after Roy and Laura's accident last year that Roy, Jemima, and she had decided not to ask their relatives for anything else. Graber Horse Farm and Roy owed everyone a debt of favors. They wouldn't accrue more. Besides, missing a full night of sleep to work in this cold barn would be too hard on the older generation, and all the cousins had little ones to tend to.

Abigail and Chris had raided every piece of usable wood, and when that ran out, they began taking apart the old shed. It was a historic shed, but Abigail would take responsibility for the decision if any of the family took issue with their using it.

When the last piece of wood was secure, Abigail tossed the hammer into the toolbox and gently tugged the cowhide work gloves off each hand. Even with the gloves, she had blisters and tender red spots that would soon become blisters.

Chris returned with full buckets of water. "This will be enough to fill all the containers and have water left over."

They'd confiscated all manner of odd containers from wherever they could find them and tacked them to the wall of each stall, one to hold water and one to hold feed. The water would freeze regularly during this cold snap, but there was no time or money to buy heated water dispensers, so this was all they could do for now.

"Ya. I agree. Denki." She brushed wisps of hair from her face using the back of her hand. There was no telling what disarray her hair was in. She'd removed her prayer Kapp and put on a much warmer white knit beanie hours ago. When the bun proved to be uncomfortable under the knit cap, she'd removed the pins but left the bun. Her guess was that half of it had fallen down.

His eyes moved to her palms. "You need to put medicated cream on your hands and wrap them in gauze before wearing the gloves again." His tone didn't hint of actually caring. He was just informing someone what needed to be done. He then went to the stall she'd just finished and shook the sides to check for steadiness. For goodness' sake, he'd put up the frame for it, yet he was inspecting her work anyway. She stifled a sigh.

"Ya"—she spoke softly, hoping to hide her irritation—"I'll get to that in a few hours." She tried not to wince as she put the gloves back on. "Right now we need to go to the farm and start leading the horses here."

Chris headed toward Pippi, and Abigail followed. To his credit, he hadn't complained once about doing all this work before the vet's test results came back. But whatever spark of interest he'd had in her when they met a few days ago was clearly gone, and that had to be for the best. His presence tugged at her entirely too much. But any man who couldn't deal with valid emotions from a woman wouldn't be suited for her in the long run. Apparently he needed a soft-spoken woman regardless of the circumstances or how the woman felt.

Whatever.

She grabbed a throw blanket from the seat of the work cart as they climbed in, praying Pippi wouldn't get sick. It wasn't likely, since Abigail lived with her parents and she kept Pippi in her parents' stable. But she rode Pippi to the horse farm almost daily, and when she didn't need Pippi for her work there, she let her out in the pasture with the other horses. Even in her exhaustion, fear kept squeezing her heart, jolting her nerves. She couldn't bear to think about any of the horses dying because of this EHV-1 virus or any other reason.

Chris tugged on the reins, turning the horse and low-riding cart onto Jemima's driveway. The wind howled and sleet pelted, and he longed to be on a couch in front of a roaring fire with a huge plate of food in hand. Abigail held the blanket over her head like an umbrella, trying to keep the sleet from hitting her face. How was she holding up? He'd never seen a woman so determined to accomplish a goal.

Jemima hurried out the door of the home, throwing a quilt around her head and shoulders. "Wait!" She ran toward them. "Is Roy at the poultry barn, or have you seen him?"

Chris brought the horse and cart to a stop.

Abigail pulled the sides of the blanket back, and he could see the concern on her face. "Nee."

Jemima's eyes widened. "Not at all since he left here over seven hours ago?"

"Sorry, Jem, but no."

"Why haven't you been answering your phones?" Jemima asked. "I've gone to the phone shanty a dozen times and tried to call each of you. Roy, too, of course."

"My cell died around ten last night." Abigail looked at Chris.

"Ya, mine lost all energy before then."

Abigail adjusted the blanket, probably to accommodate the new direction of the wind and sleet. "My phone was last charged before school yesterday, and cold weather drains batteries."

"So Roy's phone could've died too?" Jemima asked, sounding hopeful.

"Ya, sure." Abigail nodded.

But Chris had seen Roy recharge it, using a solar-powered car battery in the stable, less than two hours before he left here. Chris wouldn't volunteer that information.

"Did you call the Kurtzes' phone shanty?" Abigail asked.

"I tried, but no one answered. Should we call the police?"

"I can't see that being helpful." Chris leaned forward, peering around Abigail. "He's an adult who left of his own free will mere hours ago. Has he disappeared like this before?"

"Ya." Jemima wiped her cheeks, and although it was too dark to see well, she seemed to be crying.

"Jem," Abigail whispered, "why is this the first I've heard of it?"

"He's trying to get the farm on its feet after missing so much time after the accident. Sometimes he leaves during the night and I don't see him again until lunch or suppertime. I thought it would stop once he had more help."

"Maybe it will yet." Abigail tightened the blanket around her. "But tonight we need to keep moving."

"Something is wrong." Jemima grabbed Abigail's arm. "I can feel it." She tapped on the quilt that covered her chest. "We've got to search for him."

Abigail glanced at Chris, and he saw compassion in her eyes. She held up her index finger to him and lifted her brows, asking him to wait a minute. He nodded, and she stepped out of the cart.

"Jem, look at me." She waited until Jemima stopped scanning the surroundings for her husband. "I need you to take a deep breath and hear me."

"You're not going to help me search for your brother?"

"I can't." She gestured at Chris. "We can't. We're fighting for your livelihood, and that has to remain our focus for the next six or seven hours. There are colts, yearlings, mares, geldings, and stallions to deal with, many with past wounds and personality issues we know nothing about yet. The more stress they're under, the less their immune systems will work on their behalf.

"Roy's behavior tonight sounds as if it fits with who he's been of late. But if you're truly desperate to search for him now rather than tomorrow after we've eaten and slept, call our Daed or the bishop. Get an Amish search party if need be, but Chris and I are doing all we can and more than we should."

Jemima blinked. "You're right." She wiped her cheeks again. "You're absolutely right. Do whatever you came here for, and I'll pack some coffee and pastries for you to take with you. I'll put a charger cord and the cell power bank in with the other things. Charge your phones, and if you hear from him, call the phone shanty."

Abigail hugged Jemima and got back into the cart.

Chris's mind raced, taking his heart with it. Abigail was amazing. She had grit. And compassion. With the exception of Saturday night with Roy, she'd taken every setback in stride.

His heart pounded with a desire to know her better. But he'd backed away, and she'd accepted his retreat, so it no longer mattered what he wanted.

Nine

Jemima urged her horse to pull the buggy faster as she neared the poultry barn, the icy grass crackling under the wheels. Maybe her visit here was completely unnecessary and Roy was home by now.

She blinked, trying to clear the sleepiness and stop the tears forming in her eyes. *He's not been gone even a full day. It's not that unusual.* Then why did it feel so wrong?

She spotted Abigail coming out of the poultry-barn-turned-stable, leading Pippi, who was pulling the work cart. Chris was behind her, shoving a toolbox onto the cart.

"Hey." It was all Jemima could manage to say, but she got out of the carriage with a canvas bag that held a thermos of fresh coffee and several slices of day-old apple bread. She'd given them food the last time she saw them, but that had been five hours ago.

Abigail saw her and brought the cart to a stop. "Hi, Jem. Our phones are charged, and Roy hasn't called or texted either of us since he left the stables soon after the vet."

Jemima longed to scream her fear and rage to the heavens, but she kept her movements normal while trying to reel in her emotions. She knew that Abigail or Chris would've already let her know if they'd heard from him or seen him. But knowing that hadn't stopped her from hoping that Roy had contacted them during the night.

"You guys got a minute?" Jemima pulled the thermos and a mug out of the canvas bag she'd brought.

"Ya, sure." Abigail patted the horse.

Jemima wished she didn't need their help. They had to be completely exhausted and ready to go home and sleep.

Jemima poured coffee into the lid of the thermos. "I took Laura to school, and your substitute was there. On my way back I stopped at your home to catch a minute with your parents." She passed the lid to Abigail and then filled the mug. "Without my asking them anything, they mentioned not seeing Roy in more than a week and said they were missing him." She passed the mug to Chris. "I gave excuses and then told them about the possible EHV-1 situation and some of the work involved. They volunteered to keep Carolyn, Nevin, and Simeon for me and to pick up Laura from school. I took them up on it."

"Ya, I understand." Abigail wrapped her hands around the plastic mug, looking worn out as she took a sip.

It wasn't likely Abigail understood Jemima's goal, not yet anyway. Jemima pulled out two slices of apple bread, each wrapped in a cloth, from the canvas bag. She needed favors—big ones—but these two needed some fuel, and while they ate, she'd fill them in.

Abigail and Chris unwrapped their pieces of homemade apple bread and took a few quick bites, using the cloth to keep from touching the bread with their fingers. After working through the night, they needed extra calories, and Jemima wished she had brought them boiled eggs and bacon.

Jemima fidgeted with the straps to the canvas bag. "I went by the Kurtzes' place, too. I took them a loaf of cinnamon bread I'd made and said I was there to thank them for all the meals they'd provided for Roy this past year. I kept the conversation casual but found out he hasn't been to their place in six or seven days."

Abigail jolted, spilling coffee. She swayed, and Jemima wondered if she was about to pass out. Chris grabbed her by the arm, steadying her, and whispered something. Abigail nodded as she eased free of Chris's hand.

They didn't look like the couple who'd brought Jemima her horse and carriage three days ago. Had it been only three days since Saturday? This nightmare she couldn't wake from seemed to have been going on forever.

"*Bischt allrecht?*" Jemima poured more coffee into Abigail's plastic mug.

"Just a bit woozy." Abigail took a drink of her coffee.

Jemima assumed that the news of when Roy had last been at the Kurtzes' must've contradicted what he'd told Abigail this past week.

Abigail took another sip of coffee. "Why didn't you tell my Mamm or Daed or the Kurtzes what's going on?"

"I don't know. He's not himself. We both know that. I don't want to start anything that could lead to an inquisition by the ministers. How would getting into trouble straighten out whatever is crooked inside him?"

"I'm sorry, Jem. I am. I don't understand him of late, and I've tried."

Chris finished his last bite of apple bread. "Has he fallen off the wagon?"

"What?" Abigail asked, sounding much like her brother did when he took calls he didn't like.

"Look"—Chris shook crumbs from the cloth onto the brown grass—"I don't know Roy, but if his behavior has changed a lot over a short period of time, maybe he's dealing with an addiction, like drugs or alcohol."

Jemima's heart raced. "He was taking painkillers after surviving a bad accident last year. You think he's addicted? Maybe he took too many and overdosed and—"

"No one here was thinking that." Abigail moved in closer to Chris, and Jemima could no longer see her face. "Rather than voicing ideas of why he's acting so out of character, how about we focus on finding him? You know, avoid the whole cart-before-the-horse thing."

"Sorry," Chris whispered to Abigail. He peered beyond Abigail to see Jemima. "She's right. So where do you think we should begin looking, Jemima?"

"We should search the farm and maybe the nearby woods and the ditches running alongside the roads."

Chris looked toward the horizon. "That's a lot of acreage for three people to cover. Unless he's sitting up and making noise, we'd likely overlook him. We need a solid clue of what area to explore." He walked a few feet away, apparently studying the land, and then turned back. "Abigail, any chance you and your brother share a cell phone account?"

"Ya. We need the phones to communicate while working, and it's cheaper to share a plan."

"Would you mind if I check something?" He held his hand out.

She retrieved the phone from her pocket, put in the code to unlock it, and handed it to him.

He touched the screen a few times. "Good news. You have the app that allows finding another phone if it's on the same account." He touched the screen again. "Success! His phone is linked, and I can see its location."

Jemima stumbled as she stepped closer to see. Chris held the screen out to her. On some type of map, there was a phone pictured inside a green circle, and another place on the map was marked with a blue dot. "What does it mean?"

"The green circle is Roy's phone. This"—he wiggled Abigail's phone—"is the blue dot, and it'll move on the map as we move. It looks to me as if Roy's phone is a couple of miles from here, maybe on or near your property."

A chill ran through Jemima. *On or near the property? What if he is hurt? Why else would he not come home and not answer his phone?*

"Let's get moving." She hurried back to her carriage.

"We should use the cart," Abigail said. "The horse can pull it faster, and it can cross soggy fields."

"Gut thinking." Jemima ran to the cart.

Chris held Abigail's phone while Abigail steered the cart, moving in the direction that caused the blue dot to inch toward the green phone icon.

They drove the mile on the road toward the horse farm and kept going. If only they could go faster. *God, please keep him safe.* Was God tired of hearing that same prayer over and over again?

Chris pointed and they took a road to the right. Their large farm sat in the middle of a square with a paved county road on each side. After several hundred feet, he pointed to the right again.

"Across this field?" Jemima asked. "How far before we hit those woods?"

"Wait." He stood. "There's a long driveway up ahead. Let's use that first."

"Abigail, that leads to one of your Daed's rental properties." Not just any property, but Tiffany's property. Something akin to insecurity or maybe jealousy niggled at Jemima, but she refused to allow it. Roy cut through this property to get to the Kurtz place. That was all.

"Pippi, move it, girl." Abigail clicked her tongue, and Pippi picked up her pace. "That's my tired gal. *Wunderbaar gut.*"

The small run-down house came into view. Amigo, Roy's favorite horse, was nibbling on grass in the small patch of front yard. "That's his horse!" Jemima got on her knees in the back of the cart, holding on to the side as she peered at the grounds, searching for his phone. Had her husband fallen off Amigo? Was he sprawled somewhere nearby, injured?

Abigail slowed the rig, and Jemima jumped out while it was still moving. But when she got to Amigo, she saw no sign of Roy. Why was Amigo tethered? "Roy!" She cupped her hands around her mouth. "Roy!" No answer. Amigo snorted and pranced in place.

Abigail made a beeline for the house and knocked on the door. When no one answered, she banged on the door. "Hello? Tiffany?" She waited, but no one came.

Chris continued walking the grounds, studying the screen on Abigail's phone. He picked up something from the grass on the side of the gravel driveway. "I found the phone," he announced.

"Then where is Roy?" Jemima slowly made a circle, looking for him.

"I don't know." Abigail descended the few steps. "But he *was* here. His horse is tethered, and we found his phone. Did he tell you anything about needing to come to the rental house yesterday?"

"Nee."

Chris walked over to them and held out Roy's cell. "Can either of you unlock this?"

Jemima took it. "Ya, the password is zero, nine, one, two. Our anniversary. September twelfth." She tried it, but it didn't unlock. "My hands are shaking too much." She passed it back to Chris.

He touched the screen several times and then shook his head. "I tried those numbers twice. They don't work. I can see there were lots of texts and missed calls, but we can't see any details unless we unlock it."

Roy had changed his passcode? When and why?

Jemima went to the front door and knocked on it even though there was no car in the driveway. She had probably spoken to Tiffany only twice during her two years of renting from the Grabers. She didn't really expect anyone to answer, as no one had responded to Abigail's knocks, but she needed to try.

"No car," Jemima mumbled. Could Tiffany have had an emergency and Roy left with her? Or maybe Roy needed medical help for some reason, and this was the closest place. She was really reaching for straws here.

Jemima went down the concrete steps and walked to the closest window and peered inside. The living room was pretty sparse. Some old furniture with clothes draped over the backs. Baby clothes? And there was a bassinet in the corner. That distinct shape could be nothing else. Tiffany had a baby? Jemima didn't realize she'd been pregnant, but it'd been close to a year since she'd seen Tiffany.

Roy had to know, because he and his Daed collected the rent and checked on the house from time to time. Why hadn't he said anything? It didn't make sense. Unless he was trying to keep it from Jemima. How many times had he been called away over the past few weeks? She'd assumed the calls were for business. But if he was coming here instead . . .

No, that couldn't be. No. Jemima reeled back from the window as if she'd been stung.

"Jem?" Abigail touched her shoulder.

Jemima ran up the short set of concrete steps and tried the doorknob. Locked. "I need to get into this house, *now.*"

"Jemima!" Abigail sounded shocked. "We can't."

Jemima jerked on the doorknob. "Now!" She yanked on it again. "Now!"

"Okay." Chris stepped up next to her. "How attached are you to this window?"

"I'm not."

"Then stand back."

Jemima went down the steps. Chris took off his coat, wrapped it around his fist, and broke the window in one quick punch. He removed his hand from the coat and put it on before he snaked his long arm through the broken glass to turn the doorknob. The door creaked open.

Jemima stepped inside. Chills ran up her arms, and she couldn't find her voice. She prodded herself to walk, and she slowly moved through the living room, pausing a few times to pick up pieces of baby clothing and then dropping them. The small attached kitchen was bare except for a few empty baby bottles scattered across the countertops.

She walked down the hallway and into the bedroom. It was as scarce of items as the rest of the house. All the dresser drawers hung open and were empty. The closet was void of anything except a few plastic hangers on the bar. Tiffany certainly wasn't living here.

Jemima left the bedroom and crossed the hallway to what must've been the nursery. Why did Tiffany leave some of the baby items but take the rest of the stuff from the house? A familiar piece of cloth in the crib caught Jemima's eye, making her heart beat even faster. She reached in to pick it up.

Why was this here? Jemima had made baby Laura a wearable blanket that fastened tightly at the back with Velcro. That made it easy to swaddle a baby in the middle of the night, and it had been

Roy's go-to when, as a new parent, he rocked Laura to sleep. Jemima rubbed her thumb across the soft pink fabric. Both Laura and Carolyn had used this blanket, but she'd made a blue one when Nevin was born, which they'd also used for Simeon.

She could hear Abigail and Chris talking in the other room, trying to piece together what to do next.

Jemima brought the fabric to her nose and smelled it. It smelled like her husband. Roy wouldn't have given away such a beloved homemade baby item, and Tiffany for sure didn't come into Jemima's house and steal it. It could only mean that Roy felt a deep connection to the baby who lived here. And for this to smell like him, he'd held the baby while she was wearing it. *No, no, no!* Her mind spun as she sank into the empty rocking chair, clutching the blanket to her chest.

Ten

Pain burned in Roy's arm and neck as he fought his way out of the darkness. Where was he?

Memories rushed back to him, and he knew he was stuck, unable to get free of his seat belt. His hand touched the cloth he'd wrapped around his injured arm after the wreck. Warm and wet. He was still bleeding. Pain ran like lightning up and down his right arm. It was broken, maybe in several places, and somehow he'd sustained a gash in his forearm, probably from holding his arms over his head for protection as the car rolled. His arm screamed at him for relief, and there was nothing he could do.

It seemed that more than a minute passed as he willed himself to full consciousness before he could open his eyes.

Sunlight!

Finally it was daytime. Based on the angle of the beams of light that floated through the wooded area, he guessed it was around eight or so in the morning. Whatever the exact time was, at least ten hours had passed since the car slid down this embankment, and he ached with thoughts of what Jemima was going through. But now that it was daylight, he could see, and that meant he could get free!

He was covered in trash bags that were filled with clothes. Tiffany was too, and thankfully she was asleep. He'd leave her that way until he could get free of his seat belt and hopefully find either his phone or hers to call for help. He'd had a pocketknife in his shirt pocket before the wreck. It had to be around here somewhere, and hopefully he could reach it.

He pushed a bag off him and into the back seat. With the confinement of seat belts and the complete darkness last night, they'd been unable to do anything to free themselves. But in desperation they'd slowly and painfully moved the bags filled with clothes to the front seat to cover themselves and provide some protection from the cold.

He searched the area for a phone. He saw none, but he did see his pocketknife caught between the console and his car seat. He shifted, trying to reach it, and screamed out in pain. Tiffany stirred.

All he could manage were short breaths as he eased his uninjured arm into position to slide his hand between the console and seat. Tiffany's seat belt had unbuckled easily after the wreck, but the car was sitting at an angle, so she couldn't get out on either side without his help. Because she'd been unable to find her phone in the dark, she couldn't call for help, and she didn't think she could navigate the embankment on her own.

He craned his neck to look at the steep slope. How were they going to climb that in their injured states?

When Tiffany couldn't get out of the car last night, she had given up pretty quickly and fallen asleep easily. Maybe too easily, as he used to do when he was taking painkillers. Was she on something?

While she slept, he'd spent hours trying to break free of the seat belt or find the knife or a phone. Eventually pain and exhaustion took over and he'd given up. Then he fell asleep, the body shutting down after a trauma.

His index and middle fingers grasped the edge of the knife. *Please, God.* He squeezed his fingers, trying to hold on to the knife as he worked his hand out of the tight spot.

Yes! He had the knife. Using his teeth, he opened the blade and carefully moved it to the seat belt and sawed it back and forth, flinching and grimacing from the pain of his broken arm. Whatever seat belts were made of didn't cut easily.

What a miserable night it'd been. If staying one step ahead of unbearable guilt and shame was impossible when in full busy mode, being a prisoner in a car with Tiffany was even worse. His excruciating physical pain gave him little distraction from his constant remorse. What was Jemima going through? Had she unearthed his secrets?

The knife finally sliced through the last threads in the seat belt, and he was free!

"Tiffany." With his uninjured hand he reached for her, feeling the bags of clothes they'd managed to place over her for warmth. He touched her shoulder. "Tiffany."

"Ow!" She stirred. "What?"

"Daylight." He panted. "It's daylight." He shifted, trying to move one of the bags of clothes into the seat behind him. "We have to get out of here and climb the embankment." Saying the words was one thing. Making his body obey him would be another. While giving her a moment to wake up fully, he decided to ask again about the baby. "Where's Heidi?"

How many times had he asked her? Her response every time was that she'd tell him once he gave her money. Apparently, twenty thousand dollars in cash would do it, but he had no cash. Maybe he could get a loan for that amount, but it seemed ungodly to purchase a baby.

His thoughts moved to his wife. What she had to be dealing with caused him more pain than his broken arm. But he was alive, and that meant he could look her in the eyes and tell her the truth, including how deeply he loved her. And it also meant he could find the baby and get her to safety.

He opened the car door, and his body shifted with the movement. Pain bolted through him. Because of the shrubbery, the door opened only partway. Shifting the bags of clothing as best he could with only one arm and lots of pain, he leaned away from the door. Using his leverage with his feet, he opened the door just wide enough that he could get out. Wincing and moaning, he shoved bags of clothes out the door, trying to clear them out of the way.

Pain throbbed throughout his body. "Where's the baby, Tiffany?"

"Help me get out and up the embankment and I'll tell you."

He looked at her, praying her words were true. "Deal." At the pace of an injured turtle, he got out of the car. Then he removed more bags, clearing the way for her. "Kumm." He motioned and offered his hand.

She slid across the seat. "We have to find my phone."

"Mine too."

Once she was out of the car, he started searching the floorboard as best he could for either phone. Hers was wedged between the floor mat and the bottom of the passenger's seat. Ignoring the pain, he kept reaching deeper and deeper until he had the phone in hand. Because he didn't trust her, he planned to use her phone to call his, but her phone was locked.

He held it out to her. "Call my phone."

She seized it. "Why would I do that?"

While she unlocked her phone and made a call, he searched his foggy thoughts.

"Hey, it's me. I'm with Roy, and we've wrecked the car."

We? Even with his pain and a high-pitch ringing in his ears, he was clear on the fact that *she'd* wrecked the car, taking him with her.

She told the person what road they were on. "I'll be on the shoulder, near the viaduct but past the guardrail." She paused. "Yeah, exactly there. Thanks. I owe you."

She had just given him the words he was looking for to explain why she should call his phone. "Call my phone because I've earned it, Tiffany. I've earned your going to the great effort of touching that screen and calling my phone. That and much more, and we both know it."

She huffed but unlocked her phone again and passed it to him. He touched Favorites and his name, but he heard no sound at all. He called it two more times while moving bags of clothes around, but it was no use. His phone wasn't in hearing range. Disappointed as he was, he had to turn his attention to what was most important: getting up the embankment before they were too drained to do so. "Kumm."

"My laptop! I'm not leaving without it."

She loved that thing more than her own child, and she spent more time with it in a day than she had with Heidi in six weeks. "Then get it and come on, but I can't carry it. I have one good arm, and we'll both need my use of it to get to the top."

She fumbled through the car until she came out with a computer bag. She slung the strap over her shoulder, and they went around the car and began climbing. He couldn't remember ever being this thirsty before, and his feet dragged as he inched his way up the steep hill, steadying or tugging on Tiffany the whole way.

Finally they reached the top. He willed himself not to pass out, but the world was spinning. "Where's Heidi?"

Tiffany's eyes rolled as if she was about to pass out. He steadied her and removed the weight of the laptop. Somehow they both stayed standing. "Where's Heidi?" he muttered. He feared that if he sat, he'd not be able to get up again. As they stood there, every second was excruciating, yet time almost didn't seem to exist.

A car slowed as it came toward them and pulled onto the shoulder. The passenger door opened, and an unfamiliar woman with matted hair and wrinkled clothes was behind the wheel. Tiffany snatched the strap of the computer he was holding and wasted no time getting into the car. He grabbed the handle of the back door, but it was locked.

A burst of energy ran through him, and he stopped Tiffany from closing her door and grasped the handle of the computer bag. "Where's Heidi?"

"Got money?" the driver asked.

What was wrong with these people?

"He doesn't," Tiffany said. "Apparently none left at all."

"Tiffany!" He held on to the bag as the car rolled forward. "Where's Heidi?"

As the car drove off, Tiffany couldn't hold on to the computer bag, and as it came free, he went to his knees in pain.

Was he a fool to care this much? The value of God's great gift of innocent little ones was ingrained in him. It was entrenched in every Amish person. How a man protected the vulnerable showed his true character. Heidi had no power. And by the time she did have any power, she would be so wounded that pain and sadness would have molded her life. Without a loved one to protect and provide for her, she was at the mercy of a merciless world.

Mustering all his strength, he staggered to his feet. He moved to the edge of the embankment to toss the laptop down it. The handle of the computer bag had been his only way to hold on to Tiffany and find out where Heidi was, but now it was just deadweight. He wasn't sure he had the strength to get home, but there was no reason to carry four extra pounds in his one good hand.

Don't! The voice called inside him. He lowered his hand and looked at the computer. *Don't?* Fog and anxiety made it impossible to think, but he realized his best chance of finding answers or at least clues concerning Heidi's whereabouts was this computer. His shoulders were in too much pain from his broken arm to put the strap around his neck, so he tucked the laptop under his good arm and headed toward home.

Home was a strange concept. Even when it was filled with pressure and secrets or anger from secrets revealed, which was sure to await him, home was a haven. It would center him despite there being nearly nothing left of him to center.

The distinct sound of horse hooves on pavement grabbed his attention. He couldn't be seen like this. Rumors would spread like wildfire. He'd be questioned, first by those in the rig and later by the ministers. He'd be branded an adulterer and then shunned. He deserved that. But his children would pay the price of embarrassment for the rest of their lives. They would feel the shame of his wrongs. That shame would bring dishonor on them from their peers, and it would shape and twist their innocence, their lives.

He hurried up a hill and into the woods. He leaned against a tree, trying to catch his breath, and then rethought his decision. Maybe he shouldn't hide. If the people in the buggy could get him home an hour sooner, he could have a better jump on searching for Heidi. The rig came into sight, and he started down the hill.

Don't! Again he heard the voice. He grabbed a small tree, stopping his downhill momentum. *Don't?* He probably should do it anyway, but he stayed put, wavering on what to do. The rig passed him by without the occupants seeing him.

He began walking toward home again. He fell and sprawled out on the damp ground with blood from his arm discoloring the leaves. Birds and squirrels seemed unfazed as he tried over and over to get up. The pain was too great, and he was too weak.

Eleven

Abigail set a cup of hot tea in front of Jemima. As she returned to the counter to get her own mug of tea, she caught a glimpse of the clock. Almost one. They'd returned from Tiffany's a little more than three hours ago. She'd wanted to stay awake and comfort Jemima after they'd come home, but the body could stay awake only so many hours, regardless of what life was dishing out. Chris had gone to the guest room, and Abigail had curled up on the couch. Apparently she'd been out cold for almost the full three hours before jerking awake.

Jemima couldn't stop quiet tears from flowing.

Abigail set her mug on the table and put her arm around Jemima's shoulders. She hugged her. "We'll get through this, whatever *this* is. I'll be with you every step of the way. I promise."

Jemima wiped her tears. "Don't ever use the word *promise*. Not ever. Roy said it daily, often several times a day this past year, and like a fool I believed him."

Abigail gave her sister-in-law another squeeze and then sat at the head of the table, near her.

Jemima stared at the table. "How could I ignore all the signs that were right in front of my face?"

Abigail didn't have any answers, and Jemima had already said these things, but Abigail just let her talk.

A floor creaked and she looked that way.

Chris.

He'd seemed different, less distant with Abigail as the night had worn on without Roy returning. Not that it mattered. But even now, standing there barefoot with uncombed hair, he was quite a good-looking specimen. Handsome Amish men weren't that hard to come by. Maybe it was part of the genetic heritage. But finding a man with the right temperament to build a life with—that was challenging. Ya, she was picky, unwilling to raise beloved children with an un-equally yoked partner who had more power over her decisions than she did.

But Chris drew her. He was energetic, smart, and a hard worker. Based on their talk Saturday morning, he was pretty comfortable being honest about himself, about feeling haunted and guilty. That was a lot to say to someone he'd just met, and the fact that he didn't expound on it indicated he knew when to draw boundaries. But they each had deal breakers in a relationship, and they'd each done a deal-breaking thing. He needed a woman who walked in stoic self-denial, offering only patience and kindness no matter what was happening inside her. She needed someone who wanted emotional honesty even when it was uncomfortable. Besides that, he'd made up his mind to step back from her *before* talking to her about any of it.

"How could he do this?" Jemima asked once again.

Abigail returned her attention to Jemima. "I know what this looks like with Roy, and maybe it is as it looks, but—"

Jemima slapped her hand against the table. "He's been sneaking out at all hours and coming home at all hours for nearly two months. He was gone overnight on *business* last Friday, and it wasn't the first time in the last six or so weeks. Based on the baby clothes at Tiffany's, I'd say that's just about how old that infant is. As we learned Saturday, he emptied forty thousand dollars from our savings, and half of that money was yours. Are you really going to sit there and tell me to continue hoping it's not what it looks like?"

Abigail took a sip of her tea. "Nee."

Jemima was in no state of mind to hear Abigail right now. Earlier today Jemima had wanted to protect Roy, believing that he'd been made crooked inside somehow and that he needed help, not condemnation. But if he was guilty, as he appeared to be, it changed everything.

"Jemima"—Abigail reached across the table and gently took her hands—"however this goes from here, I'm with you. Do you understand me? You're not alone."

It didn't matter what Roy was guilty of. The church would demand that Jemima forgive him and walk in love. Forgive and let go. Abigail had seen the results of forced forgiveness in women's lives. The intense and immediate requirement didn't allow people to sort through all the facets and to slowly find healing and forgiveness between them and God or them and the person. It didn't require the person who'd caused the train wreck to help clean it up and sort through the debris of lies, shattered trust, and broken hearts. Roy would be shunned for a period of time, heaping shame on him and his wife, and that was the end of it. Jemima was still supposed to be his dutiful and faithful wife, still serve him as a humble servant.

Abigail could hardly imagine what that would do to any woman's soul. But if Jemima chose to divorce him, Abigail would stand by her, move in with her—whatever she needed.

Jemima squeezed Abigail's hands, seeming to understand what she was offering. "Denki." Without another word, she rose, put on her coat, grabbed a basket of freshly washed diapers, and went outside.

Abigail pressed her fingertips against her forehead, covering her face. *Dear God, is it true? Has my brother betrayed his wife?*

Unwilling for Chris to see the emotions on her face, she rose and turned her back to him as she lowered her hands.

"I was wrong." Chris's hoarse whisper stopped her cold, but she didn't face him. "I saw you fly into a rage with Roy on Saturday, and I thought . . ." He went to the percolator on the stove and poured a cup of coffee. "It doesn't matter what I thought. I judged who you were, and I was wrong. I'm truly sorry." He held out the mug to her even though she had her own on the table. He was offering a kind gesture.

She didn't take it. "You could've withheld making a judgment. You could've given me the benefit of the doubt. My stars, Chris, you could've asked me why I lost my temper like I did."

He pulled the mug back and rested it in his palm. "Ya, but when people are hiding who they are, none of what you just said would've been helpful or wise. I've been down that road with a woman—withholding judgment, giving the benefit of the doubt, and asking directly."

Her hurt feelings from Chris's previous sudden change of heart toward her quieted, and she saw a different man in front of her, perhaps one as cautious as she was and someone who was caught off guard by her presence as much as she was by his. But what struck her as sad was that Chris seemed to know firsthand a side to people she was just now experiencing.

He gazed out the kitchen window above the sink. "She was charming and gorgeous and deceitful. She would pull accusations against me out of thin air and then fly into a rage as if they were founded. She would tell me things people had said to her, and I was shocked anyone could talk to her or treat her that way. She'd beg me to keep what she'd told me between us, and I did, but I joined her in her anger against those people, believing what she'd said. The longer we were together, the more I realized there was a constant buzz of chaos around her, and our lives kept moving from one drama to another." He sighed and sat down at the kitchen table.

Abigail sat too. "What caused you to figure her out?"

He tapped his finger on the table, keeping his eyes on that same spot. "As blind as love is, I saw flickers of things, red flags maybe, that led me to believe she had some mental-health issues. I was determined that we would get help together and things would smooth out, so I convinced her to see a doctor. She fought it at first but eventually agreed. We saw several doctors, and she was diagnosed. It wasn't until we were nearing the end of instruction so we could join the faith and marry—a mere two months away from being bound to her for the rest of my life—when I really saw her."

Abigail had chills as he spoke, and she waited, listening to the wood crackle in the stove as it burned.

He touched his chest. "With my eyes I saw, and it was as if God Himself had opened my eyes. Mental illness was only a small part of her issues. She was stubborn beyond reason, and my gut said she wasn't taking her medication and didn't intend to. But maybe the biggest issue was that for all her humor and charisma, she had a mean streak a mile wide. In that moment, I saw that every false accusation, whether against me or others, and all her tears and outbursts of rage were her ways of manipulating me, stirring up storms just for the satisfaction of it. I understand that was partly due to the mental illness, but I know what I saw, and she had far more responsibility for her actions than she would ever admit. Seeing her true self changed me, and she didn't possess enough lies or tears or false praise to pull me in again." He turned the mug, fidgeting with it. "And I hate that I grieved over the loss of her, but I did." He drew a deep breath. "That was seven years ago."

Her heart pounded. He'd come within weeks of living with Abigail's worst fear: being bound for life to a difficult person.

"I'm sorry you went through that and grateful you saw the truth before it was too late."

"Ya, exactly."

She appreciated his opening up to her, but how could she have this moment with Chris while Jemima's heart was shattered? Life was often rays of light and laughter shining through thunderous gray clouds. She looked out the window to check on Jemima, who had gone outside to hang clothes on the line. But she was standing on the edge of the porch now, staring off.

Abigail shifted her attention to Chris. His eyes held her so close and gently she felt as if they were embracing before a first kiss. Whatever this was between them, she liked it, at least some of the time.

She searched her heart. "I guess if I'm honest with myself, I didn't really want to talk about why I'd reacted to Roy as I did. It was easier to accept your decision that we wouldn't be good together as clear evidence that another man wasn't worthy of my time." She shrugged. "No traumatic incident brought me to that cynical place with men. Just observations of various people that increased when my friends started pairing off."

"Observations?" He rose, went to the stove, and topped off his coffee.

"We can talk about all that later, but I need to be clear." She stood, facing him. "It looks as if we'll be stuck together for a while. I may have to ask Sarah, my substitute, to fill in for me at school for a little longer. As for us, we are way too early in this relationship to know anything beyond that we are attracted to each other."

His eyes bore into hers. "One hundred percent attracted."

Her heart pounded and she stepped forward, despite telling herself to step back. "Definitely."

"But I know there's a lot about me that could derail us."

She didn't step back. "That's reassuring. Thanks."

"In the words of a very wise woman, men are annoying, present company included." His tone was serious, but his smile was genuine.

"Kidding aside, I have times when I live by my own rules, not the Ordnung." He held out the mug to her.

She took it this time and enjoyed a sip before returning it to him. "Let's not discuss it now." She sounded relaxed, but she was at the end of her ability to learn truths too heavy to bear. "Let's just hold off, maybe pretend this could be a viable relationship for now."

"You sure you don't want to clear the air?" He took a drink.

She knew this dance—the one of committing to not committing. The Englisch said the man should lead in a dance, but she'd always led the one concerning relationships. The beat was different with each set of participants, but the steps were the same: one tiny step forward and two giant steps back. It reminded her of the game Mother May I. It was always awkward, and for once she wished it were unnecessary.

Maybe levity would help. "Wow, we're alone in a home, sharing the same cup of coffee, and you want to inundate me with uncomfortable honesty. You're not very skilled at sweeping a woman off her feet."

"Is that what you want, Abi? For me to ignore the truth of who I am and try to sweep you off your feet?"

"Nee."

"Of course you don't. Even I knew that."

Unlike the others she'd danced with, Chris seemed to know her well, even though they'd met only a few days ago.

"Ya, if you tried to sweep me off my feet, I'd have to deck you. I just find it a shame you didn't try."

He laughed. "I think—"

"Abigail!" Jemima screamed. "Kumm quick!"

Twelve

A man on the horizon went to his knees. He was so far away that Jemima couldn't see who it was. But she knew. Her heart knew.

He hadn't left her! He hadn't run off! Hope unleashed inside her with the fury of a windstorm.

"Abigail!" she yelled again before taking off and running toward the man.

He slowly got to his feet and put one foot in front of the other. His head was down, and he was cradling his right arm.

"Roy!" Jemima ran, tears flowing. He hadn't left her. He was doing all he could to make his way home. She didn't know why his horse had been at Tiffany's or why he'd given her their daughter's blanket, but this was the man she'd married: the one going through hell or high water to get to her.

She was out of breath and unable to speak by the time she neared him. He held up his hand, palm toward her, slowing her pace before he cradled his arm again.

"Dear God," she gasped. "You're bleeding."

He thrust the straps of a bag toward her. "The baby," he panted, barely audible.

The baby? That's what is on his mind?

"This"—he jiggled the straps—"is the key to finding her." He drew deep breaths, looking too weak to stay standing. "Don't let go of it. I have to find her." Who did he mean by *her?* The baby or Tiffany?

Jemima steadied herself despite her hurt and anger. "Ya. Sh. I've got it." She put the strap over her head and shoulder.

"Promise me, Jem." His legs began to give way.

She tucked her shoulder under his arm to keep him from falling.

Fast-paced steps were coming up behind her. She turned her head to see Chris closing the gap. "Easy." She held up a hand and then gestured at Roy's wrapped and bloodied arm.

Chris slowed and somehow swapped places with Jemima. "Abigail is bringing the cart."

"He needs to be seen by Doc Grant." Jemima had some of Roy's blood on her hands. Thank God for the kindhearted medical doctor who tended to the Amish. "Sometimes he makes house calls, but my guess is he'll want his machines and surgical room."

"Unless he's so injured that he needs a hospital."

"Doc Grant sews fingers back on and does all manner of emergency things like this at his office."

"Jem." Roy reached out and touched her chin.

She stood stock still and looked him in the eye.

"Listen to me." His body trembled, maybe from the cold or

maybe he was going into shock. "That computer is my only chance of finding Heidi. Let no one have it, not even if Tiffany comes for it. Promise me."

She didn't want to give her word or think about Tiffany or the baby. She wanted to tend to her husband, but she nodded. "Ya, I promise."

His eyes closed, and his legs collapsed. Chris kept him from falling, but Roy crumpled to the ground.

The world was black, but it was warm and there was no pain. "Roy." A warm compress dabbed across his brow. "Kumm now. It's time to wake."

He tried to pull free of the darkness.

"Kumm." Someone patted his cheek. "Wake up."

He opened his eyes and stared into his wife's face. Had it all been a bad dream? "*Ach, mei liewi* Jem." His wife recoiled at the words *my dear,* and dozens of memories pelted him. The strain on her face let him know that it hadn't been just a nightmare.

"I'm so sorry, Jemima."

She pursed her lips tight and nodded. He looked around, but dizziness got the better of him. Where was he? He wasn't at home, and he wasn't in a hospital.

Chris stepped into view. "Hey." He sat in a chair next to the little bed Roy was in. "You're at the clinic, Doc Grant's place. You know it?"

Roy nodded. Were his wife and sister not talking to him?

"Gut." Chris smiled. "The doc's busy, so I'll just tell you. Your arm has three fractures and a serious gash. He was able to set the bone, but you'll need X-rays every week or so to make sure the bones are staying aligned as your arm heals. He put stitches in the gash, but you lost a lot of blood. You also have small cuts and contusions, so you'll be really sore for a while. We good?"

"Ya." He willed himself to stay awake. "We have to find Heidi. She could be in danger." Warmth and grogginess tugged at him, and his eyes closed.

"Roy? Listen up." Chris snapped his fingers.

Roy tried to respond.

"Roy." Abigail leaned over his bed. "We've been trying, but we can't get into the laptop. It's password protected."

"Not that we have a clue what we're looking for anyway," Jemima said.

He knew the password, didn't he? A couple of months ago, Tiffany had handed him a small stack of bills to pay, and one of the envelopes had a strange word written on it, one he assumed was a password. He hadn't thought much about it at the time. What was it? Something that sort of fit the mess they were in. He fought against the fogginess and prayed to remember.

Messy, soupy . . . "Stickystew. One word, first letter capitalized. Then the number three and an exclamation point."

He heard someone tapping on the keyboard.

"I'm in," Chris said. "What am I looking for?"

"Messages." Why was it so hard to talk? "Every text she sends or receives on her phone goes to Messages on her laptop."

"I'll need someone from the clinic to give me the password to the Wi-Fi before any recent messages will download. Give me a second." Chris left the room.

He could feel Jemima's anger, and he wanted to talk to her, but it was all he could do to get information from his brain to come out of his mouth. He fought to stay awake.

"Okay." Chris was beside Roy's bed. Had he fallen asleep again? "Messages have updated, and I'm in the app and reading through them. The most recent messages are between two people. One's from Tiffany, saying she's heading for New York. She asks someone named Amber to keep the baby, and . . ." Chris's voice trailed off.

Roy didn't have it in him to ask what he was thinking.

"Okay"—Chris resumed talking—"I have a name, phone number, and address that I've put in my phone."

"Gut." A weight lifted from Roy, and tears threatened, but he reeled in all visible signs of his emotions. Jemima wouldn't understand his tears. *He* didn't understand them. "We have to get her." He tried to sit up, but nausea hit so strong he gagged and fell back.

"I think you'll have to stay here." Chris closed the laptop and set it on the stand beside the bed.

"Help me sit up." Roy held out his good hand.

"Roy," Abigail chided.

But the voice he heard the loudest was the silence from his wife.

Roy kept his hand out and Chris took it. Roy's head spun as he pushed away the covers and put his feet on the floor. He stayed put, hoping the room would stop swaying. He then stood, but his knees buckled. Why?

Chris caught him and helped him sit on the edge of the bed. "Look, man, what you're asking is a big undertaking. We can call an Uber driver and handle it ourselves. You'll just make it more dangerous if we have to watch you."

Roy stared at the floor. "Ya." He hated to put them in this position. "You and Abigail go get her." He and Jemima needed this time to talk anyway. "You do anything you have to, but do not leave without her."

Abigail was across the room, near the door and next to Jemima. "Do anything?" Abigail stepped closer. "What do we tell them? That we're at their home to get a baby? That they should give her to us because Roy said to?"

Roy pushed against the bed, trying to get back into it so he could lie down. Maybe then the room would stop spinning. "Her mother abandoned her, and whoever these people are, they don't want Heidi. You're there to take her off their hands."

"And if they balk?" Abigail asked. "I've never taken a single thing from someone's home that wasn't offered to me—not even a pencil or a cookie. But we're supposed to take a human?"

He grimaced. Was there no way to avoid saying the awful truth like this when he and Jemima had yet to talk? "You have the legal right to take her." His eyes moved to Jemima's. "There are no words to let you know how sorry I feel about all this, Jem."

His wife's arms were folded, her face was like carved stone, and her eyes were glued to the floor.

He looked at his sister. "I think the people keeping Heidi are addicts. It's the only thing that makes sense of their callousness and endless need for money."

Was there another way, some possible way to avoid his sister and Chris's having to get mixed up in the mess of his making? Regret owned him, but he didn't know another way to get Heidi to safety.

"If they're addicts, then why aren't we calling the police?" Abigail asked.

"It may come to that, and if so, I'll have to accept it." His mind was clearing, and he willed the words forward so he could make his sister understand. "If police come, they'll see that people on drugs have Heidi and they'll hear the ugly, messy story surrounding her. I don't think they're allowed to make a judgment call and hand the baby over to you or even me. They're most likely to send her to foster care, and if that happens, the courts and judges and family services will get involved."

Maybe he needed to relinquish control and let that happen, but he couldn't. Not yet anyway. His grief for his infant daughter and his desperate need to hold her and make sure she was safe was too strong right now. He needed to protect her and have a say in her future, just as he did with his other children.

"Now give me my phone. I'll forward what you need. Then take my ID."

Abigail asked nothing else and handed him his phone.

Roy unlocked it and searched through the few images. He clicked on Heidi's birth certificate and sent the image to Abigail's phone. "Since you're unsure of your footing, let Chris do the talking."

Abigail tossed his billfold into his lap.

He pulled out his ID. "Do you have your ID with you?"

"Ya, but why?"

"To prove to Amber that you and I have the same last name. Use the IDs and what I just sent via text. Now go."

Chris checked his phone. "Uber's here." He headed for the door.

Abigail stopped in front of Jemima, and Roy heard no words and saw no gestures, but Abigail then left.

Jemima came from the far corner of the room, and Roy froze. She took his phone from his hand and touched the image he'd sent to Abigail.

"I can explain it, Jem." He reached for her hand, but she backed away.

She studied the screen, enlarging the image and scrolling as she read. She seemed to stop breathing.

"Listen to me. It wasn't an affair. I don't recall—"

Her eyes seemed fixated on one thing, and she enlarged the image again. The color drained from her face. "You're listed as the father."

"This is a horrible way for you to learn this, but it's not at all what it looks like. I promise."

She thrust the phone toward his face, holding it out, eyes brimming with tears. "You're listed as the father."

"It's not how this looks." Was she able to hear anything he was saying?

She dropped the phone onto his bed.

"Jem, I need you to hear me."

She stumbled out the door.

"Jem! Just hear me out!"

But she was gone. Her heart was broken. All manner of lies were probably circling in her mind about how this could be, and he was too weak to go after her.

How had he come to this place where his wife learned the truth in the worst way possible?

Dear God, help her.

Thirteen

From the back seat of the Uber car, Abigail stared out the window as the countryside and farms disappeared and stores filled the landscape. At first the stores looked like all the ones she saw when a driver took her to a chain grocery store, but the farther they drove, the more decrepit the buildings became.

It hurt to breathe. Her brother had fathered a child with another woman? How could anything like this be happening to her family?

Chris reached across the seat and covered her hand with his. He gently squeezed it, apparently no more willing to talk about any of this in front of a stranger than she was.

They'd been in the car for nearly an hour when the driver turned into an area that looked like an array of long back alleys but instead turned out to be narrow roads with cars pulled halfway onto the sidewalks. They took several more turns, and each time the conditions got worse.

The driver adjusted his mirror. "This doesn't look like your kind of neighborhood. You're sure about this?"

"Yeah." Chris pulled cash from his wallet. "I know how Uber

works and that it doesn't involve giving you cash. But here's the thing: it would be best if we didn't have to wait for another Uber driver to get to us." He held a hundred-dollar bill over the seat. "We only need fifteen minutes. Any chance you'd wait for us?"

The driver looked at the money. "Not if something illegal's going on. No way. I got a wife and kids, and—"

Abigail shifted, catching the driver's eye. "It's not illegal. A baby. My . . ."

"Niece." Chris finished the sentence.

She couldn't make herself even say the word. This baby seemed more like an unwanted stray cat than a niece, and Abigail hated herself for feeling that way.

"Ya." How weird her hesitancy must sound to the driver. "Her name's Heidi, and she was abandoned by her mom and given to people we don't know. We're here to pick her up." She held up two IDs and the phone as if somehow that would explain it to the driver.

The man shrugged. "Not a problem. I believe you." The GPS said they'd arrived at their destination, and the driver stopped the car. "But hanging out in this neighborhood looks unwise to me, so I'll give you the fifteen minutes you asked for but not a minute more."

Chris nodded and the man took the money. "Thanks."

They got out of the car. A toddler wailed. Dogs barked. Deep voices shouted in anger. On each side of the narrow road were old buildings with broken windows and rickety stairs. Tires and mattresses and trash were everywhere.

She hadn't realized people lived this way.

"Apartment 2B should be up these steps." Chris pointed to the lengthy set of wooden steps running along the side of the building. But first"—he held up his phone—"I've set the timer to thirteen minutes. If we're still inside when it sounds, you take the baby and walk out. Get in the car and go." He motioned toward the steps, and they went toward them.

"What if I don't have the baby in my arms by that point?"

"You'll have her." He sounded so confident.

Her heart pounded. "So why isn't the plan for you to leave with us?"

"It is."

She stopped halfway up the stairs. "You're talking in circles."

"Sorry." He tapped his phone, showing her the timer, and they started up the stairs again. "I wish you could stay in the car, but for numerous reasons I couldn't say in the car and don't have time to explain now, you need to go with me. We'll follow each other's lead, but if things get off track, you do exactly as I say when I say it."

Her thoughts and feelings were as unfamiliar and unpleasant as her surroundings. "You sound as if you know what you're doing."

"I don't. Maybe getting the baby will be easy and everything I'm saying is unnecessary. But we have to go in with a plan."

What plan? For her to walk out with the baby? How was that a plan?

They came to a door with 2B spray-painted on it. He knocked firmly.

She fidgeted with her phone and the two IDs. "The plan can't be for the baby and me to get out and leave you behind."

"That's the worst-case scenario, but if it happens, once you're in the car, call the police and give them this address while the driver is leaving with you and the baby." He tried the doorknob and it turned. "We clear?"

An infant wailed. Surely it was Heidi. The cries caused Abigail to long to comfort her, yet she also wanted to pretend Heidi didn't exist.

Had she always been this shallow but had never been tested enough to realize it? And why hadn't Chris and she gone to the police? Roy's plan had seemed simple, but looking at this place and seeing Chris this uptight and alert was disturbing.

He put his hand into hers. "I need you to trust me, Abi. Can you do that?"

She certainly couldn't trust herself. She was confused by everything, including her own feelings about Heidi. "Ya."

He knocked again. When there was still no answer, he tried the knob. To her surprise, the door was unlocked. He pushed it open.

Abigail touched his arm and nodded for him to enter after her. He stepped back.

"Hello?" Abigail sang. "Auntie here, looking for Heidi."

A fortyish woman in a tank top and pajama bottoms walked into the living room. Two men, one massive and one average, followed her.

"Who are you?" Average Guy started laughing. "Look, man, some religious cult has arrived."

Abigail chuckled, determined to at least pretend to be a good sport. "I'm here for the baby."

"Good. This is our place, and one night of *that* is more than enough," Average Guy said.

Abigail forced a smile. "I'm sure." Why were they at home last night and today? Didn't anyone work a shift anywhere?

The sound of crying was coming from down the hallway, but when Abigail headed that way, Massive Guy stood in front of her. "Where's the money?"

"Oh, yeah, the money." Chris pressed something on his phone. "Good grief, man, let her get the baby and shut her up so I can hear you."

"I'm all for that," Average Guy said.

"Okay." Massive Guy stepped to the side.

Abigail started down the hallway, and Chris went with her. Squalor was everywhere. Not one clean corner. Rotted food. Trash. Beer cans. Who would leave a baby here?

Abigail looked into a portable crib. The smell hit her first. "She needs to be changed."

"Nee," Chris whispered. "Take nothing. Grab her and get as close to the front door as you can without looking obvious."

Abigail picked her up and cradled her. "Sh, little one. Sh." Abigail crooked her pinkie finger and put it in the baby's mouth. Heidi began sucking furiously and silence reigned.

"Now"—Average Guy stood at the door—"the money?"

"Yeah, about that." Chris pulled out his phone. "I've got a banking app." He motioned for the guy to enter the room, and he did.

Abigail left the room, but halfway down the hallway she heard a loud pop, as if flesh had hit flesh, and it was followed by a thud. She cringed, terrified, but she kept going.

Chris was behind her as they came to the end of the hall and into the open area. "The door," he whispered. Then he spoke louder to the others in the room. "Hey, whew. I can hear you now, so tell me about the money we owe you, 'cause I feel confused."

Abigail rocked the baby and walked nonchalantly while making her way to the door.

"There's nothing to be confused about," Massive Guy said. "The baby's mom said—"

"Uh, according to the birth certificate, the mom is Tiffany Porter," Chris said. "Is that right?"

"Yes, Tiffany Porter," Massive Guy mocked. "She said to keep the baby here and we'd get ten thousand dollars in exchange for her. She said the dad refused to pay but that she had someone else who would. So where's the money?"

"Good question. How were we supposed to exchange that?"

Abigail was a few feet from escaping, when the woman got between her and the door. Abigail smiled. "Look at this." She moved in closer to the woman and showed her the baby sucking on her finger.

"Nobody's leaving until we've got the money." Massive Guy's tone grew sharp, but Abigail stayed focused on the woman in front of her. Her pupils were tiny. Hadn't Roy's pupils been small when he was on high-powered pain meds after the accident?

"She's not so bad, is she?" There was a hint of compassion in the woman's voice. "I rocked her most of the night, not that it seemed to help much."

"Look at how red my finger is from this girl gnawing on it." Abigail showed her.

A grin crossed the woman's face, and Abigail noticed she was missing teeth.

"Do you have a bottle or pacifier?" Abigail asked.

"Yeah. Hang on." The woman walked over to the kitchen table.

Abigail opened the front door, but she turned to check on Chris. He was embroiled with both men.

Massive Guy broke free and headed for Abigail.

Move, Abigail! But her body didn't listen.

"On record!" Chris pounced between Massive Guy and Abigail. "You, confessing to the plan to sell the baby." Chris held up his phone.

Both men lumbered toward him, and one now had a baseball bat.

Chris ducked as Massive Guy swung a fist at him. When Chris came up, he hit the man hard. But Average Guy raised the bat, about to hit Chris in the back. Chris turned and managed to deflect a full blow. "Go."

His word jolted her. Although Chris hadn't looked away from the men, she knew he was talking to her. Couldn't she do something to help him? Maybe put the baby on the floor and hit one of the men with a chair? She shuddered at the thought, and the desire faded as she remembered Chris asking if she trusted him.

She scurried out the door and down the steps.

"Wait." The wiry woman ran after her, holding out a pacifier.

Something made Abigail stop.

The woman touched the baby's head. "I tried, but she's not a happy one. Not that one. You take good care of her."

This infant had touched something inside this lost woman, and Abigail took the pacifier from her filthy hands. "Denki."

The woman stared into Abigail's eyes, and it seemed for a moment that they connected.

A *pop* seemed to shake the stairs, and a moan followed. Had Chris been hit with the bat?

"Go," the woman whispered as she touched the baby's head.

Abigail hurried down the steps, desperate to put the baby down inside the car. Should she go back up the stairs and try to help? She shuddered, unable to imagine striking anyone.

Why did it seem so effortless for Chris?

She pulled on the car door, but it was locked. She rapped on the window and heard the locks click. She opened the door, climbed inside, and shut it. "Don't go." She stared at the door of the apartment, constantly clenching her hands. Should she call the police? Or would Chris get in trouble too? "Just wait. Our fifteen minutes aren't up yet."

Every second felt like ten minutes, and she prayed, unsure whether to call the police.

"I thought this was on the up and up," the driver said.

"It is. She's my niece, and the mom abandoned her. But they wanted money in exchange for her."

The man's timer went off.

"Wait. Please, just stay here. If someone other than Chris comes out that door, you can take off."

"Deal."

As she was praying, someone came barreling out the door. *Chris!*

Massive Guy followed him out the door, swinging the baseball bat. Chris used the handrails while seeming to skip four or five steps at a time, putting distance between him and Massive Guy. She opened the car door and slid out of the way.

Chris seemed to float into the car like a bubble, but he landed hard. "Go!"

The car took off and Chris slammed the door. He leaned back against the seat, panting. "You okay?"

"Me?" Abigail stared at him.

His knuckles were bloody, as was his mouth and the top of one ear. But he laughed, holding his ribs. "Scrappers. I was doing okay until the bat entered the picture." He chuckled. "That was a good fight. Wow."

He'd enjoyed it? What was *wrong* with him?

"The baby?" He leaned forward.

Heidi was still sucking on the knuckle of Abigail's pinkie. "She's fine, thanks to you. But what happens if Tiffany comes back for her?"

"I recorded the man saying Tiffany intended to *give* her to a rich couple who couldn't have kids of their own, and a lot of money would be given to Tiffany in exchange for the gift."

"What?"

"Ya, you heard me right."

Abigail couldn't imagine. "Are you hurt?"

He looked at his hands. "Maybe."

He was so nonchalant, as if pain was a routine thing. He seemed to know a lot about fighting, and she should be thankful that he'd been able to protect them, but her insides felt as though someone was scrubbing them with steel wool. The Amish didn't believe in violence, not ever. But she didn't want clarification. Not now. He got them out of there, and she was grateful. That's all that mattered for now.

She needed to buckle in, but since there wasn't a car seat for the baby, she didn't bother. "Denki, Chris."

He lifted a trembling hand and stroked her cheek with his thumb. As his eyes moved over her face, he smiled, and then he leaned in and kissed her forehead. "*You* are something else, Abi."

"Me?"

He nodded.

"I feel so confused, so lost and angry. How could Roy do this to Jemima?"

"A piece of advice?" He clutched his trembling hands and leaned back, closing his eyes.

She guessed he was trying to stop the flow of adrenaline. "Please."

"Don't go there. Put it in God's hands. Acknowledge and then dismiss all the emotions and questions that come your way. Do it a hundred times an hour if need be, but it's your brother's battle. And Jemima's. Emotional turmoil over what's happening in someone else's marriage is like us taking on the feeding and care of every horse farm in Pennsylvania."

She could clearly see his meaning. They would be exhausted by the impossibility of it.

She slid her hand over his. "That was the perfect thing to say. Denki."

"Ya, even a blind squirrel finds a nut every once in a while."

As unlikely as it seemed, he had her smiling and feeling safe and hopeful. Who was this rugged man, and how did he have such wisdom?

She tapped the driver's shoulder. "Once we're in a decent area, we need to stop somewhere to buy baby items." They needed several things. Abigail's finger wasn't going to hold the little one much longer.

How was Jemima going to emotionally cope with this infant coming into her home? And how long would it be before the community learned the truth, adding even more humiliation to Jemima's already full load?

Fourteen

Chris walked toward the poultry-barn-turned-stable. Pain shot through his right hand, a lingering reminder of yesterday's fight to get Heidi. But his hand wasn't all that bothered him. His entire body ached. He had bruised ribs, a headache, and a bloody cough, and his right eye was a little blurry. Had he really hurt himself? That fight was something different, especially when both men came at him, one with a baseball bat. He was relieved he had escaped when he did.

He opened the door to the makeshift stable. The horses were especially quiet this morning, which could be a bad sign. He walked to the first stall, shaking his aching hand.

"Good morning." Abigail's voice caught his attention, and he turned in that direction.

Did she have any idea how amazing she was? His pounding heart was fully aware, yet he hardly knew her. He'd like to rectify that—if that was possible.

She was at the far end of the barn, coming out of Houdini's stall, and Chris headed that direction. The night they'd moved the horses, they'd decided to bring Houdini here even though he was sick, as this barn provided the most distance between the horses. With twelve feet on each side of his usual stall between him and the next horse, Houdini shouldn't pass the virus to other horses. But since they could put him in a stall several hundred feet away from the others, why not take the time and effort to be extremely careful?

"Morning, Abi." He stopped outside Houdini's stall, studying him. The horse's head was hanging, and his eyes were nearly closed. "He's not looking so great, is he?"

Chris turned his attention to Abigail, wondering how she was doing after seeing him fight yesterday and catching a glimpse of who he was. How did she feel about that?

She pulled off the latex gloves. "Nee. He seems to feel worse, but his temperature and steadiness are the same as yesterday." She tossed the gloves into a nearby receptacle. "Speaking of which, you aren't looking exactly chipper yourself. You okay?"

"Rough night." He hoped she wouldn't press him, although it would be nice to talk openly about the fight and his injuries. He wanted to pour out his heart to her and tell her the full truth of what he did and why. He'd started out with good intentions to help his brother with his debt but now was at a loss over how to gain control of the mess.

His brother Dan had texted him a dozen times saying that Chris *had* to agree to another fight or the men Dan owed would lose their patience and come after him. His brother also texted that the powers that be were setting up the next fight and that he'd let Chris know the specifics as soon as he heard anything.

Was there a way out of this that wouldn't cause problems for his brother? Dan owed serious money from gambling, and Chris had agreed to help him. But since then, Chris had hurt his parents and been kicked out of his home, while Dan kept his job, stayed with his wife and children, and acted as if he were innocent and upright.

Abigail put an extra set of gloves in her jacket pocket. Her brows furrowed, and she studied his face. "Do you need to be seen?"

He certainly didn't regret that those events had led him to the Graber farm and Abigail. Should he tell her he fought, even had a trainer, and had to fulfill his commitment or else violent men would come after his brother? Apparently the world of gambling went dark really fast.

"Chris?"

He shook his head. "Nee, I'll be fine."

Between family matters and the horses, she had more than enough to contend with right now without feeling guilty for his injuries or being made aware of the mess he'd gotten himself in. He and Abigail were better off *not* opening that can of worms.

"You're sure? I can handle the workload while you go."

Her kindness warmed him, but he knew his body, and he just needed time to heal. A good bit of time probably.

"I'm gut, Abi. Change of subject, please."

She pursed her lips, looking at him for a few more moments. "Ya, okay." She grabbed a lead line off a nearby nail. "We should get the EHV-1 test results back tomorrow, and if they're negative, life gets easier. Until then the horses need exercising while we keep them apart, so they'll have to be led. That includes Houdini."

He agreed. They didn't want to exhaust Houdini, but he needed to stretch his legs. It wasn't good for a horse to stay stationary, even when sick.

He gestured at the stalls. "I hauled water last night, and it looks as if you've fed them already."

"Ya." Abigail went to another horse's stall. Chris connected the lead line to Houdini's halter and led him out of the stall and into the open air. Abigail came to the edge of the stall with her horse.

"How's Lady Belle?"

"No fever, and her cold symptoms are gone."

Chris nodded his head. "Gut."

Every step he took sent pain through him, and he imagined that Houdini felt the same: achy and stiff. He patted the horse. "We have some solidarity in the discomfort department, don't we, boy?"

Abigail went ahead of him, moving at a much faster pace than Houdini was up for.

Chris's mind reeled back to the fight with the Englisch guy the night before he came here. He hadn't known if he was winning or losing that night, just as he didn't know in any fight.

He had begun fighting years ago. He and his brother Sol had been in town to get supplies, and a man was being a jerk to Chris, knowing he was Amish and wouldn't do anything about it. His brother challenged him to pop the guy—or at least try. The man had been about the same age as Chris but was bigger. He raised his fists, daring Chris to fight him. Sol told Chris to go for it, and he did. The moment his fist connected with the man's face, an immediate rush of relief went through him. He'd never experienced any feeling that good. So when his brother Dan got in over his head with gambling debt and came up with the idea of Chris, an Amish man, boxing a ranked Englisch man, Chris didn't hesitate to give it a try. Maybe he'd started training to fight for the solid reason of helping his brother, or maybe he'd agreed because he had a hidden passion for it and, dare he think, also a talent for it. But now was he right to go against the Amish ways in order to help Dan? Regardless of the answer, he couldn't abandon his brother to violent men.

His phone buzzed, and he looked at the screen. It was a text from Dan: NEXT FIGHT SET UP! You will need training. Date of fight is March 15.

March fifteenth? That was in less than a month! The fight should set everything straight with the bookies, but after taking two hits to the gut yesterday with a baseball bat—especially given the way the strikes landed—he shouldn't fight for at least six weeks. He felt sure his spleen needed time to heal. But this fight would end his brother's troubles. Still, could he fight that soon? He certainly couldn't without proper training, and his trainer, Mike, wasn't close by. How could he train and do his job here? He needed to arrange a session with Mike. He would know pretty quickly if Chris would be ready for another fight by mid-March.

"Girlfriend trouble?" Abigail passed him, leading Lady Belle back to the barn.

He looked up from his phone. "Definitely not. Too single for that." He shoved it into his pocket. "Didn't we cover that topic?"

She turned, grinning. "Just making sure it hadn't changed."

He laughed and his insides clenched, sending aches and pains throughout his body. She was clearly flirting with him. What was he thinking? If he fought again, it could ruin all chances with Abigail. Or would she be open minded?

Meeting someone had been off his radar for so long that he'd become comfortable doing things as he saw fit without regard to how a significant other might feel. Today was only day five of knowing her, but they'd navigated a lot, and he was drawn to her. Besides, regardless of all else, Roy needed him.

He texted his brother: Too soon. I need to mend from a recent incident and I'm needed here. Maybe in a few months.

Dan: What? No! What could I possibly tell these people that they'd accept and reschedule?

He needed time to think, so he slid the phone into his pocket. He had given Dan his word—a promise to fight in order to take care of the gambling debt. That was crystal clear. But he felt uneasy for reasons he couldn't put his finger on. Was the disquiet simply a matter of guilt for stepping outside the Amish faith in order to help his brother? Or was it fear that his fighting could come between Abigail and him? And why hadn't Dan paused for a moment when Chris mentioned being hurt?

He led Houdini to a post twelve feet away from where Abi was grooming Lady Belle. He grabbed a brush and began running it over the horse. Abigail would be the perfect person to talk to about his confusion over the text, but yesterday she'd been clear that she didn't want to know his secrets or his past—not right now with so much happening with her brother and Jemima.

Maybe he could ask her a few questions without divulging anything she might find disappointing or stressful. "How do you know what you owe to someone else?"

She paused in the middle of the brush stroke. "Usually a bill comes in the mail that clarifies it." Amusement danced in her eyes before she returned to brushing the horse.

He grinned. "Not the monetary kind, but you knew that."

She nodded. "I did." She moved to the front of the horse and brushed her neck. "Everyone could use an extra set of hands in life. Some feel my time is theirs for the asking, as if I owe my free time to them since I don't have a husband and children needing me." She nuzzled Lady Belle, and the horse seemed to be in heaven. "Is that what you mean?"

He'd experienced a good bit of that himself over the years, but he imagined more was asked of single women than men because the work of getting meals on the table and tending to children was non-stop. "Sort of. I agreed to do something to help my brother Dan, and I did so because he *really* needs the help, and it's something I enjoy, and I'm good at it. But it's physically hard on the body. He texted me just now, telling me the date. When I mentioned being injured and needing to be here to help out, his response was . . . confusing, but I'm not sure why."

She studied him. "What did he say about your injuries?"

"Nothing, but I owe him the help. I agreed to it, and he's backed into a corner with no way out unless I help." How could Chris just up and leave the farm with Roy injured and unable to work?

Her eyes narrowed, reflecting concern. "He said nothing about your being hurt?"

"You're missing the point, Abi."

"Nee, I don't think I am. He dismissed your injuries."

"Because I gave him my word and he desperately needs me to follow through. We both know the teachings about swear to your own hurt."

"We do, from the book of Psalms. If we want to dwell in His holy hill, we swear to our own hurt and carry out what we agreed to."

His gut churned with anxiety. How could he use a scripture as his reason for following through on something that was against the Amish ways?

"But, Chris, life is full of give-and-take. When you and Roy worked out a deal, did he say you'd be working around the clock?"

Chris shook his head.

"So you give more than was asked, and that's fine with you, but you can't give less when the need arises?"

"I hadn't thought of it like that."

"Is someone sick?"

"Nee. He made some bad decisions, and he's repentant and getting his life in order. But he owes money and needs my help."

"You didn't hesitate to put up a boundary with me when you thought I had an uncontrollable temper, so why is it a problem to put up a boundary with your brother?"

He sighed. "I wouldn't call what I did with you 'setting a boundary.' It was more like being in full retreat mode, which comes naturally to me in dealing with single women." Why did he feel such a strong desire to tell her the truth no matter how embarrassing?

Her smile warmed his heart. Where was her judgment?

"I'm glad it wasn't a boundary, or we wouldn't be here, free to enjoy whatever this is between us."

He chuckled. "That's a positive spin on it." He moved to the other side of Houdini and stroked him with the brush. "Have you been in a bind like this?"

"Sure. I think all nice people are too agreeable at times. But we have to sort out our motivation, because until we understand that part, we'll just keep giving in."

"That makes sense. How do you know all that?"

"Our community has an Al-Anon–type group of women who are married to addicts, and since I help at the recovery home, I assist in facilitating meetings, have for seven years. I haven't been the last few weeks, but as a general rule I go. We read self-help books regularly and talk and cover a lot of this kind of stuff. If a family member is too nice to an addict, it actually supports the addict's drinking and bad decisions. It's called enabling. Are you being too agreeable?"

"How would I know?"

"There's a short list of questions to ask yourself. My favorite is this: Is it hurting your life while helping his?"

That question put so many things in perspective, and he nodded. He knew why he'd gotten backed into this corner. He liked boxing, but that wasn't the reason for the fix he was in. Dan was constantly in some sort of fix. He seemed to move from one addiction battle to another, and Chris hated what it would do to their parents and to Dan's wife and children if no one helped him.

"Seems to me that most relationship issues are solved with one thing: setting boundaries. See the problem for what it is, set a boundary, and follow through despite how hard the person tries to break the boundary and how much it hurts to hold fast."

That was exactly what he'd done with his fiancée, although he hadn't realized it until now. But this was different. Dan's wife and children were innocent in this mess, and he didn't want them to become victims of any kind. "I can't abandon Dan."

"What can you do?"

Again her question put a lot in perspective. He could see his trainer as soon as possible to find out if he was able to train safely and fight by mid-March. If his trainer said no, he had to tell Dan no. If the trainer said yes, he still needed to refuse to leave Roy in a bind. Either Dan took a leave of absence at work to take Chris's place on this farm or Dan found someone who could. "I get it. I know what I need to do and not do, until I can meet my obligation to Dan. Who knew that a man who stood his ground on so many things would have an area where he gave in regardless of the cost."

She raised her hand. "I knew. I see it regularly. I've done it myself. Even good boundary keepers will often have at least one person in their lives that they struggle to say no to."

"So, Abigail Graber, why are you still single?"

She led Lady Belle to her stall, unfastened the lead line, and closed the stall. "I told you why the morning we met. Men grate on my nerves."

"All men, all the time? That's sort of weird. You don't look like the kind of woman who is perpetually irked."

"Denki, I think." She scrunched her brows, making a face at him. "I don't know what happens." She disinfected the lead line and hung it on a nail on the wall before grabbing a fresh one. "I date someone for a few weeks, maybe up to six weeks, and I see what the future would hold with him, and then I'm done. No second chances given, because I've seen women who gave second chances and lived to regret it."

"That must be hard."

"Nah, not even a little, actually." She opened another stall and attached the fresh lead line to another horse. "I guess it could be if I didn't see what I needed to and fell in love first. But I haven't, and I really enjoy my life as a single woman. So that helps me let go each time, I'm sure."

"You've dated, what, ten guys?"

"Closer to thirty." She came out of the stall, watching the horse's right front leg, which the horse seemed to be favoring. She stopped, and the horse followed suit.

"Wow, and not one lasted more than six weeks?"

"Not that I recall."

"But some had to be good, steady guys."

"I'm sure they were, but I'm also sure each one would have created unnecessary heavy baggage that I would have had to contend with. Now I'm the one saying change of subject, please." She moved her hands down one of the horse's front legs and made it bend at the knee.

Chris put Houdini in his stall, disinfected the lead, and hung it far away from the other leads. They wouldn't use that one on any other horse. "You mentioned that even good boundary keepers often have someone they struggle to say no to. Is it safe to assume that's Roy for you?"

She pulled a hoof pick from the hidden pocket of her apron. "Ya. Sometimes." She scraped around the inside of the horseshoe and dug what appeared to be a small rock from its sole. "One time he asked me to quit teaching and work the farm. I love working with horses, but riding and grooming are only part of the job. There's too much mucking out stalls, carrying hay bales, and hauling feed sacks for me to enjoy it as a full-time job. On top of that, rather than my uncle being my overseer, my brother would be. Uh, no, but thanks." She continued cleaning the hoof.

"I can see that. So when you give up teaching, it'll be to do something you love"—he led another horse from its stall—"like cooking over a hot stove in the very confined space of a food truck."

She laughed and released the horse's leg. "Yep. And during those few months of tourist season, I'll make more money than I did working an entire school year, and I'll have lots of free time that I will not give away unless I want to. It's my life. But I know I'll give my uncle a full day of help every week, and I'll attend the women's group sessions."

"Abigail?" A man called.

"Oh." Abigail's face lit up. "My uncle."

"Hallo?" The man came around the corner and strode into the barn.

"Uncle Mervin." She hurried toward him, and the horse followed. "I'm so glad to see you."

The man's eyes took her in. "Are you okay? Is everything all right?" He looked at Chris sideways before he hugged his niece.

Abigail released him. "I'm fine. Rough few days with the horses, but everything is just fine." She nodded at Chris. "Uncle, this is—"

"Chris Fisher. I know. He's why I'm here."

Chris knew the look and the disapproving ring in words.

"Ah, here to meet the newcomer." Abigail patted the horse's neck. Her uncle's demeanor seemed to go over Abigail's head. "Chris, this is Mervin Stoltzfus, my uncle and the bishop."

Chris held out his hand. "Nice to meet you."

Mervin didn't shake his hand.

"Uncle." Abigail looked from Chris's hand to her uncle, and her expression changed. When an Amish minister refused to shake an Amish man's hand, it said everything most people needed to know. "What's the problem?" Abigail tugged at the lead, making the horse back up so the three of them could see each other.

"Chris isn't just here as a hired hand. Do you know anything about him? I heard about the new string and the possible EHV-1, but that is no reason for you to be way off out here with a man you don't know."

Abigail tilted her head. "It sounds as if you have news that's worrying you." Her smile was genuine. "But you know me and trust me, and I trust Chris."

"I got a call from one of his preachers, ya. He was forced to leave his community. His Mamm put his clothes in paper bags and sent them with his Daed, unwilling to allow him back in the house, and then he came here."

Abigail's beautiful brown eyes lingered on Chris. "I trust him."

"Abi, are you hearing me?" Mervin's concern seemed genuine. "A man who left home under those circumstances can't be trusted to work beside you like this."

Abigail's eyes met Chris's, and she seemed less confident in him already. "He's needed here."

"Then you return to the classroom and teaching and let Roy work beside him."

"Roy's hurt," she said. "The horses can't be in contact with each other. They need settling, grooming, and exercising, and some need shoeing. I can't tend to them without Chris's help."

The bishop raised an eyebrow. "Your brother's hurt? Why is this the first I'm hearing of it?"

"Happened yesterday." She looked at the ground for a moment. "Badly broken arm."

"I'm sorry to hear that. A new string of horses can be risky business."

Abigail's eyes moved to Chris's, and he could see her guilt as plain as day. She hadn't lied, but she wasn't correcting her uncle either. In Chris's few days of knowing her—actually in his first few minutes—he realized she was most comfortable with complete honesty even if it was brutal. What was *he* comfortable with?

Mervin smoothed the horse's mane. "So when will you return to the classroom?"

"Another week, maybe two, but since Sarah hopes to win that teaching spot when I quit, she's loving being my substitute. She's hoping to impress you, and the experience is good for her."

"Gut." The bishop nodded. "Look, with Roy injured that badly, I'm sure he needs his wife by his side to help him right now, so you tell her that both of them and the children are given permission to miss church this Sunday." He stepped forward, getting closer to Chris. "I've never known my niece to trust an unworthy man, so that gives you some grace, but I'm going to keep an eye on you, and if you're staying in my district, I expect *you* to be in church . . . clean shaven."

"Fair enough." Chris stroked the horse.

The bishop pointed at Abigail. "You watch your back."

She smiled and hugged him. "I love you too."

As the bishop walked out, Chris's heart was racing. What should he tell Abigail? He didn't want to ruin any chance he had of their dating.

"Are we talking about this?" Abigail seemed ready to either stay or walk the horse and drop the matter, probably not for forever but for now.

He should shake his head and let the subject drop, at least until after the pleasure of a date night or two. "I . . . I fight, and I'm good at it."

"Fight? Like you get into brawls, similar to yesterday?" The disbelief on her face said more than he wanted to hear.

"I've done that, too, but, no, I'm talking about planned fights. And I practice at a boxing gym with a trainer."

She seemed frozen, and he wasn't sure she was breathing. Organized sports were forbidden for the Amish. Martial arts were taboo. And violence of any kind, especially premeditated or for profit, was unthinkable.

Finally she drew a breath and rubbed the horse's neck. "That makes a lot of things add up, doesn't it?" Everything about her—her facial expression, her eyes, her body language—indicated disappointment. "I'm glad you know how to fight. Grateful that yesterday you had the skill to take on two men at once and get all three of us out of there. I can't condemn what you do when something that good came from it."

Her gratitude was clear. Unfortunately he expected the word *but* was coming soon, and he felt that nothing between them would be the same once she finished her thoughts.

"Abi." He crooked his fingers and put them under her chin, hoping for a kiss. She leaned in and he lowered his lips to hers. Her kiss was tender and sweet, unlike any other. She tasted of spicy Red Hots candy.

Step back!

It was several long moments before he pulled back. "But?" He didn't want to know. Still, it was the respectful thing to do: ignore what he wanted and listen to what she needed to say.

She put her hands on his face and drew him to her, kissing him again. He put his arms around her. It seemed they both wanted more time before she had to tell him the rest of her thoughts.

She slipped from his arms and lightly touched his lips, saying nothing for several moments. She lowered her hand. "When you said there were things that could come between us, I thought you meant things that were behind you. I don't know how I feel about this. You seem to be fine with going against our ways."

"I'm not always sure how I feel about it either. But my brother is drowning in gambling debt. It's serious debt with serious conse-quences. He's in a program and hasn't placed a bet in six months, but with one fight I should be able to get rid of the debt." Was that all he'd tell her? "But there is a part of me that loves boxing."

"One fight *should* be enough?"

"One fight would've taken care of all the debt if the match hadn't been interrupted. I don't know how well this next one will be pro-moted. It's possible it'll take two or three more fights."

"I can see why your Mamm was unwilling for you to return home for your clothes."

"I've got to do this for Dan."

"Just for Dan?"

She had him dead to rights. He was wavering all over the place. He wasn't doing this only for Dan. "Look, Abi, it's very clear that I have to give up boxing and fairly soon, but I can't right now."

She said nothing as she bridled the horse, apparently planning to ride it at least briefly for its exercise, which made sense because it hadn't had a cold and had no signs of EHV-1.

But was her intention to end the conversation without closure and get away from him?

"Abigail, say something."

She grabbed the horse's mane, and with a slight jump she easily pulled herself onto its bare back and straddled it. "Over the years, I've seen a lot of men decide to go their own way rather than the Amish way." She shifted her weight, settling in to ride bareback. "It does something inside them. Their hearts seem to wander to places they never fully come back from, even when they choose to stay. Many return, deciding to follow the Amish ways, but often for the wrong reasons: for a woman they loved or parents they can't continue to hurt by living out the dream. But whatever their reason for staying, their love of life is only half there. The other half is deadweight, stuck in a world they never really left behind, and their wives are the ones who have to help carry that load."

Was she right? Would following through with this one fight for Dan change who he was? The desire to box had taken hold of him through one decision to set aside the Amish ways and punch a man, sending adrenaline and the thrill of a rush through him.

"Chris."

He pulled from his thoughts and looked up at her.

The horse pranced, but Abigail's eyes stayed fixed on his. "I don't want to be one of those women, one who helps drag her man's dead-weight from another world."

Should he refuse to fight?

How could he? His brother needed this of him, and he'd agreed to do it.

Fifteen

A newborn's cry pierced Roy's haze of sleep, stirring a need to get to Simeon. The little guy didn't cry very much, and it was strange that Jemima hadn't tended to him already.

Wait, that wasn't right. The painful throbbing of his arm jolted him to reality. Simeon wasn't a newborn anymore. Which meant . . . Heidi? A wave of relief the size of a pond washed over him. He was home, and Heidi was in the house.

Then a second wave, the size of an ocean, hit: *Jemima.*

He sat up and pushed the quilt back, every part of his body reminding him exactly what had happened. The crash. Staggering home. Jemima learning about Heidi. Doc Grant tending to his injuries.

So where was Jemima? He paused to pray for her, for them, but it did nothing for the anxiety he felt.

"Jem?" His voice came out in a hoarse crackle. There was no way she could hear him above Heidi's cries. How could they help the little girl feel better? She seemed to always be crying. He swung his legs to the side of the bed and stood, feeling as if he were a hundred years old.

Following the sound of the wailing, he walked to the guest room, his arm and battered body aching more with each step. When he got there, he saw that someone had set up Heidi's bassinet in the center of the room. But the baby was in his wife's arms.

"Ah, zsh . . . zsh . . . zsh." Jemima was standing in front of the window and making long shushing sounds near the infant's ear. Jemima was such a seasoned pro at this. Heidi was wrapped in the pink swaddle blanket he'd brought to Tiffany's a few weeks ago. Someone must have found that too. Had Jemima been in Tiffany's house? Jemima shifted Heidi higher on her shoulder and patted her back.

He leaned against the doorframe on his good arm. The sight of his beautiful wife holding his child by another woman made him feel sick. He was relieved for Heidi's sake, but deep sadness mingled with his guilt.

Did Jemima hate him? Heidi belonged to the woman who'd turned Jemima's life upside down, yet Jemima was more tender and caring toward the newborn than Heidi's birth mother had ever been.

Heidi let out a huge burp and then a sigh as she snuggled against Jemima's shoulder, finally stopping her cries.

Jemima released a big breath too. "Now go to sleep, for Pete's sake." She turned from the window and noticed Roy. The pain that filled her face made him physically hurt.

He smiled at her. "Denki."

She regarded him for a moment before turning away to face the window again, still patting Heidi's back. He never imagined seeing that kind of hurt in her eyes. How could *he* be the cause of that wound in his beloved?

What could he say? He stood a little straighter. "Jem . . . this whole situation. It's not how it looks."

She turned just enough to shoot him a look over her shoulder. "My holding this baby isn't how it looks either." Her voice was eerily calm. He'd heard this tone before. To anyone else Jemima would appear serene, but Roy knew there was a volcano of feelings boiling below the surface.

Carolyn's giggle floated through the air, followed by a happy squeal from Simeon.

"Are the children okay?" he asked. "Do I need to go down there with them?"

"Oh?" She turned, fury in her eyes. "So *now* you think about the children you had with me. Of course they're safe." She walked a few more steps away from him. "It's a school day and about ten in the morning, so Laura isn't home. I told Carolyn there were two cookies for her if she watched and played nicely with her brothers in the gated play area in the living room. I was planning to come to your room after I got this child to sleep. We need to talk."

Roy swallowed the lump in his throat. He'd known this moment was coming. Would she believe him? Could they work past her rage and distrust? Or would her hurt turn to hate, causing her to live out her days detesting him?

She crossed the room and stood directly in front of him. "Tell me everything." She sounded threatening, as if she were giving a mean stray dog a final warning to get off the property before she called the authorities or got the shotgun. "Everything."

He nodded. "Ya, I will." Where to start? "Last year after the accident—"

The sound of buggy wheels on the gravel driveway startled both of them.

Jemima shifted the now sleeping Heidi to a cradle position and placed her into the crook of Roy's good arm. "Stay here. I'll find out who it is." She pointed at the baby. "*No one* is to know about her. Understand? I don't care what has to be said. No one is to know she's yours. You'll find a good home for her immediately, and then she's gone from this house."

That statement was completely at odds with the tranquil scene he'd witnessed earlier as she was calming Heidi. He blinked a few times. "Find a good home" was something a person said about a horse or a dog, not a child. "Excuse me?"

"You heard me. You'll let another family raise her. After she's gone, our home goes back to normal. You owe me and our children that much." She stepped around him and closed the door behind her as she left.

Roy looked at the sleeping child in his arms. She pursed her tiny pink lips, occasionally sucking on a phantom bottle. Like every infant, she was pure innocence. Was she not as valuable in God's eyes as any other child?

She's valuable beyond measure.

The words stole his breath. It was as if God was speaking to Roy just as He had after Laura was born. Roy snuggled Heidi tighter to his chest. No. They didn't allow strangers even to babysit their children for a few hours. The person had to be very familiar to them, usually with years of known diligence and gentleness. How in the world could he give her up now that she was safe in his arms? He couldn't.

Sixteen

Jemima drove the rig down the road toward home. She'd taken Laura to school by herself, hoping to have a few moments of solitude. Heidi had been in her home two nights, really long, tough nights and one full day. Hurt and rage simmered in Jemima continually, and she was desperate for some type of relief.

Yesterday around this same time, she'd been upstairs listening as Roy began telling what caused Tiffany to carry his child. But his Daed had arrived, and she'd had to hurry outside and cover for Roy. It hadn't been easy to keep him from going inside to see Roy, but she'd managed it. By the time she walked back inside, both babies were crying, and Carolyn and Nevin were both clingy, as if the two crying babies had shaken their world.

Jemima never got to hear Roy's tale—not that she wanted to, but it seemed necessary. She hoped something inside the story would give her relief from wanting to emotionally destroy Roy. She struggled day and night, wondering exactly what had taken place between her husband and Tiffany. Did he love Tiffany?

Clearly the woman had conceived Heidi while Jemima was an hour away by car, staying at her mother's with complications from a pregnancy. Is that all it took for her husband to be unfaithful—for Jemima to be away from home?

She pulled onto the driveway and stopped the rig in front of the carriage house. The conflict inside her chest felt as if it were going to tear her in two. She couldn't stop loving her husband, but at the same time, she couldn't shake the utter repulsion she felt because of his actions. Creating a baby with another woman!

"Hey, Jemima." Chris came out of the stables and hurried toward her. "I'll unhitch the horse and take care of it."

"Denki." She got out of the carriage, looking closely at Chris. She'd seen him when he and Abigail brought the baby home day before yesterday, but she hadn't seen him at breakfast. His face was more bruised today.

"Lunch will be ready at noon."

"We appreciate it, Jemima."

"It's the least I can do." She started toward the house and paused. "Any word from the vet?"

"Ya. Houdini tested positive on the EHV-1. But he's the only one who's shown any signs so far. The horses need to remain separated for twenty-eight days after the last horse shows symptoms. Since Abigail insisted we separate them the day Houdini showed symptoms, we have reason to hope no other horse has been exposed to it. And we're smoothing out the system of taking care of them, so in another week it won't be such a burden to tend to them."

"That's good and encouraging. Denki, Chris." It was embarrassing to chat with someone she barely knew while he knew the worst secrets between her and her husband. She nodded and went toward the house.

She and Roy still hadn't talked. By the time the children were tucked into bed, Roy was too drowsy from the pain meds to say anything coherent. He fell asleep mumbling that he was sorry. Her rage stayed just beneath the surface, even when she was nursing Simeon or bathing Nevin or praying with her girls. The fact that Heidi rarely slept only added to Jemima's inability to feel anything except fury.

She went up the steps and paused just outside the front door, her hand hovering over the knob. There were a number of unpleasant chores she'd rather do than go inside and have to be reasonably nice to Roy. But her three younger kids were inside too, and they needed her.

She swallowed and opened the door.

"Vroom!" Nevin's sweet voice echoed through the house, followed by Simeon's happy squeal.

Jemima hung her coat on the peg by the door and then walked through the home until she came to the gated play area. Roy was sitting on the floor, leaning against the wall for support. Nevin shoved a toy truck toward his father, who caught it before it whacked him in the leg. In one smooth motion he turned it around and rolled it back to the toddler. Simeon was nearby on his hands and knees, looking like he really wanted to crawl toward the rolling thing. Any day now he'd be able to, and then he'd be on the move too. Roy tried to meet her eyes, but Jemima couldn't stand to look at him.

"Mamm!" Carolyn jumped up from her spot on the floor and bounced to her feet. *"Kumm guck. Zwee Bobbelis. Zwee!"* She held up two fingers while pointing toward a soft blanket on the other side of Roy, protected from the rolling toy truck by Roy's legs. In the center of the blanket was Tiffany's baby girl. The infant wasn't currently crying, which was rare.

"Ya." What could Jemima say to her daughter? She couldn't explain the situation. "Two babies."

Carolyn grinned. "Friend Bobbeli!"

A friend's baby—the lie Roy had given their daughter, no doubt. However, Jemima was grateful she didn't have to explain to her five-year-old why they had another baby in the house. The pacifier worked its way out of Heidi's mouth and she immediately started crying. Carolyn skipped back to Heidi and replaced it.

A corner of Roy's lips turned up in a half smile. "She's put that back about a hundred times so far this morning."

Carolyn gently rubbed the infant's stomach and said in Pennsylvania Dutch that she was good at taking care of *her* babies, a phrase she often used to refer to her younger brothers.

A cold rage filled Jemima's core, and she had to bite her tongue not to say anything. Her daughter, who wanted a little sister so badly, was loving on *that woman's* baby. Jemima stepped over the gate, leaned down, and picked up the baby, saying in Pennsylvania Dutch, "Nap time for the baby. I'll put her in her crib." As angry as Jemima was, she handled the baby with care. She'd happily pick up Roy and chuck him outside, broken arm and all, but the baby was one of God's own. She turned to Carolyn and asked if she would play with her brothers for a few minutes while Jemima got the baby to bed, and she promised to make her something yummy afterward.

Carolyn's eyes lit up. "Ya, Mamm." She crawled over and intercepted the toy truck as it came Roy's way.

Again Jemima could feel his eyes on her. She barely looked at him and gestured with her head toward the guest room where the bassinet was. He nodded and then used his good arm to help himself to his feet. They both walked into the guest room, and Jemima wasted no time putting the baby in the bassinet.

Roy sat on the guest bed, where he'd slept last night, where he might sleep for years to come. He'd made the bed, but the quilt was slightly rumpled, likely due to his having the use of only one arm.

Jemima took a few steps back and crossed her arms. Being in the same room with him was bad enough. She couldn't bring herself to sit next to him. "I want to hear everything."

"I know you do. You deserve that."

Deserve? Jemima had to fight with herself to keep from yelling at him before he even began. "Go on."

He fiddled with the pattern on the quilt. "Last year was hard, Jem, on all of us."

"Spare me the descriptions of how hard life was and get to the point, Roy."

"After the accident, not long after Laura was released from the hospital and while you and the children were staying at your Mamm's, I . . . Something happened at Tiffany's house."

"You think?" Her voice sounded nothing like her, and she wondered who she was becoming.

"But I need to back up a tad first. After the horse-and-buggy wreck, while you and the children were staying with your Mamm, I hurt all the time from the injuries, and I got hooked on pain meds."

Her heart lurched and she audibly gasped. He'd become addicted to pain meds while she was gone? How had she not known that? But anger raged. "I don't want your excuses."

"I didn't mean . . ." He took a deep breath. "One evening Tiffany kept calling my cell, desperate for me to come and fix a broken pipe. She had friends over, and the plumbing in the only bathroom wasn't working. My head was spinning, maybe from exhaustion but probably from the pain meds I was popping like candy to get through the day. I guess I'd taken too many of them. I remember seeing her friends, and I remember going into the bathroom to work on the pipe. I think I fixed it. Tiffany was talking to me, maybe in the bathroom. I don't really know, but I just wanted to come home."

She gave him a good thirty seconds to find his voice, but he still didn't speak up. "I'm waiting."

He cleared his throat and nodded. "We talked for a minute, and I was surprised when we kissed. I remember backing away, saying I needed to go home. That's all I really remember. Nothing felt real for some reason. Most everything seemed black and was spinning." Roy closed his eyes. "I . . . woke up in her bed, half-dressed. Her friends were long gone."

No memory at all? Was that true or just another lie?

"Then after that forgetful night, you came home to me as if nothing had happened," Jemima spewed.

"I came home. You and the children were still at your Mamm's, and you were on full bed rest."

"Were you lonely while I was carrying our fourth child, or just bored with me?"

Roy hit the bedspread with his fist. "Don't do that, Jemima. I wanted to tell you immediately! But you were pregnant with Simeon. Remember your blood-pressure issue? The doctor had told me that if it got too high, it would put your life and Simeon's at risk. The very least of the consequences would have been your having him by C-section, which would make any future births more complicated."

Future births. That was never going to happen! But she didn't say that out loud. "So you went back to your routine life after sleeping with her just once. Are you sure you didn't return to her bed again?"

"I swear to you, Jemima. I came off the pain pills so I'd never lose another night like that. I *never* would've been with her if I was in my right mind."

Was that the truth? He'd dated Tiffany when he was a teen in his rumschpringe. "She always wanted you, and you stopped seeing her to chase after me. We chose to confide in each other all of who we were. I knew you. *I* was your confidante, not her. Now you've humiliated me by keeping this secret with her. She knew about me, about our children. I was the only one in the dark."

"I'm sorry."

"Saying you're sorry after circumstances forced you to tell me the truth means less than nothing. So then what happened?"

"Weeks later she texted me saying she was pregnant. For the

same reasons, I still couldn't tell you. I had to protect you and our child."

"And what about after Simeon was born? You couldn't tell me then? He's eight months old! You've had forever with both of us being healthy and stable to divulge this secret."

"I know." Roy took a deep breath and let it out slowly. "I thought it would be easier on you if you didn't know. I thought I could get Tiffany and Heidi set up and then things would go back to normal."

"Normal?" she shrieked. "Normal? You wanted us all to live a lie for the rest of our lives. How is that normal?" She had to fight to keep from screaming at him. Carolyn didn't need to hear her Mamm yelling at her Daed.

His shoulders slumped. "I didn't want you to have to go through any of this, to doubt what I'm telling you, to feel betrayed by something I can't recall." He paused. "You of all people didn't deserve to pay for this in any way—"

"Whoa!" Jemima held up one hand. "Speaking of paying, were *my* savings, Abigail's and mine, used for taking care of Tiffany and"—she pointed—"that baby?"

"Some was used for covering the medical bills for Laura, just like I told you, but having a baby the Englisch way is expensive, especially without their insurance."

Emotions pounded her, and her thoughts ran wild, each one adding fire to the others. "Only the best hospital for your illegitimate daughter to be born in."

Roy dragged his hand down his face. "I was doing my best to take care of her, just like I would any of my kids. She shouldn't have to pay for the mistakes of an unloving mother and a father who never meant to be with that woman, much less create a baby."

Jemima pointed at the bassinet, where Heidi was beginning to fuss. "Except she won't pay. Our children will pay for your mistake if this gets out to the community and you're shunned. They'll have to deal with it for the rest of their lives. Can you imagine living under such a stigma?"

"I don't want that."

"Then we're in agreement." Jemima went over to the bassinet and looked in but didn't pick up the squirming baby. "You have to find her an Englisch home. It's where she belongs. They won't question how she was created, and she can grow up in a loving home with a mother and father."

"Jem." His whisper was filled with dismay. "I don't think I can give her up."

"I'm not raising *that* child. You can forget it, Roy. My children will not watch you be shunned for this. There are good families praying for a healthy baby to adopt. Good people who can't have kids of their own or who desperately want another. You need to take her to social services. They'll help you find one of those families. Then she'll have a stable home life, and so will your older four children. You owe it to them and to me to keep our lives intact."

"Aren't our lives already upside down?"

"If you give her up, I'll forgive you." Even as the words tumbled out of her mouth, they felt wrong. "We'll put everything in the past and move forward." Why did her words feel as if they were more of a lie than anything Roy had said?

Then it hit her. She had no idea if she could actually forgive him. She didn't even know how much she believed of what he'd told her. But even if she believed all of it, she hated how long he'd withheld this truth from her—hated how often he'd gone to see Tiffany while lying to Jemima about where he was. Could she ever forgive him?

Did she have any other option?

Seventeen

Roy glanced at the clock on the wall of the social services' private meeting room. It was ten minutes past one o'clock, the time he'd set for the meeting. He'd called yesterday after his argument with Jemima, and he'd been surprised the woman he spoke with on the phone had been able to meet with him and Heidi so soon. But if he had to wait much longer, he'd have to fix Heidi another bottle.

A pleasant-looking Englisch couple smiled down at Roy from a poster that said in bold text, "Be a foster parent. Save a life!" The meeting room itself was small but cozy with a soft brown couch that he was sitting on, a short coffee table, and two easy chairs. Heidi stirred and began fussing in her car seat next to him on the couch. Did she need a bottle? It wasn't quite time. Maybe he could get her back to sleep first.

Roy reached for her with his good arm. He was getting better at unlatching the buckles with one hand. After he released the straps, he used his torso to keep the seat from moving off the couch, and then he scooped her up out of the plastic-and-fabric infant carrier and into the crook of his arm. "Sh." He hoped that if he bounced her gently she'd fall back to sleep. He'd rather not face this with her wailing. It was going to be hard enough, at best.

The seven-week-old sighed but didn't open her eyes. *Phew.* Heidi must've just wanted to be held. He kissed the top of her head through her pink baby hat.

He didn't want to give her up. But he'd walked the floors all night, praying. At least half of that time, he'd been holding Heidi. By sunrise he knew what he had to do. He had to put what Jemima needed ahead of what he needed. After hours of praying without ceasing, he'd realized that with Tiffany out of the picture, Heidi's life could be normal and happy inside a good home. But the same couldn't be said for his wife. If Heidi stayed, Jemima's life would never be normal or happy again. She would be forced to care for a child she resented. His community would shun him, and his children would face the stigma of an unfaithful father.

No. He had to choose his wife's needs above all else.

A soft knock sounded on the door, and it slowly opened. "Sorry that I'm a few minutes late." A woman in her midthirties entered. She had neat shoulder-length blond hair and gentle mannerisms. "I was just finishing some paperwork on another placement." She smiled at Roy and then tilted her head as she saw Heidi. "Aw, she's asleep. I'm Jenny. We spoke on the phone." Jenny sat in one of the easy chairs across from Roy.

Roy nodded. *It's time. Just stick to the plan.* He'd be okay and so would Heidi. "I'm Roy and this is Heidi."

"It's nice to meet you in person. I didn't realize you were Amish."

He assumed he might be the first Amish person, man or woman, to place a child with the state.

She looked at the baby in his arms. "Heidi looks so sweet."

"I . . . can't keep her." Tears threatened, catching him off guard. Were they from sadness or embarrassment? He had to spill the shameful details. "She's mine, but she's not my wife's. I have a copy of her birth certificate on my phone."

Jenny nodded. "I understand."

There was no way she understood, but Roy wouldn't explain it. He'd sounded like a liar to his own wife. Why would this woman believe him?

"Tiffany, Heidi's mother, abandoned her. I don't know where she is or how to contact her, but I think she's using drugs."

"It's okay. We'll investigate and take care of that." She waved a folder of papers. "I have some information for you, and we'll go over the whole process. Do you have any questions before we begin?"

Roy couldn't take his eyes off the baby's face—her perfect button nose, long eyelashes, and pursed lips.

"Mr. Graber?" The woman leaned in. "You seem to be having second thoughts."

"I never meant to be with Tiffany." Hot tears rolled down his cheeks. "I'd been injured, and I was taking strong pain medicine." Why was he telling her this? What was wrong with him? "A child from a night I don't even recall. How awful a start in life is that for an innocent baby."

Jenny sat upright, fidgeting with the folder of information in her lap. "Mr. Graber, have you done a DNA test on her?"

Roy wiped his cheeks and took a deep breath. "What?"

"Do you have proof that this child is yours?"

"I need proof?"

"For us to take her? No. Anyone with a child they don't wish to care for has the legal right to drop off him or her at an approved secure location, and this is one of those locations. But I work with people all the time, and from what little you've said, a few things are very clear to me: you don't wish to give her up, and—"

"I don't want to, no." Instant relief went through him at his honesty. Lying brought so much anxiety. He studied Heidi. "But I need to think of my wife, not me or even Heidi."

Jenny set the folder on the table. "Does your wife know about your daughter?"

He nodded. "Learned about her a few days ago."

"Are you and Heidi safe in your home?"

"Ya—yes, of course."

"She has plenty to eat, clean clothes, and a safe place to sleep?"

"Yes. Definitely."

"Good."

"My wife is angry with me, but she's good to her and much better to her than Heidi's own mother was."

"I've always heard that the Amish have a special place in their hearts for babies and children. I think I'm seeing that firsthand." She smiled. "The decision is yours, and I can take her from you right now if that's what you want. But I think you should do a few things first. One is take her home with you and think about this for a few more days."

"You don't understand. My wife wants Heidi in someone else's good home, not ours."

"I understand. She's hurt and angry, but we have resources for you if you need them. I can set up counseling for you and your wife."

"You have counseling?" Would that actually help him and Jemima? He couldn't imagine that an Englisch counselor could have anything to say that would apply to their lives, but maybe he was wrong.

"We do, and there's no need to rush into a decision about giving up Heidi. Once she enters the system, getting her back is difficult. But you can easily turn her over in a few days or a week, when you're absolutely sure that is what you want to do." She pulled a sheet of paper from the folder. "The other thing I suggest you do is have a DNA test." She held out the paper to him. "This has the location of labs that would run the test. They may use a cotton swab inside your cheek and Heidi's or draw a little blood from each of you— I'm unsure which—but the DNA results will verify if she's your daughter."

"You think she might not be mine?"

"It's a possibility."

"But if I'm giving her to you, does that even matter? You said it was legal to give up any child."

"If we verify she's yours, you can have a say in releasing her from the foster care system to be adopted, receive occasional letters from her caregivers while she's in foster care, and possibly have contact with her when she's older."

"I could have contact with her?"

"It's likely, yes, depending on a few things. But there's no possibility of it until she's eighteen unless we have verification that she is your daughter. It takes only a few minutes to run the test, but it may take a few weeks to get the results. How did you get here today, Mr. Graber?"

"I hired a driver."

"Good. I can call the lab now, just to see if they could get a blood or saliva sample from you and Heidi today. If they can fit you into their schedule, I imagine that your driver could take you by there on your way home."

He hesitated, studying Heidi. He'd come here in order to put his wife ahead of his illegitimate child. Should he bring the baby home with him?

Jenny stood. "I'll give you a few minutes to think. But there's no pressure here. The decision is in your hands." She nodded at him before exiting the room.

Was the decision in his hands? How could he upend his family's lives and return with the baby? If he did, his community would soon learn of her and have a multitude of questions, putting his family in the exact scenario Jemima needed them to avoid.

He closed his eyes and prayed as the minutes ticked by. What was the right decision here? Heidi began fussing. "Sh." He walked the empty room, swaying her back and forth and praying. One of Roy's favorite Bible verses came to mind, Isaiah 43:1: *Do not fear, for I have redeemed you. I have called you by name; you are Mine!*

That meant Heidi was His too. Roy opened his eyes and gazed

into the baby's sleeping face. It was too soon to tell his wife that Jenny believed Heidi might not be his. The results wouldn't change how many lies he'd told Jemima over the last ten months, and it wouldn't replace the money he'd taken from her. It might raise Jemima's hopes, but the results could dash them again. He knew Heidi was his, had never doubted it from the moment Tiffany told him she was pregnant.

He cupped his hand over the cap on her little head. He couldn't send Heidi off into the great unknown. Not yet.

Maybe not ever.

Jemima placed the flatiron facedown on the woodstove and removed the wooden handle. She folded a couple of towels before she put a dress on the ironing board and reattached the handle. Based on the heat coming off the iron, it should be hot enough to work but not so hot that it would scorch the clothes. The first time she'd used one as a teen, she'd burned a hole in her dress. Her mother wasn't pleased. Jemima pressed it against Laura's dress and moved it back and forth. The feeling and sight of the fabric releasing its wrinkles was always so satisfying.

She glanced at the pile of clothes waiting on the table, including Roy's white church shirts. She'd put those off until last. She felt like burning them.

The sound of a vehicle on the gravel driveway caught her attention.

She set the flatiron upright on the ironing board, went to the window next to the front door, and watched the hired driver pull toward the house. Roy was back.

His story about Tiffany was believable, if he was telling her the truth, and she wanted to believe him. She really did. But that wouldn't change how betrayed she felt by his months of lies by omission or saying that he was leaving the house for work when he was actually going to *her* house, or his decision on his own to empty the savings account, or . . . The list was too long, and it made her head hurt.

Had it been hard hearted of her to demand that he give up the baby? Maybe. But how could their lives go back to normal until he did? They had so much weighing on them already. The lingering issues of last year's accident. Roy's newly broken arm. The disaster of the EHV-1 outbreak. And it was going to take *years* to catch up financially. The emotional trauma of Roy's shunning would be beyond what they could deal with. No, the decision was right. Placing Heidi in an Englisch home was better for all of them.

The car stopped, and the passenger door opened. Roy stood, and even from the window, Jemima could see his grimace of pain. He said something to the driver and then turned to open the back passenger door. No, surely he didn't . . .

He pulled out a car seat, hung it on his good arm, and started walking to the house.

Jemima gaped, sorting through a dozen emotions. She took a deep, steadying breath and walked back to the kitchen. Something had been niggling at the back of her mind all day. She figured that it was from all the heavy emotions she'd been dealing with, but, no, it was a hunch that she didn't want to acknowledge: Roy couldn't give up the baby.

She wanted to scream, but that would wake her napping children. She spread her hands on the kitchen counter, bracing herself. In a few moments the front door opened, and his heavy steps crossed the floor. They stopped near the kitchen, but she didn't look up. She couldn't. She closed her eyes.

"Jemima." Roy's voice was gentle. It was the tone he always used when he was about to tell her something disappointing.

She looked up at him, taking in the sight of him holding the sleeping baby's car seat. He had a determined look on his face. Clearly he'd made a decision. Who was this man? Who was she? They were so far removed from the people they were when they married all those years ago.

"I wanted to. I did, but I . . . I couldn't do it. I need more time. Maybe forever. I don't know. Isn't it possible she's meant to be here with us?"

The question stung, and then it remained in the air. Jemima moved back to the ironing board and picked up the iron by its wooden handle. It still had enough heat to smooth the rest of Laura's dress, so she worked it across the fabric. What could she say to that? She set the iron down on its end and shook out the dress. "Don't ask me ridiculous questions. You know why we agreed to take her to social services. If our family existed in a bubble, it would be different. But if she stays and the community finds out—"

"Jemima, I know the consequences, and I'm ready for them. It's a horrible mess of embarrassment, and if I could take that away for you, I would. Despite how it may seem, it's not that I love her like I do our children. They are a part of you, a part of our love that began years before Laura was born. But just as God is our Father, He is also Heidi's, and her future matters."

"What about our children's futures, their emotional and spiritual security? Don't you think they're more important than Heidi?"

"Not to God."

Jemima closed her eyes. *One, two, three, four.* Sometimes she told her children to stop talking and count to four so they didn't say things they would regret.

Could she really do it? Let Roy keep his baby by another woman in the same house?

"Jem?"

She opened her eyes and faced her husband.

"Maybe we don't have to tell anyone she's mine."

The idea sounded reasonable. It would keep their children from being hurt. "The woman who was renting a home on your Daed's property abandoned her baby. Is that the plan?"

He looked uncomfortable with the idea, but he nodded. How was their family ever supposed to move past this? Would it be easier to do if they didn't tell others that Roy was Heidi's father?

Eighteen

Chris looked out the window of the Uber car. It'd been a long ride marked by rolling hills and barns.

"The scenic route is over." The driver smiled as he entered the small town square.

Soon he pulled to a stop in front of the boxing gym. Chris's coach was outside with a cigarette hanging from his mouth. Chris was halfway out of the car when Mike shouted, "Well, if it isn't the Amish Floyd Mayweather."

Chris closed the car door, stepped up to Mike, and shook his hand.

Mike took a drag from his cigarette, then flicked it. "Missed you last session."

Chris debated whether to tell Mike about all that had been going on. At times they were close, but Chris had far more practice at keeping people at bay, often through a friendliness that was silent on important topics.

"I know I missed the practice," Chris said. "Haven't been able to come here of late."

"So, what brings you back?" Mike moved to the gym door and held it open.

Chris stepped inside. "Well, I've got another fight set up."

"Still fighting bare knuckle?"

Chris nodded. "Yeah."

Mike pointed at Chris's busted lip. "Apparently not very well."

Chris swatted his hand away. "Do I pay you to bust my chops?"

Mike laughed. "How beat up are you?"

"Sore, but I think I'm good. Not completely sure. I hope I can start training for a mid-March fight." *Hope* seemed like a strong word. On one hand, Chris wanted to fight so he could follow through on what he'd said he would do and see just what he could accomplish in a fight of this caliber. On the other hand, he didn't want boxing to come between him and Abigail. "It sounds as if my opponent is quite the boxer."

Mike gestured toward his office. "Let's take a look and listen."

Chris went inside the small space and sat on a bench.

Mike grabbed an ophthalmoscope and looked in Chris's eyes. He looked in his ears. He checked his heart rate and blood pressure. "Remove your shirt and lie down."

As soon as Chris took off his shirt, Mike gestured at the bruises across his abdomen. "What happened?"

"Two guys, one with a bat, but I got what I needed from them."

"Sounds worth it to me. Any nausea?"

"No."

"Have you spit up or peed blood?"

"No, but I coughed up blood for a day after the baseball bat incident."

"That's not happening now?"

"Stopped about thirty hours ago."

"Dizziness? Heart racing?"

"Ya, but only when Abi comes into view."

Mike chuckled. "Never heard you mention a woman before."

"Never met one like her before. Aren't you about done pushing on me?"

Mike stopped and motioned for Chris to sit up. "How important is this next fight?"

"Very. It's the whole reason I came to you to start training in the first place."

He nodded. "Any chance you can postpone it?"

"No."

Mike shrugged. "Okay. It is what it is. You can start training, but we need your sparring partners to go easy on your upper abdomen for a few weeks."

Mike grabbed two hand wraps off a nearby shelf and pulled up a stool next to Chris. He jerked Chris's right wrist toward him and started wrapping it. "It's been nice knowing you."

Chris snickered. "Thanks for believing in me."

Mike wrapped his right hand tight and had Chris make a fist. "Train more and I'll believe in you." He smacked Chris's knuckles.

"I'm here, aren't I?" Chris extended his left hand.

"Yeah, but you aren't here enough." Mike wrapped his left wrist and knuckles tight. "You'll need to fix that if you hope to win the next fight."

Chris knew that was true. He'd told Dan that if Mike said he could fight, then someone had to fill in for Chris at the Graber Horse Farm or Chris couldn't train.

Mike stood and left the office. Chris followed, and they stopped at the heavy bags. "Show me what you've got."

Chris started light, throwing a straight jab followed by a straight left.

"One, two, hook," Mike said.

Chris obeyed.

"No." Mike pushed him away from the heavy bag. "You're throwing your hook too wide, leaving your chin open. It might work well on someone who doesn't box, but a boxer will pick that apart. Come in tight with it." Mike punched the bag, demonstrating.

Chris tried and looked back at Mike.

Mike nodded. "Better." Mike returned to the shelf and put pads on his hands. "About how big is this guy?"

Chris shook his head. "Bigger than me."

"Well"—Mike held up the pads in front of Chris—"you want to come forward then. Back him up. See if he can fight while stepping back."

Chris tried it on the pads. He dropped his hands for a second, and Mike slapped him. "Keep that guard up."

Chris nodded.

"You're already out of practice." Mike sighed. "If the fight is in three weeks, you need to be in this gym every single day, practicing morning, afternoon, and night. You need to room here."

"As soon as someone fills in for me on the Graber Horse Farm" —Chris panted, trying to catch his breath—"I'll be here, but not a day before then."

"If you're gonna be ready for a trained fighter, you've got to train." He shook his head and sighed. "Four."

Chris threw four punches in a row, all the while stepping forward. He couldn't leave the farm just yet. He needed at least a few days, maybe a week, even if the replacement ended up being Dan. His brother had to get through this week or he'd lose his job. But if need be, after this week, Dan could be on the Graber farm the next two weeks without causing work problems. Chris was trying to be fair and yet also insist Dan be available to work if Chris was here, getting ready for the fight. Leaving the Grabers was a compromise Chris didn't want to make, but it seemed clear that setting new boundaries couldn't be done all at once without hurting people's lives.

They spent the session working on footwork, and his trainer taught him how best to move forward on a bigger guy.

Chris's Amish clothes were covered in sweat by the time he was done. He'd forgotten to throw clean clothes into a gym bag. Usually he didn't bother bringing a change with him. After a workout he'd always gotten in his rig and driven home to shower and change. The thought made him miss home, miss his Mamm and Daed. How had *home* become a place where he was no longer welcome?

Mike threw him a towel. "That's all your body can do for today."

Chris went to the locker room and rinsed his face and hands. His shirt was drenched, and he wished he'd thought to take it off. He wasn't himself right now. Not seeing his folks bothered him, and he understood why Abigail was now unsure of him. He wasn't who she thought he was. He went through the gym and out the door. Mike was there smoking another cigarette.

Chris stepped beside him. "You think this is crazy, don't you?"

Mike shook his head. "Not my job to tell you what's crazy."

Chris shifted. He knew the truth. Mike didn't need to tell him. He was giving himself three weeks to train for a fight when he needed months to prepare for it. He was trying to do the right thing by his brother, but win or lose, if this fight didn't clear the debt, then what?

"Thanks for today. I'll be back to stay as quick as I can."

"A crappy room and I will be here waiting."

Chris had to return to the horse farm if for no other reason than tomorrow was his first church Sunday in Mirth, and Abigail's uncle, as bishop, had been very clear that Chris was to attend, clean shaven. He pulled out his phone, opened the Uber app, and requested a car. When this effort for Dan began, the plan seemed straightforward. Now he wanted freedom to reset his priorities—courtesy of his interest in one Abigail Graber—but he wasn't free to follow his heart.

Once this was behind him, could they start fresh, or would her strong opinions and even stronger boundaries stand guard between them?

Nineteen

Abigail pulled a pan of lasagna out of Jemima's oven. The little ones who weren't crying were running through the house squealing. It had felt strange for it to be a Monday and not be teaching in her classroom, but Jemima seemed to need her during the day for moral support more than anything.

Heidi was inconsolable at times both day and night. They'd changed her formula, using one for babies with extra-sensitive stomachs, but it hadn't helped. She had a few rough hours each night, and her crying woke Simeon, who fussed whenever his Mamm or Daed was holding the new baby. How did one so young know when another baby was moving into his territory? Simeon's protests woke Nevin, sometimes Carolyn too. During the day, Abigail worked with the older children to settle them. She didn't know how the workload was divided at night, but the stress level in this home was high twenty-four hours a day. Her brother wanted to keep Heidi? Abigail was doing her best not to share her opinion, verbally or through body language, but it wasn't easy.

Right now Jemima was a few feet away, rocking a crying Heidi, and Roy had taken Simeon into the other room to quiet him. Simeon cried whenever Heidi did, as if that was helpful. Each one of them took turns trying to soothe Heidi.

The back door opened, and Abigail turned to see Chris. She raised a brow. "Just in time for food. Why am I not surprised?"

As much as Abigail loved cooking—and she really did—she had enjoyed it much more since Chris had entered the picture. He wasn't shy about enjoying the food she made.

He grinned and hung his hat and coat on a peg. "My Mamm didn't raise no fool."

"That she did not." His Mamm had raised a devilishly hand-some and smart man who thought fighting was a sport, like playing a game of baseball in an open field. The disappointment of that ran deep, but at least she'd learned of it early on.

He disappeared up the stairs, and she knew he'd be back down, showered and with clean clothes on, before she got the food on the table and the children situated.

Last night, after she'd had a miserably long Sabbath with cry-ing or whiny children, he'd asked if she wanted to get a bite of din-ner in town, as friends. How could she say no? Chris was fun to be around, comfortable in his own skin, and interesting on every topic. For reasons she couldn't fully pinpoint, he was different from any other man she'd known but also dangerous in his own way. No one could live as he had—half in the Amish world and half out—and not be dangerous. Evidently he'd been really good at keeping a lid on his lifestyle when living with his parents in Scarsdale. She had to keep reminding herself that his ways were none of her business, but a part of her wanted to set him straight so they could have a real chance at being together. As a friend she didn't have the right to go there.

Roy walked into the room, carrying Simeon. "He's asking for his Mamm."

Jemima patted her lap, still holding Heidi on one shoulder. "Hi, sweetie. You hungry?"

He whined, reaching for her. Roy put Simeon in her lap, and she eased Heidi into Roy's good arm.

"Denki, Jem."

Jemima didn't answer or look at him. She simply unfastened the hidden nursing fold in the bodice of her dress to feed Simeon.

Roy swayed Heidi while walking out of the room, taking the noise and a lot of stress along with them. Thankfully his agility and mobility had improved in the last couple of days. It'd been a week since he'd staggered home. He would be in a cast for at least another month. She pretty much knew where he'd be physically in the next several weeks, but where would they be in their marriage in another month?

She bit her tongue a dozen times a day when in their home. It was hard to believe they were the same couple who'd wedded and been excited over the birth of each child.

Someone rapped on the front door and opened it. "Hallo?"

"Daed?" Abigail moved toward him, hoping to get him out of the house.

Jemima tensed up the moment he walked in.

"I need to talk to Roy."

"Now's not a good time, Daed." Abigail gestured to the door he'd just entered.

"Stuff and nonsense. He's got to be feeling well enough to be seen by now. Besides, there's an issue I need to see him about."

Chris bounded down the stairs. "Luke, good to see you."

Her Daed grinned and held out his hand. "Chris."

Well, her Daed didn't have any qualms with Chris, despite how his brother, the bishop, felt.

"Something I can help you with?" Chris asked.

"Nice offer, but not likely. By now I usually have an envelope with cash from Tiffany for rent. Since I haven't received that, I went to her place to collect it, but someone's broken into her home. She and most of her stuff are gone. I'm wondering if we might need to call the police."

"Nah. No need for that. I think she took off. Is that right?" Chris looked at Jemima.

"Ya."

Chris started toward the back door. "But why don't we go over there and take a look around. We could assess the damage. I could replace whatever's broken and clean it up for a new tenant."

Roy walked into the room with Heidi in the crook of his arm and stopped the moment he saw his Daed.

"Whose baby is that?" Daed pointed at Heidi.

"Uh, hi." Roy said, trying to stall.

"This is Heidi," Jemima said.

"Who?"

Jemima stood, her face taut. "Tiffany gave birth to her a little more than seven weeks ago, and she abandoned her last week."

"Why am I just now hearing about this?"

"The situation is complicated, and we're not saying anything about it just yet."

Daed looked from the baby to Roy. "Sure. I'll tell no one, but without your uncle giving another Sunday meeting you can miss, and he won't do that for a broken arm, then if Tiffany is still gone by the next church Sunday, it won't be a private matter after that."

The resignation on Jemima's face sent an ache through Abigail. Her Daed was right, and they'd known long before now that keeping this infant a secret was impossible. Members could not miss a church meeting without a good reason, and they couldn't lie about the reason, so Heidi would be found out come next church Sunday in two weeks. Once people knew she was staying here, Roy and Jemima would be peppered with questions they would have to answer.

"Did you want to stay for dinner, Daed?" Roy asked.

Daed shook his head. "Nee, your Mamm's got a roast in the oven. I don't suppose Tiffany paid the rent before she left."

"Nee."

Abigail knew that part was complete truth. She'd overheard Roy and Jemima arguing about the fact that Roy had been paying Tiffany's rent for the last nine months.

Daed turned to Chris. "I've talked to my brother about you, and I know he's giving you some grief, but Abigail is rather fond of you."

"Daed," she chided.

Chris smiled in a nonchalant way, as if Abigail meant nothing special to him. "We've made a good team since the horses came in, and I know she appreciates that I'm a hard worker."

It bothered Abigail that Chris seemed overly comfortable spinning reality to sound like something it wasn't.

"Well, maybe that's all it is," Daed said. "But let me be frank. If you give up fighting and want to settle down, I've got acres of land you can rent for the price of paying the property tax. I bought land years ago for my six children to divide up and live on, and only two stayed in the area. You could even rent that little house Tiffany moved out of for nearly nothing."

"Daed!" Abigail's cheeks burned. "Why not offer him a dowry while you're at it?"

Daed focused on Chris. "Would it help?"

Abigail grabbed the closest items, two empty plastic cups, and threw them at him.

Daed swatted one away with his hand, was hit by the other, and broke into laughter. "'Cause if it would help, Chris, I'll sell every square inch of land I own to come up with a dowry. She's nothing but trouble!"

Everyone was laughing as Abigail walked over to her Daed and started shoving him out the door.

"Name your price, Chris!" he called over his shoulder, his voice and laughter fading as Abigail closed the door behind him. When she moved out of her Daed's home, whether she was getting married or not, her Daed would miss her something fierce. They were two peas in a pod most evenings. A few years ago she'd insisted he learn how to cook, and much to his surprise he took to it like a horse let loose in a lush green pasture. Daed and she talked and laughed their way through most meal preps. Mamm, who'd raised six children the traditional Amish way and spent half of her day in the kitchen cooking and cleaning, now used that time to read or crochet or do whatever else suited her. Afterward the three of them washed dishes and then played board games.

The chuckles faded, but the laughter he'd stirred felt like fresh air being piped into a dank cave.

Abigail rolled her eyes. "What'd I tell you the first day we met, Chris? My Daed would throw a celebration if he saw me walking with a guy."

A moment later the door popped open. "I was just kidding." Daed winked at Abigail. "I'd pay all I have to keep her, not that she's mine to keep."

"You." Abigail pointed out the door. "Go."

He blew her a kiss and was gone.

"Chris"—Roy went to the dish drainer and grabbed a clean pacifier—"it sounds as if Daed will be even more disappointed by your leaving on Sunday morning than we are."

What? Blood rushed to Abigail's heart, making it quiver. "You're leaving?"

Chris shifted from one foot to the other. "For a while."

"When were you going to tell me?"

"You got into the buggy last night saying you were desperate for fun and uplifting conversations, but I was going to tell you tonight."

"Sorry." Roy eased Heidi into her bassinet. "I shouldn't have assumed you'd already told Abigail."

Chris seemed frustrated, but he nodded.

"Roy's in no shape to work the farm alone." Abigail looked at her brother and then at Chris. "Jemima now has two babies to tend to, so she can't fill in. The farm has two strings of horses that need tending and training when the extra work of quarantine is over. I return to work next Monday, and you've not been here two full weeks yet, but you're leaving?"

"I've made arrangements for someone to fill in for me."

"How did you find a skilled stableman and trainer this quickly?"

"He's not particularly skilled, but Roy will be on his feet enough to give instructions. It's a cousin, Aaron Fisher. He's a hard worker, and he'll learn fast."

"Great. We could have an EHV-1 outbreak, and . . ." Abigail suddenly realized why he was leaving. "You're going to fight."

Chris rubbed the back of his neck. "I have to do this, Abi."

Her heart ignited with ire. "You're still stiff and injured from the fight to get Heidi. This isn't what's best for you, Chris. This is what your brother needs, not you." She knew she sounded horrified, and she willed herself to respond calmly. "You could get seriously hurt."

"I'll be fine."

"You don't know that. You've allowed yourself to get backed into a corner, and you're hoping you'll be fine." She tried to reel in her emotions from being blindsided.

He said nothing, staring at her as if she'd spoken in a foreign language.

Determined not to voice even half of what she felt, she gave a slight shrug. It was the kindest reaction she could manage. "Makes sense, I guess." She went to the stove and began cutting the lasagna. Why was this news so bitterly disappointing? Had she been holding out hope that he'd change, even though she knew where his heart was?

"Laura, Carolyn, Nevin, *es iss Zeit esse.*" Jemima called them to come eat.

Abigail dipped lasagna onto plates, glad she wasn't facing Chris, but it didn't take her long to have the plates ready. Jemima set them on the table.

Abigail drew a breath and turned around. The scurry of getting the children settled took a few minutes, but soon everyone sat and pulled the cloth napkins onto their laps.

Chris was leaving Sunday morning before the church meeting? Her eyes met his, and she couldn't manage even a polite smile before closing her eyes for the silent prayer. She'd like to stay here, eyes closed, no conversation, but before she could gather herself, she heard movement. Prayer was over.

Just leave him alone. Eat. Pray. Make small talk. But don't look at him.

She lifted her eyes and found his. "Where will you go?"

"There's a room above the gym. It makes sense for all the training I'll be doing."

Roy passed the basket of bread to Chris. "I can see the attraction for Englisch to see an Amish man fight them."

"Ex-Amish, apparently," Abigail corrected.

"You're jumping to conclusions, Abi." Chris held the basket out to her. "I have to do this. That's all I know."

She made herself take the basket. When people were shunned, no one could take anything from their hands. He wouldn't be shunned, at least not officially. He would simply be unwelcome in most Amish homes and ignored if seen somewhere, like in town.

She dreaded this for him. It was the one thing she hated about the old ways. If he chose to leave, he should be hugged, given going-away gifts, and told to return to visit as often as he could. But all she wanted to do at the moment was throw the basket of bread at him.

"When and where is the fight?" Roy asked.

Chris buttered his bread and answered him. "March fifteenth, at an abandoned barn on Englisch property this time. The people in power feel that an Amish person fighting an Englisch person in a barn will garner the kind of attention they're looking for. But this isn't a fight to attend, if that's what you were thinking. It'll be brutal, and it's doubtful I'll win."

"Would you actually consider going?" Jemima asked.

"No." Roy shook his head. "That's for youth who haven't been baptized into the church yet. The rest of us would get into too much trouble for going, but I can see the allure, even for the Amish." Roy cut up small pieces of food on Nevin's plate. "With this untrained guy coming in, I'm going to need your help next week, Abigail."

"I can give you an hour before school and a few after, but I've got to be back in the classroom on Monday."

"But you're needed here."

"My substitute has made it clear that she has plans for next week."

"Then find someone else."

Abigail dug her fork into the lasagna despite that she was not hungry. Her temples ached as blood pounded from her heart. "Funny, isn't it? I don't see you telling the men—not any uncles or brothers or Daed or even ex-Amish Chris over here—how they need to give up their days because it suits your needs. Care to explain that one, brother?"

"I just thought that since you're single and good with horses, you could give me a few more weeks."

"Hmm. So if I were your brother who was single and taught school, you'd ask him?"

Roy stared at her as if startled by a revelation. He pursed his lips and gave a nod. "You're right. I'm sorry. I'll find someone else."

The win did little to ease her frustrations.

"Abi, I'm not ex-Amish. I'm not leaving."

She nodded, trying to keep her words in check. "You sure about that? Seems to me that wherever your body lands, the rest of you may or may not follow."

"Abigail!" Disbelief rang in Jemima's voice as she fed Simeon a bite of lasagna.

"It's fine," Chris said. "She was very clear on how she felt about men who sort of stay and sort of leave."

"Yeah, no worries. Right, Chris?" She stared at him. "You were even in church yesterday." Her tone held far more accusation than her words. She closed her eyes and rubbed her forehead. "I'm sorry," she whispered. "I'm too out of sorts." She stood. "I'll go on home now, but starting tomorrow I'll be good as gold until you're gone. I won't complain or snap."

No one said a word as she grabbed her coat and left.

If she'd hoped to end things with Chris on truly friendly terms, she'd just ruined it. Right now she didn't care.

Men.

Twenty

Jemima used a pitchfork to toss fresh hay into the stalls. Earlier she'd mucked them out while Roy brought bails of straw and hay from the barn behind their home. He could do that with one good arm, but it took two hands to muck out stalls.

Chris had left yesterday, and Abigail was back at school today, but their new help, Aaron, wasn't here. He was supposed to have arrived yesterday afternoon, but his Mamm called to say he had the flu. It sounded as if he'd be in bed all this week and maybe next week too.

This old poultry barn was a surprisingly effective makeshift stable for keeping all the horses separated. Fortunately Houdini seemed to be gaining strength daily, and no other horse had come down sick.

They would need to keep the horses apart for just two more weeks. With or without Aaron's help, that shouldn't be too difficult. But it would require at least one week of her working with Roy. After that he should be out of the sling and able to work on his own. Could she hold her tongue and work beside him? Did she have a choice?

Today was their first day, and Jemima's thoughts railed against her husband.

She understood why Abigail had been so upset when Chris made plans with Roy and told her nothing. She could feel Abigail's sense of displacement when she learned that Chris intended to fight regardless of whether he was up to it or what that decision did to them as a potential couple. Chris's decision made no sense to Jemima.

The one thing she could credit Roy with was that keeping his secrets had made sense. But she still had issues with the secrets. Lots of them. Even if she could fully believe his story of spending only one night with Tiffany, a night that he didn't even remember—and she was torn between wanting to believe him and fearing she was being naive—she still had nine months of lies to wade through. She cringed when she thought of him leaving the house as if he were going to work and instead going to *her* house to help parent Heidi. Of all the people, Tiffany Porter! Jemima had been so jealous when he was going out with Tiffany, an Englisch girl, that she'd later been tempted not to date him. But he'd convinced her that there was nothing between them, that he hadn't sown any wild oats with Tiffany on their few dates as teens.

Had that been more lies? Was Jemima playing the fool, a trapped-with-no-way-out fool?

Roy walked by, pulling a hose. He had deep dark circles under his eyes from getting up with Heidi at night. And the baby had fussed for several hours every night since she'd arrived at their house, so they were trying another new formula for sensitive stomachs. Thank goodness Roy's Mamm, Naomi, had agreed to take care of the little ones. Still, Jemima would have to stop work at times to go there and nurse Simeon, and she also had a pump she could use. She would pick them up after she got Laura from school. The number of children and the workload didn't bother her. She and Roy had hoped to have at least six children. But Heidi's presence was just about Jemima's undoing.

She sighed and stabbed the pitchfork into more hay and slung it over the rail of the next stall. At least the physical work with the horses should make the time pass quickly. After Roy and she fed the horses, they would attach a lead and walk them and then groom them. She just had to get through being near Roy until the kids were tucked into bed. Then she could escape with Simeon into her bedroom while Roy kept Heidi in the guest room. But not even her bedroom brought peace since Heidi was in her home, crying sporadically throughout the night.

Roy started to fill the water container in the stall where Jemima was shoveling hay. "I need to send Chris a text thanking him for setting up this hose. I can't imagine hauling water all the way out here like he had to do the first few days."

"Ya." She recoiled when Roy's arm brushed hers.

His brows knit together, but he didn't say anything.

She dug into the hay bale and carried it to the next stall. Every day since she had found out about Roy's secrets had been completely devoid of joy. She had no hope of chasing her dreams of a food truck anymore, nothing to look forward to, and no expectation of feeling again the joy of just being alive and loved. Would things ever get better? Probably not with Heidi as a constant reminder of her broken marriage, of her commitment to Roy with no way out. There would be at least eighteen years of raising her, pretending, and hiding things from everyone, including her own children. Was that even possible? When Heidi was no longer a crying baby, she'd be a toddler, and then a child, and then a teen—each stage with new demands and needs. Could they really keep this secret from the community that whole time?

What would she give to go back in time and not get married? She couldn't wish for her children not to exist. But maybe if she'd never married, their souls would've been put in the children of another couple who didn't make each other so miserable.

Roy turned the hose nozzle to off, and the sound of water stopped. "Jemima, you're crying."

Was she? "No, I'm not." But when she brushed her sleeve against her eyes, it was wet. She turned so he couldn't see her face. "It doesn't matter."

"It matters to me." Roy walked a few steps closer to her.

She kept looking at the ground and saw his feet stop, leaving a gulf of a few feet between them. Was he afraid to close the distance?

"I know this is hard. If you could believe me about what took place, it would help both of us. But, please, you *have* to believe that I love you."

"The magic words, right?" Jemima turned away and stuck the pitchfork into the bale of hay. "It doesn't really matter how either of us feels. There is no choice here. We're stuck together until death. Apparently that's fine with you. But it's not with me, and I have no say and no choices." She turned around, facing him. "I'm trapped like these horses. Grab a lead, Roy, and you can trot me out for some air on church Sundays before penning me up again."

Roy's eyes were huge with dismay. "That's not who we are. It's how you feel right now, but it's skewed, Jemima. We have our whole lives before us, with hope and joy just beyond this darkness."

"Ya. Gut. I feel so much better now. Why don't you spell it out for me, tell me how I *should* feel?" How could he not see her side in this? "This marriage came with a lot of promises from you, but it's taken away any control I ever had over my own life. I love our children. I'm not going to run off and abandon them. And what would be my other option? Take our four children somewhere when I have no money and no ability to make money? I have less autonomy in this mess than a child."

He dropped the hose, blinking at her. "You'd take our kids and leave our marriage if you could? Over something that wasn't even an affair? I didn't mean to sleep with Tiffany. Do you believe me?"

That was a good question. "Lying would still serve a purpose for you, wouldn't it? I'd still be angry about all the other lies, but if I could simply believe your version, I'd have my feet under me much sooner, and my anger wouldn't engulf everything between us that ever mattered."

She met his eyes as she'd done tens of thousands of times, and she saw what appeared to be honesty. Was he *really* telling her the truth?

His eyes remained steadfast on hers. "It happened as I said, Jem. Before God, it did."

His words mingled with the truth she saw in his eyes, and

something inside her, something real between them that was beyond her rage, saw the unvarnished honesty.

He was being completely forthright about what took place between Tiffany and him. She could feel his frustration from being forced to deal with Tiffany, his anger that had grown until he was on the edge of hating her. Maybe he did hate her. Yet, even with that full insight, Jemima was tempted to pretend she was unsure what had taken place and lash out at him with renewed anger.

God, help me! Where was her integrity? Her sense of decency and mercy?

She instantly knew where it was: buried under her rage.

She wanted to hurt him, but she had to admit what she now knew for sure. She sighed. "I was wavering, but, ya, I believe you. I believe that it was a single night with Tiffany, and unintentional, and that you don't remember any more than what you've said."

His body seemed to deflate with relief. "Gut. Wunderbaar gut." He remained in place, and his relief quickly seemed to wane. "But you'd still leave if you could."

"I can't leave, so what difference does my answer make?" She raised her hands, palms up, before turning to grab the pitchfork. This whole conversation was pointless. They needed to finish their work with the horses so they could get away from each other.

"Tell me what you need, Jem. How do I help you forgive me? We have to find our way through this somehow or eventually everything between us will be ripped apart."

She turned around and faced him. "I can't forgive. I just can't. You spent months lying to me and stealing money. Where did I think you were when you were with Tiffany? What lie did you tell me so you could be with Tiffany at the hospital as she gave birth to your daughter? After Heidi was born, how many times did you lead me to believe you were dealing with horse business when you were actually going to Tiffany's house? I'm sorry if I'm not getting over the loss of trust in our marriage fast enough for you." She jabbed the pitchfork into the hay again and dumped the load into another stall.

She kept moving, but had Roy even blinked?

"What?" she scoffed.

"You're grieving the loss of our marriage?"

"If I'm being honest, I started that grieving process long before I found out about Heidi. There's been a distance between us, and it's not a new feeling."

"If you're talking about this past year, surely you know now why I was trying to keep it from you. I was trying to protect you."

"It goes back before that! Your idea of being partners in marriage is to protect me as if I'm a fragile child, one with a chronic illness."

He was silent for a moment and then tilted his head slightly. "I don't think I understand."

Would he ever be able to? "The horses." She gestured to the stables around them. "I know it's hard work, but you ask and depend on your sister to work with you. Not until now, when you had no other choice, have you asked me to be a part of your business. You've always gone to the auctions alone and made all the buying decisions without me. Ever since we've been married, you've held total control over our finances while I've cooked and cleaned for you. And I'm always there for you whenever you return. Just me there, waiting to be informed. Even if the Amish ways were different and I could ask for a divorce, I couldn't leave, because I have no power and no money. You've created a cage for me. It was a beautiful cage in many ways until this thing with Tiffany, but it is a trap." Her face was hot, and she fought to keep back her tears. Not wanting to bare any more of herself to him, she turned and walked out the door of the make-shift stable.

The cool early-March air helped her stop the tears from forming, and she took several deep breaths as she looked out over the fields. He'd never understand. She would have been better off to be like Abigail and never marry, never be so vulnerable.

She heard Roy's steps approaching.

"I don't understand, Jemima. How can you feel trapped? Both of us have responsibilities to each other, the children, the community, and God—not necessarily in that order. Didn't we make our life choices when we decided to marry? It's the Amish way: the man provides, and the woman stays home with her young children. How is it not freedom to be at home, protecting and nurturing the gifts God gave us?"

She looked over the hills of the property. There was a deep river at the bottom of a large hill, and she sometimes took the children there to dip their toes in the water. "The only way I could find freedom would be to walk into the center of the river and let it sweep me away until I no longer existed on this planet. But our children need me, so I can't do that."

There. She'd said it. Her dream of late was to end everything. That would be freedom.

Twenty-One

Roy's insides were in knots as his Mamm passed him a cup of coffee. Jemima wished she could walk into the river and let it sweep her away? He felt as though he'd go crazy if he didn't talk to someone. He'd left the stables and come straight here, to the home he'd grown up in, to tell his Daed everything. A fresh jolt of emotion shot through his nerves.

Everything.

Roy managed a nod of thanks to his Mamm. He ran his hand over the familiar kitchen table and inhaled deeply, trying to calm himself. The fragrant aroma of the coffee stirred memories of sitting at this table through his growing-up years and talking as his Daed sipped on coffee. It was six in the evening, but his Daed could drink coffee at any time without it affecting his sleep. Caffeine too late in the day usually kept Roy awake at night, but no matter how potent this delicious brew of caffeine was, it wouldn't begin to touch his exhaustion.

He had no desire to burden his Daed with information, but he had to talk to someone before he imploded and became of no use to anyone—his family, his community, God, or himself. He needed advice, and no one seemed as wise or understanding as his Daed. Jemima had gone home to fix dinner and tend to the children, including Heidi. All the things his wife had said rolled through his head like constant storms churning the sea. Did her words come just from her pain and anger, or from a hidden place in her heart she'd never shared before?

His Mamm set another cup of coffee in front of his Daed, who was at the head of the table, making small talk about the job Abigail and Chris had done turning the former poultry barn into temporary stables.

"I'll let you two talk." Mamm smiled down at Roy. He hadn't said he was here to talk, but she knew her son. She kissed his forehead and left the kitchen.

Roy held his mug firm, gathering his thoughts and his courage. "Daed," he began, and he had to force the next few sentences out of his mouth, telling him about getting hooked on pain pills and the confusion. His voice cracked as he confessed going alone to Tiffany's that one night.

Daed closed his eyes and rubbed his forehead as he took deep breaths. Roy waited, not wanting to make his Daed go into shock. Daed lowered his hand and gestured to Roy to continue. Roy stumbled as he told him all the embarrassing details of waking in Tiffany's bed, her coming up pregnant, and now Heidi living with them.

Daed stared at his mug, fidgeting with it for nearly a minute before he cleared his throat. "Son"—his eyes misted—"you've carried this by yourself all this time?"

Roy's head pounded. His Daed had no words of condemnation? "I thought—"

His Daed's hand came across the table and grabbed Roy's forearm. "I know what you thought, but you were wrong. No man can carry the weight of something like this on his own without its injuring his view of himself and life and God."

Roy hadn't expected compassion, and he couldn't make himself look up.

Daed leaned forward. "Look at me, Son."

Roy lifted his eyes.

"I speak for myself, for your Mamm, and for God. We forgive you. Do you hear me?"

Roy wiped moisture from his eyes.

"Whatever this family goes through that's embarrassing or problematic," Daed continued, "I forgive you. Whatever you need that's inconvenient or displeasing, I forgive you. God forgives you. Now you forgive you."

Roy's heart threatened to beat right out of his chest, and he could almost breathe again. "Denki," he whispered. But it would be a while before he could forgive himself. That night shouldn't have happened. How had he let himself get so hooked on prescription pain pills that he opened the door to this monster that was now eating his wife's heart one slow bite at a time?

Daed took a sip of his coffee. "I had a suspicion about that baby when I saw her and no one wanted to talk about it. Actually, the look on Jemima's face pretty much said it all."

"She's struggling." Roy swallowed hard, fighting tears. That was an understatement. He tapped his fingertip against the rim of his mug. "It's been an awful year, Daed. I never knew that life could feel so dark and confusing, but I just kept lying to everyone, thinking I could fix all the wrongs somehow and Jemima wouldn't have to suffer like she is now."

"Ya." Daed nodded. "But that's only part of why you kept this from everyone. You were also trying to stay in control and lying to yourself that you could handle everything."

Was that true? "Well, I'm ready to come clean. I need to ask something of you and Mamm. There's a possibility I'm looking at a divorce."

"What?" His Daed sounded offended.

"Jemima needs freedom, but I can't stay at the rental home. It'd be like reliving a nightmare just to enter that house again, much less try to make that place a home. Besides that, Heidi sleeps so little, and each caregiver needs a break to get a few hours of sleep. I'll figure out a safe way she can stay with me as much as possible while I work, but I'd need four to six months of her staying here at least part of each workday."

"A divorce?" His Daed seemed far more upset about that than the fact his son had been with another woman and that his wife's heart was broken.

"I know that neither Jemima nor I could ever marry someone else, but it's the most freedom I can give her."

Daed leaned back against the chair and crossed his arms. "Roy, she *has* to forgive you. God demands it."

"Is that why you wasted no time forgiving me just now?" Roy already knew the answer.

"Nee. It's fully yours from my heart. I know God has that forgiveness toward you too."

"You offered it to me because it matched what's in your heart?"

"Ya."

"But it's not in Jemima's heart to forgive me."

"But God said we must forgive. And it's your home. What else is she possibly going to do with four children to feed and clothe? They need a father in the home."

Something akin to fire skittered up and down Roy's skin, running to one spot: his chest. No wonder Jemima hated him. She'd told him she felt completely powerless, but in this moment he saw it—his beautiful, loving wife trapped, as if she'd been dragged into a cave and bound and gagged by the man who'd promised to take care of her.

His thoughts reeled. Unlike his sister, who'd stayed single because she refused to give up her own dreams and hand over her power to another, Jemima had chosen to put all of who she was in Roy's hands. Once their choice was etched in stone, they slowly began to see each other without those rose-colored glasses. But he had other outlets through work that she didn't have, ones that allowed him to pursue dreams and feel fulfilled while she washed the same dishes three to five times a day every day, year in and year out. He had accolades and outlets that went beyond their relationship while she waited on him to return home.

Daed tapped his index finger on the table near Roy. "You listen to me, Son." His eyes reflected pure stubbornness. "She has to forgive you. She took that vow when she joined our faith before she married you. Forgiveness and being Amish are one and the same."

He saw it! Jemima's only refuge was their home life, who they were to each other. For her, it was as if an atomic bomb had gone off, because her sole refuge was their home and he'd brought his lies and deception into it. He'd brought in his child who was born of another woman. She was trapped.

"Roy?"

He scratched his chin through his beard. "I kept this secret from her of my own free will. I came to a place of knowing I had to keep Heidi of my own free will. Someday—perhaps just between her and God—Jemima will forgive me of her own free will. But forgiveness does not mean taking someone back. Even God does not demand that of her in this sort of thing."

"It's not as if you chose to be with Tiffany, but even if you had, Jemima would have to forgive you. Our community has faced this before, and you will be shunned, and she will forgive you and allow you back—completely back. It's how our faith works."

Roy knew that his father was right, because he had seen it happen to a woman when he was a teen. She had complied with the ministers: weeping in front of the Sunday gathering for church, saying the right words about forgiving her husband, although anyone could see that her heart was so broken she could hardly speak. The husband was shunned for a month, and his wife went on with life as though her husband hadn't chosen to commit a sin against her and

God. From the outside, it looked like she'd forgiven him. Her husband continued to live at home, and she continued going to church meetings and tending to their children, the garden, and the laundry. After a year had passed, she was unable to get out of bed. She was just a shell of the person she had been. He'd gone with his Mamm to visit her one time. She stared into the distance, looking lost as she mumbled about being unable to enjoy her children or pray to God or love her husband.

Had she really forgiven her husband? That took time, and when forgiveness happened, it stirred love and grace and acceptance. Had her husband worked to rebuild what he'd torn apart, or had he demanded she bury her pain so he didn't have the inconvenience or guilt of facing it? Or, in obedience, had she simply said the words and then buried all her hurt and anger until those things buried her?

"But isn't it your life too, Roy? You made a mistake, but won't this plan to give Jemima whatever *she* wants put you in a prison for it?"

That was exactly the problem, wasn't it? One of them had to be in prison over this—a jail that had nothing to do with taking care of Heidi and everything to do with being confined by one's spouse's decisions and needs. "I won't force her to be a prisoner in her own home. She already feels trapped. I won't let the ministers be her warden, telling her how to feel and behave toward me. I refuse to be her warden, too, for that matter. I'll keep working the farm. I'm unsure what I need to do to get the money for her to buy a food truck." One idea he'd had made him feel sick. He could sell his prized stallions. Was that even viable? They sired healthy, good-tempered foals that became excellent trained horses. After saving for many years, he'd bought his first stallion on his eighteenth birthday. They were a part of him and an invaluable part of this farm. In order to have enough money to buy the food truck, he'd need to sell both stallions, and that would be a horrible business decision.

"Roy"—his Daed rose quickly—"do you have any idea what you're saying?"

"I think so."

"What about your children?"

Again insight hit. "I won't put their needs above Jemima's." He'd even been putting his children above his wife. But not anymore. "The church and the children will be just fine as I put my wife's needs above theirs. The children are young, and it won't be so very hard for them to forgive me. I'll stay close by and see them often." He also needed to put Jemima ahead of Heidi. He'd chosen to do just that, but once he talked to social services, he'd changed his mind. He clearly wasn't good at putting Jemima first and sticking to it. He had good intentions but not sufficient follow-through.

"I'm not sure a woman should ever be given that much power."

His Daed meant well. He loved his wife and children, and he was a good Daed, but that didn't stop him from seeing women as less important than men. Hadn't Roy been similar in many ways until Abigail called him on it? He wasn't as fully indoctrinated into that thinking as his Daed because the men Roy's age weren't as old school as their Daeds were. They did the dishes sometimes, and they took their restless children out of church at times, not always leaving that up to the women. They changed diapers, picked up a few groceries once in a while, and even helped weed the vegetable garden on occasion. His generation was making a few strides. Roy had thought he was one of the more progressive men among the Amish. He'd agreed to tend to the children one day a week so Jemima could run a food truck stand on Saturdays while Abigail ran it Monday through Friday. But after the plan was made, he'd emptied the savings account for another woman's sake, and Jemima no longer could purchase the truck.

He sighed, disgusted with himself. "Daed, a man who does wrong and then uses his power and status in the church and community to make a woman behave as he needs or wants her to—as is convenient for him—is a weak man, taking advantage of the status God gave him. Jemima needs freedom, and I intend to give it to her." Roy pushed back from the table and rose. "I need to see the ministers."

It seemed curious how he'd come here for advice but as he talked he knew what he had to do: set Jemima free.

"Whoa, Son. Slow it down." Daed stood. "I doubt that what you're saying is right, but clearly I can't change your mind. What I do know is that once the ministers learn of this, everything that happens afterward is written in stone. If you want to give Jemima the freedom to choose, then let her choose. Are you sure she wants the ministers to know?"

He wasn't, actually. He'd just assumed. Was it natural for him to come up with a plan and try to control how things played out without involving Jemima?

"You're right." He hugged his Daed, glad he'd come here to talk. "Denki."

His Daed held him. "We'll say nothing to anyone, but your Mamm and I are here for you."

"I know the deal of buying the farm from you was that I'd never get in a bind and need your help, but if you could give me a week or two until Aaron, Chris's replacement, is over the flu . . ."

His Daed nodded.

"Thanks." Roy walked out the door, just as he had so many times in his life, and now, just as then, he knew one thing for absolute certain: his Daed loved him unconditionally.

He longed to give that to Jemima.

Maybe she needed to talk to someone, to vent to a therapist who wouldn't shove the need to instantly forgive her husband down her throat. That might be more helpful than talking to anyone else. He didn't know. Maybe they needed a marriage counselor.

But he now understood that he was stubborn and willful, making decisions *for* Jemima rather than *with* her. He loved his wife. He couldn't imagine loving her any more than he did. The desire to protect her wasn't wrong. But doing so at the expense of treating her as an equal—different but equal—that was wrong.

Twenty-Two

From inside the vehicle of an Englisch driver, Abigail stared at the front of the boxing gym. It was a narrow brick building with really dirty windows. Butterflies fluttered their wings in her stomach until she felt nauseated. Why hadn't she said what needed to be said before Chris left Mirth yesterday morning? She'd been cold and moody toward him for the last week, and it wasn't until a few hours after he was gone that she realized how wrong she'd been. Her conscience had kept her awake all through the night, whispering his name, urging her to look him in the eye and talk to him.

"I won't be more than thirty minutes, Teresa."

"It's a long way to come for such a short conversation." Teresa held up her cell phone. "Ever heard of one of these?"

Abigail waggled her cell. "Nope." She chuckled and slid it into the pocket of her apron before getting out of the car. What was she doing? She opened the door to the gym and slipped inside. A dozen men were working out, all in shorts and very few with a shirt. Some were talking with trainers and other men faced each other, swinging their gloved fists and hitting each other.

The men slowly stopped until most of them were gawking at her, and the awkwardness of the moment threatened to steal her resolve. How long had it been since a woman had entered this place? It was possible that she was the first Amish woman to enter this old building, at least since it had become a boxing gym.

She scanned the men, trying to see beyond the shock of shorts and bare chests.

A man came toward her, smiling. "You in the right place, miss?"

She nodded.

"Then my guess is that you're looking for Amish Chris."

Again she nodded.

He pointed to a set of stairs. "Go up those stairs, last door to your right."

"Denki."

The man laughed. "He mumbles those strange words at me sometimes too."

She went up the stairs, down the dreary, smelly hallway, and knocked on the last door to the right.

"Enter."

Was that Chris's voice? She knocked again. A few moments later the door opened as slowly as if pushed by a breeze. Chris no longer had the pageboy haircut of an Amish man, and the bridge of his nose was red, maybe swollen. But he had on his typical Amish pants and suspenders over a brightly colored T-shirt.

"Abi." He looked down the hallway. "What are you doing here?"

"May I come in?"

"Sure." He stepped back.

The room was sparse and dingy with a lone dirty curtainless window. It had scratched wood floors and a tiny sink filled with dishes. A misshapen navy blue couch faced a television no bigger than Tiffany's laptop. Should she offer to make this room a little homier? He'd only been living here since yesterday morning.

"Is everything okay?" Chris asked.

Why would he be willing to stay in a gym or fight another human to keep his word, to help his brother? She'd thought coming here would help them in some way, but seeing him living like this was really hard.

"Nee." She hadn't come here to judge him, and she prayed for grace to understand him.

He motioned toward a kitchen chair. "Care to sit?"

"Ya." She sat. "I've been thinking." She'd told him Monday a week ago that she would finish out the week with kindness and no cold shoulder, but that's not what she'd done. She'd stopped talking to him and being kind. She'd been disappointed in his decision, and she'd used silence as punishment. But after he was gone, as she reflected on how she'd behaved, she saw her flaws, her unkindness.

"You've been thinking."

She licked her bottom lip. "Uh, ya. See, I'm demanding in my opinions of how things should work in relationships while criticizing men for being demanding in their opinions of how things should work in relationships. And I'm sorry."

His brows furrowed, and he looked confused. "You're here, in an Englisch boxing gym, to apologize?"

"Is there another kind of gym other than Englisch?"

He chuckled. "True."

"I was disappointed in your opinion of what you needed to do, and I ruined our last week together by being silent or stiffly polite while I was internally browbeating you." Why had she felt so compelled to come here? It had seemed as if God wanted her here, maybe to finish destroying all romantic myths about this man. Still, she wasn't here about his future, only about how she'd behaved last week. "Added to those things, I like to think I'm modern in my thinking, broad minded and filled with grace, and every bit of that is true"—she teasingly shook her finger in his face—"until someone does something unexpected that challenges my broad-minded views."

He smiled. "That was really nice. Thank you. I get how this must look and feel to you, so I didn't hold your responses, or lack thereof, against you." He sat. "An Amish man fighting is really hard to accept."

"You can't be in this situation and call yourself Amish."

He shrugged. "I'm living Englisch right now, but I am Amish."

She longed to ask, *Ya, for how long?* Instead she nodded. "It's your life, and I'm sure you'll figure it out. I didn't come here to dish out my inner struggle onto you."

"That's gut, ya?" His crooked smile tried to steal a piece of her heart, but it couldn't. The reality of who he was continued to sink in as she remained in his dreary apartment above a smelly gym.

He unfolded his arms. "Friends?"

She shrugged. "Our being friends is hard and awkward."

"I know, but we could move past that, couldn't we?"

She shrugged, unsure whether she could. What they felt for each other was deeper than friendship, yet who they were separated them.

"Abi, could I buy you dinner or at least coffee and dessert?"

"That's kind of you, but I have a driver waiting. I needed to see you, to look in your eyes as I apologized for my behavior." But it hurt to be here, to realize how wide the gulf was between them.

"You could send the driver on her way, and I'll pay for your Uber ride home."

"Is the idea of us spending an hour talking a good one?"

"I don't know. Can't we just enjoy it for what it is and ignore what it isn't?"

She wanted to stay for a while. She longed for him to choose to give up fighting and leave this place and go back with her. She wanted him to kiss her and say she was the one. But apparently fighting was the one, and at least half of his heart belonged to it. If she stayed, she'd end the time longing even more for things that couldn't be. Her Daed used to tell her that when she did care for someone, she'd fall fast and hard, and she had.

He stepped closer and gently lifted a string of her prayer Kapp. "This place, me in this place—it's too much, isn't it?"

She nodded. "You've known me well from the first day." She kissed his cheek. "I'm sorry."

"Denki, Abi."

She opened the door. "Bye, Chris."

If his leaving yesterday morning hadn't severed all dreams of who they could be, this visit had. Maybe that's what God had in mind when she felt impressed to come here.

"I'll walk you out."

They went down the stairs and out the door of the gym, saying nothing. She got in the front seat of the car, and he stood on the sidewalk. If he had a girlfriend who had pulled him back home and away from her, she could understand that. But boxing to clear a debt? Living in a hole in the wall because he couldn't go home? It made no sense at all.

He waved, and she returned the wave.

Jemima stirred awake, hearing faint sounds of movement in the house. It had to be Roy. Last night, after their blowup in the stables, she got all the children asleep, including Heidi, before he arrived home. Jemima had been desperate not to see Roy, so she'd put Heidi in the bassinet in the guest bedroom, where Roy slept. Then she went to the master bedroom with Simeon and closed the door, hoping Roy wouldn't disturb her when he arrived home. Maybe he got some sleep. Maybe not. But even as angry as she was with him, she was also mortified at her behavior, at all she'd said.

He hadn't come to her room.

She pulled the quilt higher on her shoulder, thinking of the dream she'd just had of Roy and her on a train, laughing and talking, holding hands as beautiful scenery whizzed by.

A few months after they were married, they'd taken a train trip and had slept in an old-fashioned sleeper car. The beds were stacked and super small, but they squeezed into one, practically on top of each other. They'd spent most of the night laughing about silly things, enjoying each other, and sharing dreams for their future. She remembered being so very thankful to God for the blessing of Roy. They'd talked of their hopes for at least six children, of Jemima's food truck that she would work in on Saturdays during tourist season, and of Roy's desire to buy his Daed's horse farm and turn it into something more, something that included teaching Englisch children how to ride. He'd hoped also to include special-needs Englisch children, but that part of the dream took extra money and licensing that hadn't worked out yet.

When morning came and they went to the dining car for breakfast, they'd gotten so many stares and winks from the other passengers, who were mostly retired Englisch couples, that Jemima had blushed through most of breakfast.

Now, waking in her marriage bed alone, she was so removed from that happy, in-love newlywed. After a decade together, their train had derailed and that perfect bubble of love had burst. But she still cared for him and always would. Maybe the derailing of the dream marriage was inevitable. Adult life was filled with unexpected stresses, so many of them. Because their way of life was designed for the husbands to have the reins, maybe she should've expected to feel powerless, but that never entered her mind until it was too late. Did most women feel that way but never talk about it?

The stairs squeaked with slow footfalls. The footsteps came closer and stopped outside her room.

Please, just keep going.

He tapped on her door.

"Kumm." She sat up.

He opened it, although she wasn't sure how, since he had a kerosene lantern in one hand and a cup of coffee in the other. She closed her eyes, longing to go back to that dream.

He walked into the room and sat on the end of the bed. "Morning, Jem. The children are still asleep, and I was hoping we could have a few minutes to talk." He held the mug out to her.

Jemima sat up a bit more and took the coffee. But there was nothing left to say. After getting the children fed and lunches packed, Jemima would take Laura to school and the others to Roy's Mamm's. Then Roy and she would go back to working physically side by side but emotionally hundreds of miles apart.

"I spoke with my Daed last night and told him everything. I asked if Heidi and I could stay at their house, and he said yes."

"Oh." How was she supposed to feel about that? She'd made it clear she didn't want their children to have to deal with his being shunned. Had he made this decision without her as well?

He put a hand on her quilt-covered leg and looked into her eyes over the flickering lantern. "Jemima, you're not powerless. I'm willing to follow your lead on everything. I'm ready to tell the bishop and move to my parents' house with Heidi if that's what you choose. Or we can say the baby is Tiffany's and she's run off, not telling who the baby's dad is, and we can keep her here."

Was any of this new? "Neither of those is a good option."

Roy nodded slowly. "I know. I know you're in a terrible place either way. But here's the rest. You don't have to help me with the horses anymore. Daed will lend a hand until Aaron can be here or I can hire someone else. I'm not sure how to go about getting a food truck, but I'll figure it out soon, and you'll have your dream, I promise."

No part of her heart believed him about the food truck. She wished she could believe him.

"I think Heidi should stay with us at least a few more weeks while we pray about what to do, but if after that you feel she'd be better off being raised by a different loving couple, then that's what we'll do."

What? The weight of his words brought as much pain as it did relief.

"Jem, you said some scary things about wishing you didn't exist and not wanting to live."

Embarrassment crawled over her. "I would never, ever disappear or do myself serious harm. I wouldn't. It's just thoughts that hit when I feel overwhelmed with all of it and see no escape."

"If the thoughts continue or become more than momentary thoughts, you tell someone, and you make them hear you. Promise me?"

She nodded.

"No matter what happens, Jemima, I'm on your side in this battle. If you need us to divorce, I'll give it to you and take the blame with the church. You're not stuck. You're not powerless. But I insist on one thing from you, okay?" He looked intently at her, and she saw tears in his eyes. "You have to take care of yourself. Don't let thoughts of wishing to die go unchecked because you feel trapped. You just tell me what you want, and that's what we'll do. Do you understand me?"

Tears stung her eyes. What *did* she want? All of his ideas were terrible options. The bottom line was that whatever she chose, it would be permanent, and she'd be powerless to undo it.

Powerless.

She hated the word, but dozens of scenarios of good, God-fearing people caught in powerless situations pounded her. Was she asking more of life than it could give?

Her mind moved to her children. A shunning would hurt them, not just for the present but also throughout their childhood as others reminded them of what their father had done. As much as she wanted Roy and Heidi out of the house, she couldn't do that to Laura, Carolyn, Nevin, and Simeon—at least not until she was sure what she truly wanted. It wouldn't be fair to them. If Roy moved out of the house with Heidi, everyone in the community would immediately know what was going on, and there'd be no changing her mind later.

Jemima looked down at her mug of coffee. "Thank you for hearing me. Just knowing that you listened helps. But this situation is still impossible. I don't know what I want, but I won't be able to figure it out with you constantly here as a reminder of everything that's wrong."

Maybe he was right that they should keep Heidi for a little while longer. Giving her away amid this turmoil would do more damage than good.

"I understand. I'll pack up Heidi's stuff now."

"No, I want you to stay in the guest room and leave before I wake or stay in the hayloft. You can eat with your folks. I don't want to see you for a while. I *can't* see you right now. I'll take care of Heidi."

Even in the lantern light, the pain on his face was obvious. "I'll do it. I'll give you the space you need."

Space. Wasn't that one of their issues that had her feeling so lonely before all this started? Now everything was out in the open, yet she was unable to put her arms around him and pull him close. But what else could they do now except live separately under the same roof? Seeing him brought nothing but anger and resentment. Maybe if she could have some time away from him to process her new reality, she could let go of her anger.

Or maybe not.

She lifted her eyes to meet his. "How did we get here?"

His faint smile wavered and faded. "I don't know, Jem. It seems to run deeper and go back further than the mess with Tiffany." He shrugged. "As much as we love our children and enjoy raising them, their needs get between us. Their conversations overtake ours until we forget what we wanted to tell each other. The buggy accident was so hard on us—all that time of being separated, of pushing our emotional needs aside while we dealt with everyone's physical needs. Sometimes marriage is like being in the same room but miles apart. Maybe I knew more about how you felt than I realized, but I walked out the door for years and buried my heart in what I could accomplish and feel good about."

A moment of silence passed. Were they both thinking about what had pulled them apart? Then Heidi's piercing cry filled the house, and Simeon woke, wailing.

Twenty-Three

March winds blew as Abigail pulled back on the reins, slowing Pippi. Early-morning sun dazzled against the dew. She took a deep breath as Pippi walked onward. This was where Abigail and Chris had met a mere three weeks ago. Had they known each other only that long? Maybe it felt like more because they'd spent nearly every waking minute of that time together. Clearly he'd been capable of stealing her heart, which she'd never actually believed was a real possibility for any man to do. But it wasn't meant to be. Even though he'd felt that connection too, none of it was enough. It all came down to who a person really was, and evidently he was actually more Englisch than Amish.

Maybe there was nothing wrong with that, but it made them unequally yoked, and the only thing left to do was walk away from each other.

She'd realized how deeply rooted he was in the Englisch ways five days ago when she went to see him at the boxing gym. It did her heart a lot of good to apologize in person, and it had helped her see the bleak reality of what was in his heart. It was disappointing to feel a deep connection to a man and for it to be nothing more than a false alarm. It would take a while to move past that. But time was on her side.

"Abi!" The faint voice of a man yelling caused her to bring Pippi to a halt. She pulled one rein, and Pippi turned in a slow circle as Abigail searched the area. A man on a white horse was galloping straight for her.

Chris? If it was him, he had on Amish clothes.

Pippi pranced, wanting to race the oncoming horse, but Abigail kept her still. "Whoa. Stand firm." Abigail leaned in, patting her. "Pippi, stand firm."

Pippi shook her head and snorted, but her hooves stayed put. There wasn't a better-trained horse on this farm. Abigail and her Daed had begun working with her when she was a colt fifteen years ago.

She recognized the white horse as Lightning, and when the horse stopped, she could see the rider's face clearly.

"Chris Fisher, what are you doing here?"

His eyes didn't move from hers, but he said nothing. He'd had a similar reaction the day they met.

She snapped her fingers. "Hallo? Fisher?"

He lowered his eyes to her hands. "Sorry. Déjà vu."

"Ya, we've been here before."

"It feels as if I've been here a thousand times." His eyes met hers again, and he said nothing else for several moments. He sat up straighter. "I hope you don't mind that I'm here today."

How did she feel about it? "Nee, it's fine, but it's strange. Why *are* you here? And why are you wearing Amish clothes?"

"To answer your last question first, they're comfortable and a part of who I am. To answer your first question, Jemima called me a few hours ago and asked if I could lend a hand. That's when I learned that Aaron's been out sick all week, and I feel really bad about that. Had I known that, I would've gotten Dan to fill in for him. So they're in a bind for today. But I called Aaron, and he's on a round of antibiotics and will be here first thing Monday."

"In a bind? Why is this the first I'm hearing of it?"

"Do you always have this many questions?"

"Ya, pretty much."

"Jemima called, saying something about Roy forgetting to cancel today's lessons for a group of Amish special-needs kids coming in."

"Ach." Abigail pulled out her phone to check her calendar and realized she'd missed numerous calls and texts. "Why is my phone on Do Not Disturb?"

"Again with the questions." He chuckled. "All I know is I didn't do it," he teased. "But I was sent to find you."

"Okay." She turned Pippi in the right direction, and they rode side by side toward the horse farm. "You know, that was the perfect time for you to have yelled, 'I'm coming for you, Graber,' as you raced past me."

"I considered it, but it seemed too playful and flirty."

"Ya, I guess so. How is a moment of flirting wrong, but years of punching men isn't?"

He didn't respond.

"Sorry." Abigail sighed. "I'm still adjusting, I guess."

"Friends don't have to agree with a decision, you know. They just have to learn to keep their mouths shut. Apparently that will take you a while."

She laughed. "It's not my strong suit."

"Tell me something I don't know, Abi."

"Um, Jemima's doing a little better."

"I know. I heard it in her voice when she called me. Try again."

"Not one other horse has shown any symptoms of EHV-1."

"I know. Roy told me that when I arrived."

"We have only ten days left before the quarantine is over."

"I know that too. You're not very good at this, are you?"

"Well, if you're so smart, why don't you tell me something you don't know."

He laughed. "How am I supposed to tell you something I don't know?"

"Most often when people lack knowledge on a topic, they ask questions. There, I just told you something you didn't know."

"I think you won, unless I come up with a good retort before leaving today. So, Teacher Abigail, how do I give equine lessons for special-needs children?"

"The info is specific but easy to do. It can be exhausting on occasion but always extremely fulfilling by the time everyone goes home."

"It will be Amish kids on a horse. How fulfilling can that be? The two have gone hand in hand since the dawn of Amish-hood."

"Your reverence for the Amish overwhelms me."

"Was that irreverent?"

She rolled her eyes. "Circling back to today, if Roy did what I think he did—canceled several Saturday classes and told everyone we'd begin again today but didn't call back to schedule specific people on specific Saturdays—we'll be double-booked all day. That will mean the three of us will each have one horse in a separate paddock while working with one child. We'll also each have an easel with laminated pictures on the front and Velcro on the back. You'll ask the child to choose which task comes first." She continued giving him instructions, explaining about some of the children and their rumblings and stimming actions and how best to deal with those and many other things. "Encouragement and lightheartedness are very important. We're not testing them to see what they know. We're offering them a chance to enjoy life on their terms in a casual but organized way. The hardest issue is if a meltdown happens. If you see hints of it through the rumblings I talked about, remember redirection is key. But if it happens, Roy and I will be close at hand. The parents, too, although we try to keep them from jumping in, if possible."

"And it'll be just for Amish children?"

"Unfortunately, ya. The Amish come here as friends and family, even if we don't know them before they arrive. But for us, as Graber Horse Farm, to reach out to the Englisch community, we would have to be certified to work with special-needs children, and that's time consuming and expensive."

"But you give the Englisch riding lessons."

"Ya, getting certified and licensed for that was easier and more affordable than getting certified to work with special-needs children." Paddock one and all that was in it came into clear view.

"There's only one parent here," Chris said.

"For now. In an hour we'll have several." She gestured. "The one parent is Elam, a widower who's very helpful on our therapy days."

"Widower? He's young."

She nodded. "Thirty-three. And he has been raising two children on his own for five years. One is special needs. His story is heartrending, but it does not define him. You stick close to me and learn. When other parents arrive, you can move to your own paddock. If you still need pointers after that, Elam can give them, but he can't take over for you. He has two boys to watch, and Kyle has no sense of what's dangerous."

"If Elam knows how to do all of it, why does he bring his child here?"

She didn't answer since their horses had stopped at the split-rail fence outside paddock one. Kyle was inside the fence with a stick in hand, squatting as he played in the dirt.

"*Guder Marye,* Kyle." Abigail dismounted and unclipped the cinch center ring, beginning the process of removing the saddle.

The little boy didn't look up or speak, but he tapped the stick against the ground as acknowledgment that he'd heard her. She removed Pippi's saddle and hung it on a fence railing.

She laid the breast collar across the saddle and unbuckled the flank cinch. "Chris, you'll need to get Lady Belle or Skunkweed. Lightning gets flighty around children, especially ones who are stimming."

"Okay."

Elam came out of the stable, carrying two saddles for special-needs children. Both were child sized with a full back brace and safety belt that went around the stomach and buckled.

"There she is." Elam smiled.

"Hallo, Elam."

He was a good man, kind and gentle, but she wasn't attracted to him.

"Hallo. The easels are set up in each paddock, and I need to grab one more saddle and the bridles." He put one saddle on the fence and then the other in front of it. "Kyle is one excited little boy today." He held out a halter to her. "For Pippi. Lady Belle and Skunkweed have their halters on."

"Denki, Elam." She gestured at Chris. "Elam, this is Chris. He's come from the other side of the Cumberland Narrows to lend a hand here."

Elam dusted off his hands and held one out. "Hi, Chris. I heard you were gone."

"Ya, I am." Chris shook his hand. "Just here today as temp help."

Elam nodded. "Roy said he'd be back just as soon as he tended the horses at the old poultry barn. I didn't get a chance to talk to him yet. Any more horses come down with EHV-1?"

Abigail opened a gate and led Pippi into the paddock. "Thankfully, no. If we can go ten more days without another horse showing symptoms, it'll all be behind us."

"I know you'll be glad when those ten days are up. And none of your horses at the Kurtzes' place came down with EHV-1?"

"Not a one," she said.

"It sounds as if things went as smoothly as possible, then, except for Roy's injuries. Since you had a new string and you weren't in sight when I arrived, I was sure I'd walk into the stables to find you with a fire in the forge, your blacksmith hammer in hand, shoeing horses."

"That's got to happen soon, but we had our string shoed, and the new string arrived with decent shoes—at least good enough to get us through this super busy time."

"You shoe horses?" Chris asked.

"I do." Abigail shrugged. "But it's far from my favorite way to expend energy."

Elam dusted off his hands. "I better get the rest of the gear."

Chris entered the paddock and closed the gate. "He seems nice."

"He is. Too nice for me, I think."

"You're kidding, right?"

She shrugged.

"But there are plenty of others, I'm sure." Despite Chris's warm smile, she saw concern.

"If you're afraid I'll die an old maid, don't be. I may die one, but it'll be by my choice. Some think less of me for remaining single this long. Too many look at me with pity or judgment, as if I have less value until I'm married. Tell me you'll never become one of them, Chris."

"Never," he whispered. He went toward Kyle, stopped several feet back, knelt, and used his finger to draw in the dirt.

Abigail observed as Chris slowly made his way into Kyle's world. Not long after, he and Kyle went to the easel with its two columns— "To-do" and "Done"—and when Kyle picked up the picture with the saddle, which should be one of the last things they did, Chris said something so softly that Abigail couldn't make out a single word, but Kyle broke into giggles.

How could a man so adept in rescuing children, whether it was Heidi from danger or Kyle from being held prisoner within himself, be so violent as to face another man made in God's own image and hit him?

Twenty-Four

Jemima's shoulders ached with tension, and she longed to fade into nothingness. She struggled to take a full breath. The wooden bench beneath her was unforgiving as she cradled Heidi in her arms and watched the preacher as if she were an upstanding godly woman.

Hypocrite!

She'd arrived at the Millers' about thirty minutes ago, carrying a fussy Heidi in the car seat. This was the first church day she'd had to attend with Heidi. Jemima softly mumbled that the baby's mom had disappeared, leaving Heidi behind, which was true. And now the other women treated Jemima as if she were a selfless saint taking care of a poor, abandoned baby. But she was the opposite.

She knew it.

Roy knew it.

God knew it.

Still, here she was with Heidi in her arms, longing to pass her to Roy and insist he take her back to social services. She looked across the Millers' living room to the men's side of the church gathering.

Roy had both Simeon and Nevin. Soon it would be Roy's and her turn to host church. How was that supposed to work?

As the bishop preached, Jemima's mind kept drifting. *Focus.* She surely needed to hear what God was telling her, as the emotions she felt daily were overwhelming. Her baby, Simeon, was asleep on Roy's shoulder. But if she took Simeon and Roy held Heidi, the community would be suspicious, wondering why Roy would be the caregiver for some other woman's newborn? So she held Heidi, pretending to be something she wasn't. The whole situation made her sick.

She wanted to stand up and tell everyone the truth, but the fear of what that would mean, of the chaos it would set in motion, was paralyzing. Roy caught her looking and gave her a half smile. She averted her eyes.

Laura pulled on Jemima's dress sleeve. "Mamm, the baby."

Jemima glanced down to see Heidi stirring and starting to fuss. Laura's crutches were peeping out from under the church bench. During the opening songs, Laura and Carolyn had somehow pulled a miracle and got Heidi to go to sleep by gently swinging her back and forth while she was still buckled in the carrier. But it didn't last, and within seconds the baby's stirring turned to screeching. Typical. Jemima had leaned down, unbuckled Heidi, and cradled her in her arms. She'd gone back to sleep for a bit.

Now a foul smell filled Jemima's nose. She leaned toward her girls and whispered in Pennsylvania Dutch, the only language Carolyn fully knew, that she needed to change the baby and probably feed her again. She promised to be back as soon as she could.

"Kann Ich kumm aa?" Carolyn looked up at her, hands clasped

prayerfully, asking to go with her. *"Ich bin gut at Bobbeli diapers. Daed saages es. Ich kann helfe."* Carolyn assured her she was good at changing diapers, because Daed said so, and she could help. Before Jemima responded, Carolyn picked up the diaper bag from its place under the bench and paused, her big eyes begging to stick close to the baby.

Jemima paused and then nodded. "Kumm." She stood. Heidi fussed louder, and Jemima knew she would be wailing within two minutes. Unwilling to mingle with the other Mamms in the crying room and chance questions or praise coming her way, she walked toward the washhouse door.

Anna Miller stood, a gentle smile on her lips. She gestured behind Jemima. "You take the baby upstairs, just as you've always done with your own."

Anna had misunderstood, apparently thinking Jemima considered it improper to mingle legitimate children with an illegitimate Englisch one. Being alone and free to talk put Jemima at risk of needing to lie outright or do so through redirection and silence.

Is this how Roy had felt—sickened to keep the truth hidden while desperate to do so? Is that why he had pulled away from Jemima more and more as time went by, even when they were near each other at mealtime or in the same bed?

Jemima shook her head.

"Ya, you will," Anna whispered. "We feel no different just because of whose she is. If you need more privacy to soothe her than with your other children, use the guest room upstairs, last door on the left."

"Denki." Jemima breathed a sigh of relief to have a room to herself. She hurried up the stairs, Carolyn on her heels. Why was her daughter so attached to this child?

Once in the guest room, Jemima closed the door and motioned for Carolyn to put the diaper bag on the bed. Doors were typically left open so caregivers could still hear the preachers, but Heidi wailed during diaper changes. Jemima methodically pulled out all the changing items. How many hundreds upon hundreds of diapers had she changed, scrubbed, and hung out to dry in her life? She laid Heidi down on the wool blanket with waterproof backing that she always used as a changing pad. Heidi ramped up her screams even more.

"*Ich hab des,* Mamm." Carolyn assured her Mamm that she had this as she climbed onto the bed and got in front of her Mamm. Carolyn leaned her mouth close to Heidi's ear, humming and shushing softly. Heidi's shaky cry quieted for a moment and she blinked. Jemima watched as her own small child undid the pins, stuck them in the bedding, wiped the baby down, and put a fresh diaper on her. Jemima drove the sharp pins through the material, and Carolyn fastened each one. When did she learn how to do all that? Carolyn had helped some with Simeon, but Jemima hadn't seen her as able to do this much. Jemima put the dirty diaper in the waterproof bag and tucked it away.

"*Ach, wie wunderbaar Bobbeli* Heidi." Carolyn cooed about how wonderful a baby Heidi was as she finished redressing her.

Jemima pulled hand sanitizer and a clean diaper out of the bag.

She put the clean cloth on her shoulder and squirted her hands and Carolyn's. They rubbed their hands until they were dry.

Heidi's face scrunched, and she let out a cry. "Sh, *es iss gut.*" Carolyn kissed Heidi's forehead and then looked up. She told Jemima that Heidi needed extra love sometimes. Then she asked if Heidi missed her Mamm and Daed and if that was why she cried so easily.

Carolyn's empathy jabbed at Jemima, making her heartache fresh while sparks of anger flew heavenward. Heidi *was* with her Daed, had been since the start. Jemima caressed Carolyn's sweet face and kissed her, but she didn't answer her daughter's question.

Heidi squirmed and cried louder, her face reddening again. Jemima picked her up. She'd given her a bottle before church began. Could she be hungry? Was this new formula no easier on Heidi's stomach than all the others they'd tried?

"Kumm on, child." Jemima stifled a sigh and rolled her eyes. *Good grief.* Enough was enough. She sat in the rocker, holding Heidi on her lap. "What do you want?" Jemima pushed back the emotional resistance she felt against this little one and cradled her and rocked back and forth. Heidi cried louder. "What?" Jemima stared at the baby's face, hackles raised. "What do you want?"

A voice whispered, and chills engulfed every inch of Jemima. She quieted her thoughts and listened, trying to make out what the whisper had said.

Then she heard it loud and clear.

To be loved.

The truth penetrated Jemima's anger and pierced her conscience. Her movements were the right ones: gentleness, cradling, rocking. But her actions didn't come from a place of love or caring; they came from a sense of duty to God as anger raged within her.

She studied the infant's tiny features, and for the first time, she saw the pouty lower lip of hurt feelings. But Jemima couldn't pull her truly close, the snuggly kind of embrace that happened naturally between a Mamm and her babe. She tried to make herself relax and cuddle, but thoughts of why this child shouldn't even exist turned up the heat underneath her anger.

Love . . .

Thoughts of what love was and wasn't flooded her.

She knew it to be gentle and bold. Quiet and loud. At times it had filled her with such force, it seemed to be more physical than abstract. Every time it entered or was stirred or was awakened anew, she was never, ever the same again.

In this ever-changing world when life was calm and steady one day and torn to shreds the next, three things were steady: faith, hope, and love. But the greatest of these was love.

She knew that God said that love is patient, but what she had given her husband and Heidi of late was more like a wall of silence than patience. She hadn't been kind. Her responses to Heidi were measured because she longed to free her life of her without anyone knowing who the baby truly was.

Jemima thought about the verses on love. If love didn't dishonor, was not self-seeking, and kept no record of wrongs, who was she?

If love always protected and persevered, what did that say about who she was? Love was an emotion, but it was so much more than that. She'd known that since she was a girl. Her Mamm taught her that it started as an emotion but that in every long-standing relationship, when life turned emotions on their heads and the only thing one felt was the opposite of what he or she used to feel, love became a decision and it stood the test of time. Her Mamm said that if she didn't believe it, ask God.

Jemima pulled Heidi close, tears brimming.

Wasn't this what God did with all His children? Adopt them? Love them the way Carolyn loved, without prejudice or anger?

"I'm sorry, little one." Jemima brushed her finger along Heidi's cheek, taking note of her puckered lip.

Heidi's stomach rumbled and growled. Poor thing was miserable.

A difficult thought seemed to shake all the other thoughts, much like a tremor in an earthquake.

Jemima inwardly shuddered, but maybe she could . . . She cringed as she unfastened the nursing fold in the bodice of her dress and lifted Heidi to her breast. As she helped her latch, Heidi's blue eyes locked on hers, and the rock-hard misery of resentment began to melt from Jemima.

Hadn't she been just like this baby of late—crying, whining, and miserable no matter how hard Roy tried?

The poor man. The blockhead. She sighed at her opposing opinions of her husband.

Through it all, God was there, always forgiving her, nudging her to trust Him no matter her sin. If He could love her, she could love this innocent child.

"Mamm, bischt allrecht?"

Carolyn's asking if her Mamm was all right caused Jemima to realize her cheeks were wet with tears. "Ya, Ich bin gut. Denki, Carolyn." And she *was* good. She cradled her daughter's face with her free hand and told her that she'd taught her something good today: how to love Heidi.

"*Loss uns lieb meh,* Mamm." Carolyn nodded her head.

Her words weren't perfect, and Jemima wouldn't correct her. "Ya, let's love more," she whispered while tears spilled down her cheeks.

Carolyn moved to a basket of toys and sat down. Jemima drew a deep breath and relaxed into the new feeling. She knew that the anger with her husband was still there, just beneath this flood of love for Heidi. She was so weary of anger. It was no longer welcome, but she'd nursed every dark, miserable thought that had come her way until anger was an oversized living thing inside her that she didn't know how to get rid of.

Heidi soon stopped nursing. She was fast asleep with a drop of milk on her rosy lips and a contented little smile. Could Heidi sense the change in Jemima, or did the breast milk sit easier on her stomach? Either way, Jemima smiled too, although the tears were still falling. She put Heidi on her shoulder and burped her before cradling her again, rocking her.

Someone knocked on the door. "It's just me," Roy whispered. "Simeon woke up and was looking for you. May I come in?"

"Ya." Jemima jerked the clean diaper off her shoulder and swiped it across her face and nose, but she didn't really care how she looked.

Roy brought Simeon in. The baby reached for her, and she held both infants on her lap. Simeon patted her face. "Mamm." He grinned.

"Simeon, look!" Roy pointed at the basket of toys in front of Carolyn.

Their son reached toward the toys, and Roy put him in front of the basket. The services were so long for little ones. She had no doubt that Simeon had been far more anxious to get down than to see his Mamm.

Roy sat on the bed. "Are you doing okay?"

Since Carolyn didn't understand much English, they could talk freely in front of her. "The day you were missing I went into Tiffany's place. It didn't take long to make sense of all the things that hadn't made sense for months. She had a newborn you hadn't mentioned. Your phone was on her property, you had a few belongings in her house, you'd emptied my account, and you and Tiffany were missing. Those were the facts. My trust was broken. But despite everything else, somewhere deep inside me I knew you'd come home to me—come hell or high water . . . or come Tiffany and the baby. I knew that if you had breath, you'd come home."

Roy studied her, seemingly at a loss for words.

"It's why I spotted you so quickly once you were on the horizon, stumbling toward home."

"I love you with all my heart." He scooted forward on the bed and placed his hand on her hand. "We can start again, Jem. I know we can."

"Maybe. I don't know." She moved her hand over his and squeezed it before pulling free. "I just don't know if what's left of us is enough. I can't see my way past my anger with you. Pray for me, Roy." Tears fell. "Please."

Twenty-Five

Chris stood in a makeshift locker room with four walls of hay. He could hear the crowd cheering for the undercard fight that was happening just thirty feet from him. The guy he would fight was bigger and possibly a much better boxer. Chris paced back and forth on the straw-covered floor. His trainer, Mike, had told him that there were boxing scouts here today and that if Chris won the fight, he could begin a boxing career. Is that what Chris wanted?

Thoughts of Abigail and the horse farm distracted him. How were they doing? At least Aaron was there now, had been there five days. He knew that much because he'd called Roy to ask.

Mike threw him a jump rope. "Just to get your blood pumping."

Chris nodded. He was too much in his head to respond. He began with single jumps. Was he here because of his brother Dan? Or did he enjoy this and was he looking for an excuse to fight?

"Switch," Mike said.

Chris began to do double jumps.

His mind wandered to the overly energetic Abigail Graber. What was she doing today? Whatever it was, it was bound to be very Amish. She could outmatch anyone with her energy and ability to move from one volunteer task to another even when working full time.

"Time." Mike clapped his hands together. "One round of shadowboxing."

Did he like this—the anxiety before a fight, the feeling of getting hit and keeping on the move, the thrill of hitting his opponent and seeing the look of surprise in his eyes? Was that what drew him? He knew the answer. The adrenaline rush was addictive. After the embarrassing breakup with his fiancée many years ago, his willingness to go outside the Amish world came with some fun and powerful emotions. But he also had put himself in a place where he wasn't welcome in his home, and he'd ruined all chances of a lasting relationship with Abi.

"Time." Mike slapped Chris on the back. "You're ready."

Chris couldn't let his thoughts rattle anymore. His head wasn't in a good place. He was wavering before a fight. No half-decent fighter did that, so why was he? He liked winning. That he knew for sure.

The crowd grew louder, and he knew the undercard fight was over.

Mike stepped toward Chris, standing chest to chest, and pinned Chris with a stare. "Never in my life have I met a boxer more naturally gifted than you. But you have a decision to make, a simple one. Do you want to give this fight your all? If so, you have to set every thought aside that isn't about winning. There are no two ways about it."

One of the walls of hay came crashing down. A burly bearded

man ushered Chris forward. The crowd cheered. In that moment, he saw his opponent for the first time: pale skin, perfectly muscled body, and a thick beard. He was smiling and had a massive hand raised over his head. Chris stepped forward. The crowd stood in a circle around the area where Chris and his opponent were to fight.

The referee brought them both forward. "All right, gentlemen, I want a clean fight. No kicks, knees, or biting. You break when I tell you to. Touch hands if you want to."

Chris put his wrapped fists out.

His opponent slapped them away. "That's the last time you'll ever touch me."

They went to opposite sides of the circle.

Ding, ding, ding.

His opponent ran forward, throwing a wild hook. Chris ducked and stepped back, trying to keep his distance. His opponent was the aggressor, coming fast and hard. He caught Chris with a jab, and a jolt of reality about how powerful this man was ran through him. Two right hands to Chris's body, followed by another straight jab to the face, had Chris covering up. His opponent fought with such tenacity that Chris didn't know how to match it. He covered up and moved around, keeping his head dodging about, while he waited for the round to end.

The bell rang, and Chris went back to his corner. "That's not what we talked about." Mike squirted water in his mouth. "Focus, Chris. Protect your ribs. He's heavy on his left foot. Move around him. Get him off balance and move in."

Chris looked at his opponent.

"Chris, a house divided falls. You're here to win, not debate with yourself whether you should be here at all."

The bell rang again. Chris stood and moved forward, eating a few punches on the way in. He clinched and then jabbed, catching his opponent on the nose. The crowd grew louder. He could hear the sound of his own heartbeat.

His opponent had a wild look in his gray-blue eyes. He came forward, swinging at Chris's body. Chris threw a straight jab and felt the soft skin flinch under his fist.

"Hook!" Mike shouted.

Chris obeyed, throwing an immediate hook after the jab. His opponent stumbled back for a moment, only to rush forward swinging wild haymakers. Chris backed up, but he was greeted by a hard right hand.

Chris fell to the floor. The ref was standing over him, counting. Chris's vision blurred. He saw something through the spots popping in front of his eyes. Abigail was facing him, motioning for him to get up. Chris stood up, searching for her.

The ref grabbed his hands and pulled tight on them. Chris snapped back into reality, knowing that he was in the fight.

"You good?" the ref asked.

Chris nodded. He put his guard up and marched forward. The ref told them to fight. A right hand and a left hand hit Chris's chin. Now was the test. He could give up. There was no shame. He'd landed a few good blows against a much bigger opponent. He shook his head. No, that's not what he came here to do.

Chris remembered what Mike had said about seeing if his opponent could fight while backing up. Chris jabbed twice, and one landed flat on his opponent. He threw a hook to the body, followed by another one. His opponent swung wildly, missing and misjudging the distance. Chris attacked him with an onslaught of punches. It was clear that his opponent didn't know what to do. Every time the guy tried to establish distance, Chris rushed forward, digging in body shots. His rival dropped all orthodox technique and tried to clinch. Chris pushed him away and swung as hard as he could, connecting with his opponent's chin. His opponent collapsed to the floor, spitting out his mouth guard. The ref cut the count short when Chris's opponent went limp.

Chris raised his hand to the wild, cheering crowd.

Mike ran up and gave him a pat on the back. "You did it, and if you want a career in fighting, this win will open every door you need."

But the victory felt wrong. It felt like an assault on his inner man. Fighting wasn't immoral, but apparently it was completely out of sorts with his inmost self. How could he stand here on the threshold of everything he wanted and be completely baffled by the simple question, *Who am I?*

Abi was right. He wasn't Amish. He'd walked away from that. He wasn't Englisch either. He'd stepped into the lifestyle, but it hadn't stepped into him. Standing here now, he realized that his choices that got him to this place felt out of place, like wearing a winter coat in summer.

Part of him was a fighter, but he was just now beginning to realize that it tore him up inside more than it filled in the missing pieces.

Mike put a hand on Chris's shoulder. "You ready to move up in the boxing world?"

Chris pulled away from searching his heart, but he knew he was far from looking for answers. "I'm sorry. I'm done with fighting, and I need to go home."

Mike smiled, his resignation clear. "Good for you, Amish Mayweather. Good for you."

Despite Mike's words, Chris knew he was disappointed. "I'm sorry, Mike."

"We each get one life, Chris. What's inside here"—he jabbed Chris's chest—"has to match what you're doing with your life. You've been mismatched for too long. Figure it out and get busy living who you are."

He'd done a lot of damage with his parents and community, but he had to go home and try to set things right. Had his very public and difficult breakup all those years ago splintered him like this? Or had the fascination and adrenaline rush of being good at something that was so foreign to his upbringing seduced him?

He didn't know. But unsplintered time at home, living Amish in every sense of that faith, would answer his questions.

Twenty-Six

The bank seemed unusually quiet as Roy sat across the wide mahogany desk from the loan officer as he explained why Roy didn't qualify for a loan. Roy tapped the folded newspaper in his hand against his leg. He'd found what seemed to be an ideal food truck. The desire to take Jemima and Abigail to see it was strong, but first he needed to know that he could come up with the money for it.

"Mr. Graber, we're a small-town bank, and we have to consider the big picture." Brad Jones looked at his computer screen. "Right now your accounts are depleted, whereas a year ago you had two savings accounts with us, one for your business and one with your wife and sister. Those totaled seventy thousand dollars. You've borrowed money to buy more horses than usual."

"I was injured"—he held up his arm with the cast—"and that slowed things down, but I'm doing better, and I have good help." Aaron had arrived eighteen days ago. He was young and green, but he was a hard worker and learned fast, just as Chris had said. "I've begun training the new string, and half will be ready to sell in a couple of months." This rejection gave him a sickening feeling of having been kicked by a horse, and it sent a wave of despair over Roy.

"Yeah, I understand, but . . ." Mr. Jones shuffled through the papers inside a folder on his desk.

When had Roy stopped feeling like himself? He used to feel confident and hopeful. Now he often just felt stupid. Life after the driver ran into the back of his horse and carriage had been unfamiliar. But the emotional upheaval aside, his only way of being able to work the farm had been to consume pain pills. Worse, he kept having to increase the dosage regularly in order to get the same relief he once had. Looking back, he realized the pills had begun stealing pieces of him but he'd been too busy striving forward to really notice.

Another bank employee brought something to Brad. "Excuse me. I hate to interrupt, but could you look at this information concerning the Lee account?"

Brad reached for the papers in the man's hand, and Roy sank into his thoughts. Jemima had no idea what she meant to him. Women seemed funny that way, or at least Amish women did. His wife's value was just as the Word said: "She is worth far more than rubies. Her husband has full confidence in her and lacks nothing of value. She brings him good, not harm, all the days of her life."

But that's not how Jemima or most Amish women saw themselves. Even before any of this began, Jemima had quietly voiced unrest with herself. Condemnation and loathing were common feelings. Why?

Was it because life made her feel helpless, like he felt sitting at this banker's desk? Or maybe she was mired in unrealized dreams, unable to bring creative business ideas to fruition because no one backed her the way she backed him.

The other bank employee took the papers back from Brad. "Thank you. Very helpful."

Brad returned his attention to Roy. "I understand that things haven't gone as you'd hoped this past year. Business ventures go south for myriad reasons, and often those reasons aren't the fault of the owner. But we . . . I feel that it isn't in the bank's best interest to loan money, especially not for this new business venture."

"What needs to happen for me to be able to sell ten to fifteen acres of land?"

"Since it's not legal to sell a mortgaged piece of property without paying it off first, you'd need to refinance your mortgage. You'd need to have a new survey done, and the closing cost would cut into any profits you'd make selling that land. Added to that, if the buyer intended to use the land to build a house, the property would have to be rezoned, and water and electricity lines would have to be run out, lessening the value of the land. And when it sold, you'd owe capital gains tax."

"That's a lot." Making it worse, Roy knew that the problem with selling land went deeper than what Brad had just explained. Roy had horses on the Kurtz farm and now on his grandfather's land. He needed more land, not less. He rose. "Thank you."

He walked out of the bank and toward his horse-drawn carriage. Maybe the answer was to sell some of the horses earlier than he'd planned. He'd begun training the new string a couple of weeks ago, and he'd been working with the older string for several months. If he sold the best trained in the older group, he would improve his cash flow, giving him money for a food truck. But none of the horses was trained enough to resell. Horses without proper retraining were problematic for the new owners, putting his and the farm's reputation on the line and causing buyers to look elsewhere for their horses.

He sighed, weary of every idea hitting a brick wall. Defeat ate at him as he climbed into the rig. He stared at the newspaper. *Dear God, how can I make this work?* He tapped the paper against his forehead, longing for an answer.

An idea hit for a second time, only this time he knew it was the right thing to do despite the lasting effects it would have for the horse farm. He pulled out his cell phone.

Spring's cool air rustled Abigail's dress and the strings of her prayer Kapp as she went out the side door of her Uncle Mervin's recovery house, carrying a laundry basket of wet clothes. With the EHV-1 scare behind them and Chris's cousin Aaron working at the farm, Abigail's schedule was finally returning to normal.

For the Amish, Monday is laundry day. But here at the recovery house, Abigail's washdays were Friday afternoon or Saturday morning because that's when she had time. Other women volunteered time throughout each week too, and they could choose their laundry day when it was their week to do the wash. The men did a lot of the work themselves, including laundry, cooking, and cleaning.

She let the tub thud to the ground and grabbed a wet pillowcase, feeling grateful for the warmer weather. As she snapped each wet item in the air before putting it on the clothesline, tiny droplets of water flew, causing a flash of something akin to a scattered rainbow. Since she hadn't gotten the laundry on the line before school, she hoped the steady wind would dry everything before nightfall.

Her uncle and his friends, as he called them, were in a circle of chairs in the side yard, coffee and cigarettes in hand. A few had an open Bible propped on their legs or lap. The men ranged in age from midtwenties to over sixty, but no one in this group of sixteen was currently from Mirth. Six states were represented among these Amish men.

Because of her years of helping out at Endless Grace, she knew that smoking and drinking loads of coffee were part of the addicts' lives, but she didn't really understand why. The addicts said it took the edge off, making their desire for drugs slightly less monstrous, and alcohol was considered a type of drug. But smoking, although also addictive, was acceptable while dealing with drug addictions because it helped people win the battle and didn't immediately ruin lives, relationships, and jobs.

Her uncle was an addict, but he hadn't had a drop of alcohol in thirty-five years.

Her phone vibrated. She stepped behind the line of wet laundry and pulled her cell from her pocket. Uncle Mervin didn't allow the residents to have personal phones, so she used hers discreetly. It was a text from Roy.

Hey, LS. Have an idea. Where are you?

LS stood for *little sister,* but she bristled at his using a term of endearment. Her loyalties were with Jemima. Still, she replied, Uncle Mervin's. Doing laundry.

K. See you in a few.

What did he want now? She returned to hanging laundry. She couldn't hear what the men said, but she knew this was a rough time of life for each of them, a battle some would not win. Even if they did win for a period of time—weeks, years, or decades—addiction was a relapsing disease. Some would stay clean for life, while others would be clean for years and then need to get clean again. She hurt for them, but she hurt worse for their spouses and children.

The round-robin conversation went on uninterrupted as she returned to the house and washed and wrung out another load of bedding. She hauled another heavy basket to the clothesline and plunked it onto the ground.

The familiar sound of a rig coming down the road and onto the driveway told her that Roy had probably arrived. Soon he was at the clothesline. "Hallo." He grabbed a few clothespins out of the sack on the line and held one out. "I have a way to get what I think is a good food truck, but I need you to go with me to see it."

She took the clothespin. "Does Jemima know about this—whatever it is you're talking about?"

"Not yet."

"Then I'm out."

His brows furrowed. "Abigail, I appreciate that you've remained steadfastly quiet this long, not making me fight to win back your trust while I'm focused on Jemima. I know my months of silence while dealing with Tiffany hurt you too, especially as I relied so heavily on you without being up front about why I needed your help."

"Ya, explain that one, Roy." She flapped a twin sheet in the air and slung it over a line. It was a good thing this clothesline was long, with six rows of line.

He put two clothespins on the sheet. "I don't need to." He shook out a towel and hung it.

"Excuse me?" She pushed the basket down the line with her foot.

"You know why I didn't say anything, Abigail."

He was right. She did know. If he'd said anything to her, she would've had to choose between keeping his secret and telling Jemima. "Did you have feelings for Tiffany?" She picked up another twin sheet.

He hesitated. "You won't like the answer. I stay in turmoil over it."

"Roy, no." She studied him, waiting.

"I had a lot of feelings for her, and I resisted every single one or I'd be held accountable to God and be in jail for hitting her. Is that honest enough for you?"

He was wrong. She liked that answer, although she probably shouldn't. She dropped the sheet into the basket and hugged him. "I'm sorry." She was sorry he'd had to carry everything alone, without the aid of his beloved wife or best-friend sister or supportive Daed or stalwart bishop-uncle.

He embraced her. "Me too, Abigail. So very sorry I hurt you." He backed away and held her shoulders firmly. "When the truth came out about Heidi, you deserved for me to make time to talk to you and apologize before now."

"Ya, maybe, but I get it."

"Gut, and now I need your help again."

She freed her shoulders of his grip. "I can't hide anything from Jemima. It will undo her if anyone else she trusts withholds something. It's a sensitive topic—for like the next decade."

His eyes closed, and he nodded, as if realizing on a deeper level the battle in front of him. "But what I'm asking is totally different from that kind of secret. Just hear me out."

Roy pulled a folded newspaper out of his pants pocket. "I've found a food truck that may be very close to what you and Jemima have been hoping for." He tapped the red circle on the newspaper.

She took the paper from him and read the description. "Ya, it looks good."

"I thought so too. I want to pay you for all the work you've done over the years, and the payment is Lucky and Thunder."

"Your prized stallions?"

"They're yours now. Sell them and buy a food truck."

She knew whom to sell the horses to. Their vet would buy them in a heartbeat. He'd said so on a few occasions.

Abigail read the description of the food truck again. It looked promising. "Why are you giving the stallions to me to sell rather than selling them yourself?" She tightened the sweater around her. "I don't understand this plan."

"Because I don't want the truck to be from me, as if I'm giving it to Jemima. You and she earned the money, so let's get your money back and you be the one to present it to her. But the truck is for sale today, so let's go see if it's right for you and Jemima, and if it is we'll go from there."

"I can have them sold before the day is out. But selling your prized stallions?"

"I should've had it in me to do this much sooner. The idea came to me almost four weeks ago, around the time Chris left the farm."

"But without Lucky and Thunder, your profits will take a hard hit over the long run."

"I know, but I don't care. I want to do this."

His sacrifice, as well as his plan to keep himself out of the middle for Jemima's sake, was one Abigail understood and respected. "It's about time you paid me an unbelievably hefty price for all my work on that farm."

He grinned. "Thanks, LS."

She pulled her phone out of the hidden pocket in her apron. "I'll call the seller to make arrangements to see the truck." She smacked her brother in the stomach with the newspaper. "You're not so bad, you know that?"

Twenty-Seven

A mixture of aromas wafted through the house. Dinner was in various stages of being done, with the entrée still in the oven. Jemima buttoned the nursing flap in the bodice of her dress, rose from the rocker, and set Simeon on the floor near Nevin inside the wide circle of gated play space. The fact that she'd had a gliding rocker in her kitchen for the last eight years pretty much said it all. It allowed her to pause from meal prep or cleaning up to nurse a babe. She pushed away sentiments of feeling like a milk cow and chose gratefulness instead.

When her babes were hungry, she could cuddle with them and meet numerous needs—emotional, spiritual, and physical—in one sitting. Still, providing that for two little ones each day was taxing as well as heartwarming.

She chose to be thankful. Deciding what to pick up and hold on to in one's mind and emotions was a powerful thing and one she wasn't super skilled at, which felt like proof that she was a little spoiled and lazy. Life had been good to her, and she was fairly used to allowing whatever emotions came her way. She had made some choices throughout life. Who hadn't? But when it came to the really important things, she'd been passive, letting circumstances dictate what she would think and feel.

"Mamm, guck." Laura was at the kitchen table, her crutches resting beside her. She held up a picture she'd drawn and colored. Heidi was in her bouncer on the floor next to Carolyn as the five-year-old played with her dolls. Heidi kicked her little feet, making the bouncer do its thing. Heidi opened and shut her hands with excitement as Carolyn talked to her and pranced a doll lightly across her belly. It was hard to believe that Heidi would soon be three months old. Harder still to realize she'd been in this home for almost six weeks.

The back door slowly opened, and Roy came inside. "Wow, it smells great in here," he whispered.

She knew why he was entering quietly. He wanted a few minutes to chat with her before the children realized he'd entered the house. She glanced at the back door, looking for Aaron.

"I gave him a chore so we'd have a minute of just us."

She suppressed a smile. "Gut."

Each day that had passed since the church Sunday almost three weeks ago when she asked him to pray for her, she was a bit less angry.

He was in a half cast now, no sling, no stiffness to his movements. Despite their nights often being interrupted with one or both babies, he looked better than he had since the accident he and Laura were in more than a year ago. Even though Jemima was nursing Heidi now, he was still sleeping in the spare room next to Heidi.

He'd bring her to Jemima, and Jemima passed her back to him for everything else: burping, changing, and rocking. Some nights and early mornings when Simeon woke, Roy tiptoed into their bedroom and patted him back to sleep or took him in the other room, as if he understood that a little extra sleep for her went a long way during the day.

Five children, two of them babies less than seven months apart, was a handful, partly because of the hows and whys of Heidi's existence. Even so, Jemima had grown to love her. She didn't fool herself into thinking she could be at this place emotionally if Heidi had been the result of an affair. But she wasn't, and Jemima was healing from all the lies.

Roy closed the gap between them, and their eyes locked. Her heart jittered. He smiled in his gentle way that was only for her, and his eyes caressed her the way they had since before they married.

She turned from his stare. "Ya, dinner is almost ready." She opened the oven door to check the color of the pastry on the beef Wellington.

His presence was welcome, although every ounce of the familiar comfort and encouragement that was her husband was sprinkled with resistance from deep inside her. They talked during the night sometimes while up tending to babies. It seemed easier to share insights in a quiet home lit by a candle or kerosene lamp. Apparently when great emotional wounds were prayed over, great insight entered, bringing a little healing with each one. But sometimes being vulnerable with him was impossible, and she had to excuse herself and leave the room or ask him to.

He came closer, peering into the oven. "My favorite."

Part of her wanted to grin and nod, rather giddy to make him happy through the kindness of preparing his favorite meal. But instead she shrugged. "It's been a while since we've had it."

That wasn't at all the reason she'd made this. He was winning her heart back, which was as terrifying as it was encouraging. She'd made this meal especially for him, so why couldn't she admit it? She had French green beans ready to sauté, oven-baked home fries cooked to perfection, and fresh rolls.

"Geh." She shooed him. "It'll be ready in ten."

"I'd rather stay right here." He folded his arms, standing mere inches from her. "You look like you've had a good day . . . emotionally."

"I hate when you read me." She sighed, forcing herself to say the rest of her thought. "I love when you read me."

He brushed his fingers down her arm. "I know that feeling quite well, Jem."

She longed to lean in for a real hug, but she just wasn't ready. He'd been with her during labor with Simeon, knowing that another woman was carrying his child. He'd looked her in the eyes as they fawned over their newborn, all the while knowing he would leave her side six months later to share a similar experience with Tiffany. What had the birth of Heidi been like? That question was like many others: she wanted to know, and she never wanted to know.

But greater understanding had come to her daily since she'd asked him to pray for her three weeks ago. She now understood that if she wanted to refuse to walk in anger in order to walk in love, she had to learn how to be angry, work through it, make peace with God and herself over it, and then let it go.

Much easier said than done. Anger was like cockleburs attaching themselves to people as they walked life's path. She'd discovered unyielding anger with him over things that earlier in their marriage had been only minor aggravations or slights.

Today she'd learned that Roy wasn't the only one who needed her forgiveness. *She* needed it. That had been a deep revelation, and she'd spent hours thinking and praying about it.

She brushed flour from her apron. "Tell me something you know today that you didn't know yesterday."

A spark of joy lit up his eyes. "Now I know that whatever our greatest strength is"—he pulled her hand to his lips and kissed her fingers—"loyalty or kindness or protectiveness or whatever else, if we don't keep it in check, it will do harm instead of good." He kissed the back of her hand. "A giver can give too much. A protector will be overprotective, like I was, taking too much control."

"That's gut, husband." She slipped from his embrace, but his kisses sent fire through her veins. She turned on the burner under a cast-iron skillet, added a pat of butter, and waited for it to melt and simmer.

One of her insights this week was that this planet was a magnet for chaos. Abigail called it entropy, meaning left on its own, everything on this planet was in gradual decline, leading to disorder. If every part of this home was repaired and cleaned and then they left it, with no one entering it again, it would soon be covered in a layer of dirt. Spiders would build webs. Rodents would find their way in to get out of the cold, and they would bring food with them and gnaw through cabinets or walls to make nests. Eventually the windows would crack and break due to cold and storms, and birds and flies would use that space to fly in and out. The bedlam would continue to expand unless someone put effort into reversing the natural progression.

With the butter simmering, she tossed the already prepped French green beans and onions into the pan and stirred.

Was every relationship like a home, and every home needed effort and work?

Wasn't it mankind's place on this earth to keep pandemonium at bay? It took constant work to keep the house in order: meals, laundry, the finances, the business, and, most important of all, relationships.

Evidently it also took work to understand one's self and to prevent unwanted critters from entering through some craggy hole and roosting in the soul. It took work to keep the mind, the heart, and emotions clean and orderly.

On one level, she'd known that for a while, but after all this turmoil with Roy, she understood it on a much deeper level now. Hopefully it wouldn't always take the amount of work it had of late, but before she'd learned about Heidi, she'd been confused and lazy concerning the entropy inside herself and between her and Roy.

"Did you realize something new today, Jem?"

The muscles across her shoulders tightened as she forced herself to tell him. He'd bruised her, and being open didn't come as easy as it used to. She missed telling him everything and feeling one hundred percent safe in who they were.

She turned the burner off under the skillet. "I figured out that a portion of my anger hasn't been with you or Tiffany or God." She opened the oven and pulled out the beef Wellington. "It was with me, and I realized that if I didn't forgive myself, I'd always be angry with you. The revelation struck me so hard I think I forgot to breathe for a full minute."

"Could you tell me why you would need forgiveness?"

She had to forgive herself for being too naive and too trusting. She'd seen the red flags with Roy for months, and rather than pressing him for answers, she'd made it easy for him to avoid her. Not only had she needed to forgive herself, but she also needed to take responsibility. Months before Heidi was born, she'd felt powerless to keep her and Roy from drifting apart. Rather than fight with him about it or work her way free of the lie that she was powerless, she simply let the hurt and sense of helplessness take up residence within her.

But that was too much to share, at least for now. "You had shut me out, and I let you. In light of all I know now, your actions make sense. Mine do not."

"Jem." His singular word was as much a gasp as it was a whisper of relief. "I'm grateful for the understanding and appalled that you blame yourself."

"I'm not blaming me. I'm taking responsibility for my actions and inactions. Without realizing it, I was angry with myself for all I knew but didn't act on. Angry for all I didn't know but should have." She shrugged. "Just angry for not being smarter, wiser, a better judge of what was going on inside my family and inside you."

She turned from the stove to grab a bowl, but her husband was right there, toe to toe with her.

"I overprotected." His matter-of-fact tone hardly hinted at what she knew to be true: he was taking full responsibility.

She held his gaze and nodded. "I forgive you."

"Ya?"

She nodded. "Boundaries are in place, and I don't really know their exact location, but ya."

"That's gut." He put his hand against the small of her back and leaned in, his lips almost touching hers, when the back door popped open.

"Jemima"—Abigail held up a newspaper—"are you ready for good news?"

Twenty-Eight

Chris startled awake. Abigail. She felt as close as his next breath.

The smell of coffee rode on the air. He sat upright, and the open Bible on his bed shifted. A soft glow of early morning took the edge off the darkness. The sun would peep over the horizon soon, and he had to help his Daed in his furniture shop. He slid into his clothes.

Chris's Daed didn't need his help, but working together had been good for both of them. Staying with his parents had been good for all of them. Healing after all he'd put them through. It helped that Dan had come clean with their parents and his wife. The bishop knew the truth, and he'd set up parameters and discipline for Chris and Dan.

If the bishop agreed to it, maybe in a month or two Chris could find his own place and start building toward his new dream. But the thing about making amends and building bridges with his ministers, community, and Amish family was that he couldn't do anything without the bishop's approval, not even visit Mike at the gym or a coffee shop.

The bishop said Chris was proving his intentions. But for all intents and purposes, Chris had agreed to be grounded since he'd come home two weeks ago right after the fight. In many ways it was ridiculous to be twenty-eight and yielding to someone else like this. He *could* walk off. But this temporary curbing of all freedom was a small price to pay to be accepted by his people. It was a small price to pay for having spread his wings and soared for years—behind most of his people's backs—determined to use his forbidden skill of fighting. Dan was going through a four-week shunning for withholding the truth from the church.

But for all his years of living his way, Chris now knew who he was and who he wasn't, and he'd do it all again to come to this deep place of understanding life and faith. It seemed a favorite old saying might be true: "We are not human beings having a spiritual experience; we are spiritual beings having a human experience."

"Chris!" his Mamm called.

He opened the bedroom door. "Coming." He went down the stairs, pulling his suspenders over his shirt, and then stopped short. The bishop and his Daed were at the kitchen table, each with a cup of coffee in hand.

"You're out early today." Chris went to the percolator on the stove and poured a cup of coffee.

"I am." The bishop took a sip of his coffee. "I have some things on my mind."

"Okay."

The four of them had talked almost nightly for two weeks, being open and honest about Chris's desire to join the church. He was glad for that amazing moment at the end of his last fight when Mike assured him he could make good money boxing. In that moment, life made sense. Chris saw himself. He also saw fighting for what it was. He loved the adrenaline rush and the training. The training goals had been really cool for someone raised Amish—to punish his body, demand it do as he said, and see amazing progress. But that wasn't who he was. It was something he could do but not something worth giving up his family and community for. A man his age might have seven or eight years of boxing. Who would he have been by the end of that time? He didn't want to find out.

But Dan's gambling debt was paid. The air was clean between his parents and their two wayward sons. As for the other four sons, well, they'd been coming to the house often, and they talked about real life—the difficult, messy realness of life as men on this planet—and compared that to the struggles of men in the Bible. Something about this mess made them want time together.

"I don't think it was rebellion," the bishop said.

Chris took a seat. "What wasn't?"

"The issues that caused you to stop going through instruction seven years ago. I think having to break off the wedding shortly before you were to marry changed you."

"The breakup did a number on my head, that's for sure."

She'd dragged his name through the mud after the breakup, saying untrue and hurtful things about him. He'd kept his mouth shut, although even now he wasn't sure that was the best way to handle it. It had taken a long time to heal from all she'd said about him. But he wouldn't say any of that out loud.

"You asked to go through instruction this spring and summer, and I've made my decision. I see no reason for you to prove yourself for a year before being allowed to become a member."

"Denki." Chris took a sip of his coffee.

"And you may have your freedom back."

"Already?"

"With the exception that we'll continue meeting once a week for a while longer, but ya." The bishop stirred sugar into his coffee.

From behind Chris, Mamm patted his shoulders, showing her approval.

"What will you do with your newly given freedom?"

"I'm still unsure, but one thing I enjoyed on the Graber farm was working with special-needs kids. I could see that being part of the picture."

"That's different"—the bishop smiled—"so I'd say it fits you to a T. Are you talking about doing that here or in Mirth?"

"Here." His life in Mirth was as much in his past as fighting was.

The bishop tapped the spoon on the rim of his mug. "I know the bishop in Mirth well. He runs the recovery house there. Good man. I called him a few days ago while trying to sort out how strict to be in my decisions concerning you. He said that you had worked beside his niece Abigail and that you were very helpful to the Grabers."

"I'm glad he feels that way."

"He also said that Abigail thought well of you and that she's one in a million."

"She is, no doubt. But"—he shook his head—"no one is more disappointed with the fighting than Abi."

The bishop nodded. "You'll find the right woman." He rose. "Denki for the coffee."

His Daed got up too. "I'll walk out with you."

Mamm moved their mugs to the kitchen sink. "I've heard you mention her a few times."

"And thought of her a gazillion." He drummed his thumbs against the table. "I'm not sure she's left my thoughts for even a second, whether I'm awake or asleep."

"And you're sure there's nothing to hope for?"

"Ya, Mamm. I've done nothing but think about this for weeks, and the conclusion I've come to is part of her being one in a million. She sees and thinks about situations completely differently than the nine hundred ninety-nine thousand, nine hundred ninety-nine other women in that same situation. In her mind and heart, I crossed a line, and it's not what I did as much as what she sees will be baggage from it that she would have to help me carry for the rest of my life."

"So she's walled off?"

"Apparently." How had he not seen this before now? "But it's in a unique and subtle way. Still, that wall is thick and tall."

Mamm clicked her thumbnails together, thinking. "Well, if nothing else, you two have that in common."

"The difference is I'm cautious. I think she's unattainable." He thought of the information he had, trying to piece things together. "She's open and honest and caring, so that hides the wall. And the wall seems to be there only for potential life mates."

"For every single man who crosses her path?"

"Probably." Chris imagined that it might take her a few weeks to see an issue with some men, but she'd find the issue and be convinced of the baggage that would go with it.

"Chris, honey, that is just a different way of coping with the same issue of being wounded. Part of being a couple is helping each other heal from the wounds."

He shook his head. "No ex has wounded her."

"Never?"

"Never."

"And her relationship with her Daed?"

"Excellent. Those things aren't the issue. She goes on a few dates with someone and sees something that makes her call it off." Everything he knew about her said she should've had at least a few serious boyfriends by now. "She's incredibly creative and smart and irresistibly cute, and her energy level is a force she has to contend with daily. She should've found someone long ago that she bonded with, right?"

"Sounds right to me." His Mamm sipped her coffee, and they sat there in silence.

"Wait." Mamm slapped the kitchen table. "She *has* been wounded. Secondhand wounds or secondhand trauma, which I was reading about the other day in one of my daily devotionals, not sure which one."

"What?"

"It usually happens to children when one parent cheats on or abuses the other. The children take on the hurt as if it happened to them. The pain and fear from that can be far more intense than it is for the person it happened to, because children are so tenderhearted and are completely powerless to process the events and emotions the way an adult is capable of doing."

This was so like his Mamm. She loved to analyze people and had spent years reading devotions that paired the spiritual with the psychological. She tapped on the table. "The question is, who had that kind of trauma in their lives so that she became a sponge for the pain?"

His heart skipped a beat. "The recovery house," he whispered, chills skittering across his skin. "But why would strangers matter enough that it caused secondhand trauma?"

"When I was a girl, I saw a teenager—a kid I didn't know—fall from a roof he was repairing. I couldn't eat or sleep for days, and I had nightmares for months. The article said it can even happen to therapists who just listen to someone else's trauma."

"She's been helping her uncle in that recovery house since before she was a teen. She's witnessed addicts as they fell apart, often sobbing with remorse as they saw who they were and the damage they'd done to loved ones. Since her teenage years, she's been in a group with the spouses, comforting those who carry unbearable pain. I can see how she would've absorbed the trauma with them and absorbed regret from those who felt it for marrying that person in the first place."

"That's a lot of other people's pain to take on as her own, Chris."

Was he on the right track? Obviously his actions had separated them. But maybe he was onto something they could work through. Or was he simply piecing things together in a way that gave him a story he wanted to believe? Did Abigail have a wall around her, or was she being reasonably cautious and wise concerning men and marriage?

"Thoughts?" Mamm asked.

"In every other area of life, she's open and loving. *If* there's a wall, it's just in that one area. Still, it could mean she's terrified of becoming one of those women, so frightened she can't let herself fall in love. But if she feels that leery of good, steady men, where does that leave me? Despite the Amish ways, I've been actively pursuing violence, enjoying it, and making money off it."

"Is there something inside that rebelliousness that might work for her instead of against her?"

"Mamm." He couldn't believe she was thinking along those lines.

"Honey, part of what makes a marriage good is taking our faults and shaping them into something that works on our spouse's behalf. Can you think of anything in your rebelliousness that would work for her?"

"I don't know what it would be. Some women would be intrigued with the so-called bad boy turned good, but not Abi. I just don't know that I can get past the wall she's been building for the last fifteen years, maybe longer." Was Abigail aware of the walls she'd built around her? "I know plenty of other men have vied for her attention."

"But they weren't you." Mamm tapped her finger on the tabletop.

"True. They were probably better."

"Chris," she chided, "is that even possible?" Her smile said she was teasing, sort of.

He laughed. "I checked, and it is." His mind searched for something he had to offer her that others couldn't. "She values independence. She needs someone who understands her desire to follow her heart and to have equal say in decisions and to continue in a career. Not just earning money through acceptable Amish ways, but a career." He could give her that. He didn't mind if the church leaders or the community thought less of him because of his stance. He would be proud to sacrifice part of each day so she could build a career.

His Mamm looked perplexed. "That's a man's place."

"Not solely, not according to the Word. Proverbs 31 describes a woman whose husband is honored through her industry and wisdom and strength, not his. Her husband is esteemed because of her skill in work and decisions and love of family. In the New Testament, God and the apostles trusted women with important work and decisions. To Abigail it's not an either-or proposition—either remain single and have control over your life or get married and put all power in your husband's hands, hoping for the best. She wants a balance of power. No one's desires are more or less important because of that person's gender."

"And this mind-set works for you?"

"It does."

"Then?" She held out both hands, palms up.

What was he doing here? He and Abi had said their goodbyes, and she'd meant it. Then again, when he was in the ring, his opponents told him they would win, and they'd meant that too. He won some. He lost some.

If he could get inside that wall with her, it would take time. Worst-case scenario was that he'd fight for her and lose, but at least he would've fought. "I'd have to live in Mirth."

"I'm sure if her bishop allowed that, our bishop would agree to it," Mamm said.

"I need to see Mervin face to face to talk to him about this."

"Mervin?"

"Her bishop."

"Oh ya, I remember now. You said he's also her uncle and that he adores her, so your getting permission to live near her could be rather sticky."

"Definitely." Chris rose.

"Where are you going?"

"To shower and call an Uber." He'd wasted entirely too much time as it was. She wanted someone she could trust, someone who wouldn't blindside her with the truth of who he was *after* they were married, someone who wasn't carrying the deadweight of wanting to be elsewhere, of wanting life to be something it wasn't.

He could do that. Despite his past actions and who he appeared to be to her, he could give her everything she was looking for, because it's what he wanted too: sharing an Amish life with a unique and exceptional spouse. "If I can get permission to live in Mirth, it could take a long time to prove to her that my decision is a forever one."

"Jacob worked seven years for the right to marry Rachel, and another seven to finish the debt."

He chuckled. "As a kid, I thought the man was ridiculous. Why not move on and find someone else? Now he sounds wise and patient and I get it."

She grinned and hugged him. "You go tear down those walls and win Abigail's heart. I'll be praying for you."

Twenty-Nine

The sounds filling the air made Roy smile as he raked onto a plate the leftover scraps of food from their picnic in the side yard. His wife's laughter mixed with his sister's while the children played. Jemima and Abigail were sitting on a quilt with the two babies. The red-and-white-checkered cloth covering the picnic table rippled in the late-afternoon sunshine.

Even though it was a mere two days into April, the earth was warming nicely, giving hope that it would be a sunny, snow-free spring this year. Nice weather was always appreciated, especially by Jemima, who had high-energy preschoolers to wrangle on cold, rainy days.

A horse snorted, drawing Roy's attention. He looked up. The buckskin mare nodded her head at him, and he went to the fence and rubbed her fuzzy nose. "What's the matter? Do you feel left out or something?"

Abigail had sold his prized stallions several days ago, and it would take him a while not to miss them. All the horses were doing well, but even with Aaron's help, training them was going slowly.

One might think there would be more Amish teens and young men ready to snatch a job on a horse farm, but those who weren't needed at home on their family's farm were taking jobs at the local plant.

"Roy," Abigail called. "Just as an FYI, a late-afternoon picnic should happen more often when Laura and I arrive after the school day."

"Ya?" Roy plunked flatware down on a messy but empty plate. "Then stop dawdling when school is over and get here to prepare it."

Abigail laughed. "Not what I had in mind, but thanks."

"Would you mind watching both babies for a few minutes?" Jemima said.

"I've got this," Abigail said. Simeon was on one side of her, sitting up and playing with toys. Heidi was on the other side of her, having some belly time while scratching at the patches of color in the quilt.

Jemima walked toward Roy. His heart raced. She took him by the hand and led him toward the food truck. "Time for another tour."

The truck had arrived yesterday, Monday morning, and Jemima had already filed for the necessary permits to set it up in town. They might not have all the necessary permits before midsummer, but all progress was a process. What was most important was that his wife was happy. Maybe he should've pushed to get a truck years ago, but at the time they felt it was best to wait. It wasn't as if she were hoping to work full time. She'd work one day a week during tourist season until the children were older. Abigail would do the rest and still be off much more than with her teaching job.

"A private tour," Roy said. "I've not been on one of those yet."

"Ya, privacy is hard to come by around here. I can't imagine why, unless it has something to do with our five children."

He loved how she'd begun speaking of Heidi as one of their children. He'd first noticed this shift about two weeks ago.

They stepped into the truck. It was efficient, with minimum space to walk and move around but lots of space for cooking and storage. It had a closet of a bathroom, but that was much better than having to leave the truck to use a public restroom in town. She ran her fingertips across the silver cooktop. "I intend to make us dinner from here tomorrow."

"I look forward to it."

She turned to face him. "You knew about this truck before Abigail arrived with that newspaper in hand."

"Ya." He couldn't lie.

She moved in closer. "I thought so." She cupped his face with her hands and leaned in.

"Roy!" Abigail yelled, startling Jemima, and she released him and took a step back.

"Man, she's supposed to be the reason we get a moment," Roy mumbled, ready to ignore his sister and kiss his wife.

"Laura," Abigail said calmly but firmly, "you do as I said immediately. Get Carolyn and Nevin inside. Move it." Abigail's teacher tone had his full attention now. "Hello." She pounded on the side of the food truck.

Roy's heart lurched, and he hurried out of the food truck. "What's going—"

Tiffany. She was a passenger in a car that was on his driveway and heading toward his home.

Abigail had Simeon and Heidi. "Gut job, Laura," Abigail said as Laura nimbly moved despite her crutches. "In the house, little ones. Hurry along."

A broad-shouldered man turned off the car, and Tiffany stepped out of the passenger's side. Roy's older children were scurrying into the house.

"Jem, help Abigail get the babies inside."

Jemima lifted Heidi from Abigail's hip, relieving her of one baby. "She can't have her, Roy." Jemima paused, looking him in the eyes. "She can't."

"I won't let that happen. You go inside and lock the doors."

Jemima's face reflected concern, but she hurried away, ushering Abigail ahead of herself, clearly protective of Simeon and Heidi.

Roy walked toward the car.

"I came for what's mine: Heidi and my laptop."

It made sense to give her the laptop, maybe convince her to take it and be on her way, but a check in his gut said not to turn it over either. "I can't do that."

"Both are mine, and I want them."

"Not happening, Tiffany. Get in the car and leave."

She motioned to the driver. He got out, carrying a baseball bat.

Tiffany crossed her arms. "It doesn't have to be this way."

"Apparently it does."

The man came closer, tapping the bat against his palm. Roy had no idea what to do, but he was grateful that his sister had hustled the children inside. If need be, she'd use her phone and call the police. Roy straightened his shoulders and stepped toward the man, hoping to catch him off guard, maybe cause the man to back up or think twice.

The man raised the bat, looking as big as that green man the Englisch called the Incredible Hulk.

"Hey!" Jemima called.

Roy didn't take his eyes off the man with the bat, but when Jemima hurried in front of him, he saw that she held Abigail's phone out in front of her, turned sideways. "I'm recording every bit of this— livestreaming it to the police station's Facebook page, actually."

The man lowered the bat and pulled his baseball cap down farther on his head, casting a shadow across his face. "Hey, I'm just here to play some baseball with Amish friends. They play ball regularly. Everybody knows that."

"We're not in the mood for that today," Roy said. "You and the bat, get in the car."

The man hesitated, and Tiffany nodded. He got in the car, and Roy breathed a sigh of relief as gratitude welled up for the smart, strong woman his wife was. And his sister. He was sure she had a part in coming up with this plan. The two were a powerhouse of ideas.

"What do you need, Tiffany?" Jemima asked.

"Put that thing down." Tiffany pointed at the phone.

Jemima lowered it, but Roy doubted that she'd shut it off. They didn't have an internet provider, so she couldn't be streaming the encounter. Recording a video, yes. Streaming it, impossible. But Tiffany and her hulk didn't know that.

"I want Heidi and my laptop."

"As I've already said, you'll get neither," Roy countered. Anger from nearly a year of putting up with her nonsense stirred. He'd been so focused on holding his family together and making sure he was doing his best by his wife that he'd stuffed the anger with Tiffany away into a dark room and locked it.

Tiffany scoffed. "I will get Heidi."

"You abandoned her," he said.

"I had postpartum depression, and I left her in good hands. The law would understand that. Besides, you have no claim to her at all."

"You abandoned her."

"No, I left her with friends, and you took her from them. You had no right to do that. She's not yours."

Roy's brain seemed to freeze. Was she saying he wasn't the father?

"Please, just get in your car and go home." Jemima's voice jarred him back to reality.

"I won't. She's not his, and I have a legal right to her, so I'm not leaving without her."

Jemima's eyes met Roy's, looking for answers. He understood how she felt. Why would Tiffany show up out of the blue and say that Heidi wasn't his? Did Tiffany simply say whatever suited her at any given moment? If so, what was going on that it now worked for her to say Roy wasn't the father?

Surely that wasn't true. He'd been completely positive that Heidi was his. Where were the results from the DNA test he'd had more than five weeks ago? The lab said to expect them within a few weeks, but he hadn't thought about them until now.

Tiffany folded her arms. "You're a smart man, Roy. How long will it take for you to put the puzzle pieces together? She's mine, not yours. If you don't want trouble with the police for kidnapping her, go into the house and get her and the laptop."

Jemima's face showed bewilderment. She looked from Roy to Tiffany.

"Oh." Tiffany leaned in. "I bet he told you the story he and I made up if you discovered we'd been together—that he didn't remember anything. But he does, and we had our good times, far more than he'll ever admit."

Jemima's eyes moved to his, searching for truth.

"Jem, she's willing to say anything that would make you walk into our house and hand over Heidi."

"He's smooth, ain't he?" Tiffany added.

Roy pointed at the car. "Get in and go. Now."

Tiffany angled her head, studying Jemima. "You know what I'm telling you is true. We spent all that money, your money. We had a great time. The plan was he'd leave you. Then guilt got the best of him and he chickened out."

Jemima's face was taut as she moved to the car. She opened the door. "You need to go, please." She gestured into the vehicle. "We need time to think and adjust to this news."

Tiffany stayed put.

"I'm asking you to please leave and give us some time."

"I've got a right to her. She's mine, solely mine."

Jemima drew a shaky breath. "But you said she was Roy's, and we've taken good care of her. I'm asking for time out of respect for the naive wife you've put through so much." Jemima's voice was soft, maybe in hopes of gaining what they needed: time.

Tiffany chuckled. "Okay." She looked at Roy. "I'll give you one day"—Tiffany held up her index finger—"but I'm not leaving here without my laptop."

Tiffany stared at him, but Jemima didn't look his way.

He shook his head. "No."

"What?" Tiffany narrowed her eyes.

"We need time to find it," Jemima said. "We have no use for it, and lots of things were boxed up when we rearranged the house to make room for Heidi."

Tiffany seemed to believe Jemima, but they knew right where it was, didn't they? Typically his wife was a stickler for telling the truth. Maybe she felt fudging was God's way of working against evil, like in the New Testament when godly men were sneaky in avoiding soldiers for the greater cause of doing God's will.

"Fine." Tiffany flipped her perfectly done hair behind her shoulder. "You have twenty-four hours, and then I'll be back for both." As she got in the car and it went down the driveway and onto the road, Jemima didn't budge.

"What she said isn't true, Jem."

"Don't," she hissed. "Don't give her words merit by defending yourself, and don't muddy the waters of what we have to get through." She turned, arms folded tight. "What's wrong with her? Seriously."

"A bad childhood, one so damaging that she was hardly the

same person from one month to the next. Then she followed that with years of drug use."

"She's so jealous of me she can hardly see straight, and she was telling lies left and right, all in an effort to hurt us. Do you think she's lying about Heidi?"

"I don't know. But at the suggestion of the social worker, I had DNA tests run."

"Where are the results?"

"Again, I don't know. They were supposed to arrive by mail about two weeks ago."

"I bet it looked like another medical bill and we didn't notice it. But we're good at keeping up with bills, so if it arrived in our mailbox, it's in our house somewhere and we can find it."

"If not, we'll call the lab tomorrow, and hopefully someone can read us the results. Or if they will print them, we'll take an Uber to pick them up." He looked at the clock on his phone. "They're closed now for the day. There has to be a self-serving reason for Tiffany wanting Heidi back."

"Hey, Roy!" Aaron called from across the fence. "Are we about ready to work with Skipper again?"

"Not now," Roy hollered back. "Just make sure the horses are fed and watered, and then go stay with my folks tonight."

Even on the nights Aaron ate with them, he often slept at Roy's parents' place, where it was much quieter.

"You sure?" Aaron asked.

"Ya. Something has come up that we need to tend to, so finish and go straight to my parents' place."

"You got it." Aaron waved and headed back toward the barn.

Jemima intertwined her fingers with his, holding tight. "And her laptop. What's with that?"

"No clue, but she's cunning and manipulative. My guess is that it has some sort of information on it and it's dawned on her that she needs it."

"If you're not the father, what she's done is criminal, isn't it?"

"I would think so. But if I'm not Heidi's father and we have to go through the court system, they'll take Heidi from us."

"Roy"—Jemima moved in close and looked up at him— "whether you're the Daed or not, we can't turn Heidi over to her. You know that, right?"

He gazed into his wife's eyes, falling in love anew. "I agree. But we'll need to figure out a way to keep Tiffany from trying to take her."

"Exactly. But how?" she asked.

"I don't know." He put his arms around her, and she rested her head on his chest and embraced him. "But what I *do* know is that I love you and together we can figure out anything with some time and prayer."

"We don't have much time, so we may need more heads and hearts involved than just ours."

"True."

The back door slammed, and Roy and Jemima separated. His sister strode across the lawn, Simeon on her hip. "Heidi's in her bed, asleep. The older ones are playing. What's going on?"

"Here's one of the people we need." Jemima put her arm around

Roy's waist, and he did the same. They were clearly in this together, and for that he would be forever thankful.

Roy explained the situation to his sister in short order but cringed as he said that Heidi might not be his. What a grueling, embarrassing journey this whole thing had been. Jemima tightened her embrace, letting him know she understood and that nothing Tiffany said or did could come between them.

Abigail hiked Simeon higher on her hip. "Chris has a video on his phone that might help. He recorded the people who had Heidi saying Tiffany intended to give Heidi to a rich family who would in turn gift her with a lot of money."

"Why didn't you say anything before now?" Jemima asked.

"You guys had enough to contend with. Besides, it's all hearsay. It's not as if Tiffany is saying it, just some people she knows. But since she's back and trying to take Heidi, it might be helpful."

"Is she right?" Jemima asked. "Does that recording prove nothing?"

"Not on its own, but if we had a piece of real evidence, it could be more support. I need to talk to Chris. He knows this situation, and he knows his way around a computer. Think he'd be willing to hit pause on whatever he's up to and help?"

Abigail shrugged. "I think so."

"Would you call him?" Jemima asked.

"Me?"

"Because"—Jemima lifted Simeon from Abigail's arms—"if *you* call him, he'll pick up even if he's in the middle of a fight or at an Englisch church in the middle of being baptized."

"He's not going to be in church on a Tuesday."

"No, but he'll be busy doing something, and we have only twenty-four hours to find what we need." Jemima kissed Simeon's head.

"Fine. I'll call." She pulled the phone from her apron pocket and walked away.

Roy and Jemima headed for the house, walking hand in hand. He couldn't imagine giving Heidi up even if she wasn't his. Hadn't God impressed on him time and again to keep her and raise her?

"Jem." Roy tugged on her hand, and she stopped. "If Heidi's not mine—"

"She's ours, regardless of what the tests say. Our goal is to get Tiffany to sign her over to us, but if the officials have to get involved and they take her, we do all we can to get her back. Ya?"

He raised her hand to his lips and slowly kissed it. "I don't deserve you."

"Nor I you, husband." She pulled his hand to her lips and kissed it.

Thirty

Abigail ended the call, confused but grateful. Jemima had been right. Chris answered his phone on the second ring. Why was he in the area, and why did he sound honored to have heard from her? She sighed and shoved the phone back into her pocket before hurrying into the house. The children were loud and running around, maybe feeding off the energy of the upset adults.

"Chris is close by, and he'll get here as quickly as he can." She left it at that, but she'd like to know if all men gave mixed messages or just Chris. He liked her. He cared about her. He'd left to participate in organized violence for money. It didn't add up unless he was fractured about who he was.

Jemima was rummaging through stacks of mail. "I knew that if you needed him, he'd come. It's what the good ones do."

Abigail wouldn't point out that apparently Roy had often hurried off to help Tiffany despite how much he just wanted to be left alone. Men's actions often didn't match who they said they were or even who they believed they were. They didn't lie just to the women they cared about; they also lied to themselves.

That aside, she needed to ask Roy a question. Keys rattled in the living room area, and she went that way. "Roy?"

"In here," he called from the closet.

She went to the doorway of the closet. "Should I take the children to Mamm's?"

"Nee, but we do need to keep them close until we have some resolution with Tiffany." He unlocked the gun cabinet and pulled out his hunting rifle.

"What are you doing?" Abigail couldn't believe her eyes.

"Jemima and I talked while you were outside calling Chris. It's not against our ways to fire a hunting rifle at the ground."

"Sure it is. You would be threatening violence."

"I have no intention of using it on anyone. But firing it will scare them off. That's not violence; it's a bluff."

Someone knocked on the door. Roy started in that direction, gun in hand.

She grabbed his arm. "You put the gun away. Bluff or not, *that*"—she pointed at the gun—"isn't how we do things."

He ignored her and pulled free.

"Hey." Chris stood inside the door near Jemima.

"Hallo." Roy motioned. "Kumm. You got here fast."

Chris's eyes moved from the gun to Abigail. "Ya, like I told Abi, I was in the area. But we didn't have a good connection. What's up?"

The home was filled with tension and it was suffocating. Abigail's face felt warm from the turmoil of it all.

"Let's sit and talk," Roy said.

"First"—Abigail reached for the gun—"get the bullet out of the chamber, put the gun on safety, and lock it in its cabinet, Roy."

Roy's hand tightened around the gun. "A man showed up at my house, threatening violence against me in order to take a helpless child from safety into danger, probably for the almighty dollar, Abigail. I will fire this gun, and Jemima will call the police."

"This house has only moments of calm where the adults aren't diverted by the needs of one or more children. Distraction is constant, and it's far more dangerous to everyone you want to protect for a gun to be out and loaded. You forget about it for a few seconds during some minor, normal mishap, and the chance of an unwatched child causing an accidental death far outweighs the chance of anyone rushing inside to snatch Heidi. I won't stand for it, Roy."

"He came to my home, baseball bat in hand. Do you understand what Tiffany said? She's been manipulating me this whole time concerning Heidi, which says she has no sense of boundaries or of right and wrong. What is she willing to do to get Heidi back or hurt me, Jemima, or our children?"

She hadn't thought of it like that, and she had no comeback.

"So, this man who came here"—Chris sounded warm and friendly—"is he a big guy?" Chris held his hands apart as if telling a fish story. "Massive shoulders?"

"Ya."

"Really daunting guy, huh?"

"Very. But the plan isn't to shoot him, just fire the gun and run him off."

Chris sat in a chair at the kitchen table. "Everything you're thinking and feeling is justified, including your desire to have a loaded gun on hand. But we need to find the tools that will help us solve the problem, like paper, pens, and brainstorming." He held up his cell phone. "I have the recording Abi asked about, and she said something about information on Tiffany's computer."

The knee-jerk anger seemed to drain from Roy. He looked at the gun and opened the chamber. "I'll unload it and put it away. Chris is right. We need to focus on figuring things out while taking care of a houseful of little ones."

Jemima looked at Roy. "I didn't find it."

Roy grimaced. "Let's check near the desk where I pay bills."

Jemima turned to Abigail. "We'll be back in a few. We need to search through the mail upstairs. We'll grab the laptop, pens, and paper too."

Just like that, Abigail was alone with Chris, something she would've preferred to avoid at this point of having closure with him. Still . . . "Denki." She searched for more words, but his presence unnerved her. She took the percolator off the stove, filled it with water, and put coffee grounds into the silver basket. "I'm glad you came to help, and I'm sorry there's been constant drama in this home since we've known you. Tiffany seems to be a walking hurricane, leaving chaos and destruction in her path."

"Not a problem."

"But it is above and beyond." She turned on the burner and set the percolator on it.

Chris seemed unusually quiet.

"Why were you in our neck of the woods?"

"I-I needed to see a man about something."

That was oddly vague. She chose to change the subject. "You're still dressing Amish. That's usually one of the first things people give up when they leave the Amish, so I take it you're having trouble deciding whether you'll stay Amish or live Englisch."

He looked down at his blue shirt and dark-blue pants. "About that—"

Jemima hurried down the stairs and into the room, holding the laptop. "We haven't found the missing piece of mail yet, which makes no sense. If it was supposed to be here a week or so ago, where is it?" She held out the laptop to Chris. "Here you go."

Chris took the laptop, set it on the table, and opened it. "So, what's going on?"

Simeon started crying, and Jemima pointed at Abigail. "Fill the man in. I'll be back."

Abigail shifted the conversation to the point of his visit: what Tiffany had said about Roy not being the father and demanding he hand over Heidi.

"Wait. He's not the father?"

She shrugged. "That's what she says. I'm unsure what the truth is, although I have some suspicions. But my opinions aside, she seems to run with whatever emotion hits, and she likes to stir up drama simply for the sake of it."

Chris looked sickened. "After all your brother's been through, she shows up here with a thug and says that?"

"Ya. He's one upset man. Jemima somehow got Tiffany to agree to give them twenty-four hours to find her laptop, and then she's returning for it and Heidi. If Tiffany hadn't agreed to that, they would've called the police, and Heidi would be in social services while this mess is straightened out. The missing piece of mail with the DNA results isn't helping anything. We need to know Roy's legal rights *before* we make a plan."

"So what's the goal with the laptop?" He turned it on.

"To see if we can figure out why she's desperate to get it back. Look for incriminating evidence that Tiffany's goal is to sell the baby. If that can be proved, Roy and Jemima hope to convince her to give her parental rights to them, no authorities involved. If we can't find the kind of incriminating evidence that would cause Tiffany to cooperate, Roy and Jemima will take any lesser evidence to the authorities and do what they can to keep Heidi from having to live with Tiffany. That sounds cruel, but she's not fit to raise a child."

"She's not fit to take care of herself, but that's not our problem." Chris entered the password, but it didn't unlock the computer.

Roy walked into the room, holding Heidi. "Tiffany is panicked about getting that laptop back, so I think it's dawned on her that there's info on the computer that could be damaging to whatever her plan is."

"Ya."

Jemima entered, carrying Simeon. She set him in his high chair, buckled him in, and got some blueberries out of the fridge.

Chris studied the laptop. "What was the password? 'Stickystew'? One word, first letter capitalized. Then the number three followed by a dollar sign." He tapped out the password again on the keyboard.

"You asked a question and then answered it yourself." Abigail chuckled, watching the screen from behind him.

"Ya, I do that a lot." He frowned. "With pretty much the same response from life as I'm getting from the computer. I'm wrong. No access granted."

"You had most of it correct. You were only off by the last key-stroke." Roy strapped Heidi into her bouncer and set it on the table. "It should be an exclamation point at the end, not a dollar sign, although I can see why you'd remember it as a dollar sign. Tiffany and money go hand in hand."

Chris typed in the password again. "I'm in." He typed a few words into fields that said Search. "I don't see anything useful right off, but here's the problem: any recent messages aren't going to sync to the computer without an internet source."

Jemima placed several sliced blueberries in front of Simeon before sitting hard in a kitchen chair. "How are we supposed to make plans if we can't find the letter from the lab and if nothing on the computer is synced?"

"Mamm." Carolyn stood in the doorway of the room, her hands and her big sister behind her.

"You and Laura go play, sweetie." Jemima pointed to the play-room. "The adults need to talk."

"I'm looking through what I can." Chris clicked on the trash can. "But I don't see anything pertinent."

"Mamm." Barely using one crutch to steady herself, Laura came to the edge of the table. "Is it still true that if we tell the truth, we won't get in trouble, no matter what?"

Jemima pursed her lips. "Not now."

"Jem," Roy whispered and nodded at Carolyn.

Carolyn's eyes were brimming with tears.

"Ach, Liewi, kumm." Jemima's voice was soft as she called her dear daughter to come. She motioned and Carolyn came closer. *"Was iss letz?"* Jemima's faint smile seemed reassuring as she asked what was wrong.

Carolyn slowly put her hands in front of her, and she was holding several pieces of mail.

Jemima looked through the mail and slid an envelope to Roy. He ripped it open while Jemima talked to Carolyn, assuring her that it was okay and that she was proud of her for telling the truth. But she also told her not to pick up mail and play with it unless her Mamm gave it to her. After a tight hug, Jemima sent her on her way. "Geh."

Carolyn skipped off, and Jemima turned to Roy.

He shook his head. "I'm not her father." Roy sat there rubbing his forehead. "What is wrong with her?"

No one answered. They didn't need to. The woman had serious issues.

Jemima moved to stand behind him, and she rested her hands on his shoulders. "There are things to be grateful for, and one is that what she intended as evil in Heidi's life, God is using for good. Heidi doesn't have to take on her mom's issues, not if she is raised in a loving home with a good Daed."

Roy shifted and looked up at Jemima. "Are you sure you want us to raise her? *Sure,* sure?"

"I'm sure. I don't love her like our own yet, but I already love her more than I thought possible, and I know the fullness of love will come as the trauma and heartache surrounding her fades. You?"

"Logically it seems I should feel different about her now and wash my hands of the whole ordeal. But I know that giving her up would be a terrible mistake."

Abigail could see the depth of sincerity inside her brother, and it was clear why she loved him even when he was on her last nerve, asking too much of her and taking her for granted.

A new thought hit her. "You know what? Tiffany listed Roy as the father on the birth certificate. You couple that with the fact that she abandoned her and has known where Heidi has been for six weeks but has not called, texted, or returned for her before now. Those things should count on your behalf if you have to turn her over because you're not the biological father."

Chris pulled his phone from his pocket. "I have an idea of ways to narrow the search, but I need to know an approximate date of when you think she would've sent or received anything incriminating."

Roy looked at Jemima. "I'm sorry."

Jemima kissed his cheek. "Me too."

He drew a breath. "The night I went to her place and can't recall what happened was mid-April of last year."

"That narrows it down." Chris slid his phone across the table. "While I begin searching and skimming, you can listen to the recording."

The three of them—Jemima, Roy, and Abigail—went to the far end of the room, away from the noise of the older children playing.

Abigail found the video and turned on the speaker, and they hud-
dled near the phone, listening. Chris's voice on the recording was
calm as he led one of the men to share what he knew about the plan
to receive money in exchange for the baby, and at that time the man
thought Chris was one of them, out for money. A couple of minutes
later everything changed. Loud bangs and moans, and the fight
seemed to go on forever. It sent chills through Abigail as she realized
anew what he went through to help them.

While Roy and Jemima settled something between the older
children, Abigail went to the countertop and cut Chris a piece of
cake, put it on a plate, and grabbed a fork. Then she poured him a
cup of coffee and set both near him. "Denki."

He looked up from the laptop. "For?"

"Being here to help us no matter what we've needed. For knowing how to fight and not being afraid to do so. For taking the injuries
in stride as if they were no big deal. For coming back when we've
asked although we had no right to ask it."

"You're welcome for every ounce of it." He looked up, his eyes
boring into hers. "Abi, we need to talk. I—"

"Find anything?" Roy entered, carrying Nevin this time.

"Ya." Chris shrugged, looking torn.

Jemima walked back into the room and went straight for the
fridge. She got out a bowl of sliced fruit and put a few pieces on a
plastic plate. Roy set Nevin in a chair.

"Chris said he found something." Roy put the plate of fruit in
front of Nevin.

Chris tapped the keyboard. "Roy, maybe we should talk in private."

"I appreciate it, Chris, but I'm not keeping any more secrets. We'll keep talking in Englisch so the little ones nearby don't know what we're saying." He glanced into the other room, probably to make sure Laura wasn't within hearing range.

"Okay, so she gets messages on her laptop."

Jemima moved in closer. "You mentioned that when we were at Doc Grant's clinic. But I don't really know what it means."

"Whenever she sends or receives texts on her phone, those also go to her laptop and download into an app called Messages. Since you don't have an internet provider but Doc Grant did, nothing has downloaded since the day we were there. With the exception of the last few days before Roy and Tiffany were in that accident, there are hardly any messages, which probably means she deleted them."

"But it can't all be gone," Abigail said. "Why would you need to talk to Roy privately if everything is missing?"

"See, I knew you'd catch that," Chris said, smiling. "Messages keeps a backup copy of everything in a well-hidden archive on the computer, and deleting the original doesn't remove the copy."

"So you do have all the texts she's written or received?" Jemima asked.

"Probably. Glitches can always happen, but we have plenty, that's for sure. Go to Finder, click on Go, and then on Go to Folders. It has thousands of texts she's sent and received while owning this computer. Unfortunately they're not really stored by date. They are stored by numeric order, which works well only if she's had the computer just a year. Otherwise it has all the January texts grouped together, even if there are ten years of Januarys." Chris paused. "I think you should probably sit down for this."

"Why?" Jemima took a seat.

Roy remained standing. "Nothing would surprise me at this point, so you can just say it, Chris."

"From what I've reviewed, it sounds as if she came up pregnant on purpose, thinking the dad, who is apparently rich, would support her. When that didn't happen, she set up Roy. She wrote of actually caring about you, thinking you were handsome and a good guy. But she and her friends put something in your drink, and it scared them. They thought they'd killed you."

"Something in my drink?"

"Ya. It was intended to lower your inhibitions so she could seduce you, but instead it put you out cold."

Jemima's eyes flooded with tears. "He was on high-powered pain meds from the horse-and-buggy wreck he and Laura had. It's amazing that stunt didn't kill him."

What would it have done to Jemima if Roy had died in Tiffany's bed? Abigail's blood pounded at her temples. "Jesus, help me. Even I want to load the gun about now."

"But we won't," Roy said. "She meant this as evil against me, but God meant it for good for Heidi."

"I agree," Chris said. "Heidi's innocent, and despite who her biological parents are, God is pulling for her, just as He's done for me time and again."

"And me," Abigail said.

"And me," Roy added.

"And me." Jemima grinned. "We sound so corny, but it's completely true. If God be for us, who can be against us?"

Abigail sat next to Chris. It'd been a hard road for Roy and Jemima, but God was helping them while working on Heidi's behalf. Greedy and disturbed liars and manipulators were against her brother, and they'd won a few battles, making life so much harder for Roy and Jemima than it should have been. But none of Tiffany's deceitful plans were stronger than God's good graces.

Jemima got Heidi out of the bouncer and held her close. "We need to get those things printed out. Is that possible?"

"I don't know if they can be printed straight from the archives. I would have to ask someone more tech savvy than me, but I know we can make screenshots and print those," Chris said. "Here's the thing: if I get this laptop to a place with a speedy internet and get connected, I think every message she's sent or received via text since we last connected at Doc Grant's will download into Messages, although it could take a while if she texts a lot."

"Could you do that? Could you take the laptop to such a place and see what downloads?" Jemima asked.

Chris nodded. "Of course." He turned to Abigail. "Care to go with me?"

How could she say no? He was once again coming to the rescue of her family. "Ya. Call us an Uber."

"Would you mind if we took a rig? There's a café in Mirth with free Wi-Fi."

Whether the Amish hired a neighbor or Uber to transport them, it was expensive. He'd probably paid more than a hundred dollars just to get from Scarsdale to Mirth one way. But rather than offer to pay for the ride, she nodded. "It's a beautiful evening for a buggy ride."

Thirty-One

Chris went to the stable. Abigail seemed more open to seeing him than he'd expected, but he was sure she was just grateful for his help.

He got Houdini from his stall. "How are you doing, fella?" He removed the halter and put on the bridle. Houdini nudged him, wanting more pats. Chris chuckled. "You look good, and you didn't share EHV-1 with any other horse. Good job on that." He patted him as they walked out the stables and to the carriage house.

The sights, smells, and sounds of Amish living in Mirth filled him with satisfaction. He'd always enjoyed this part of being Amish: the pleasure of traveling by horse and buggy, and the sense of being grounded in and connected to nature.

Once Houdini was hitched to the carriage, Chris lit a kerosene lantern and hung it in its spot. It would be dark before too much longer. He drove the carriage to the house and hopped out. He was headed for the front door, when Abigail came outside. He opened her door.

"Well, thank you, kind sir."

He closed the door and went around to the other side. He clicked his tongue, and Houdini began walking.

"Will you return home tonight or tomorrow?"

Nervousness gnawed at him. He'd faced opponents in a ring with less apprehension and less at stake. "Uh, I'm not sure."

"You're welcome to stay. Aaron's been sleeping at my folks' house, and Roy and Jemima would be pleased to have you."

"That's kind, and I'll think about it." They rode onward, and he couldn't think of how to tell her all he needed to.

"You're very quiet for a man who said we needed to talk."

"I am." He wouldn't tell her up front that he thought she had walls. If she had them, they would show themselves, and then they could talk about it. He had a lot of proving to do first because right now she was justified to wall him out.

"What's going on?"

"I . . . I messed up." He fidgeted with the leather straps, willing himself to say the rest.

She shifted to face him, and the soft glow of evening illuminated her face, making her look more heavenly than earthly. "You regret that your leaving to fight undid us. That's it, isn't it?"

That was Abigail, and he loved this about her—straightforward.

"Ya, but I don't regret what I learned about myself and that I gave my all to help Dan get a fresh start. But I do regret the timing of it. I've come clean with my parents and bishop, and I returned home to live two weeks ago. The bishop has come by almost every night since so we could talk, and I'll begin instruction this spring."

"That's good, Chris." Her heart was sincere. He knew that, but she also sounded like a teacher telling a pupil she was proud of him. Perhaps that kind of distant affection was all that was left between them.

"Abi, I know I didn't handle us well." He slowed and made a left turn. "And I've damaged your ability to trust that I know who I am and what I want, but I know both now. I saw it clearly after I won the fight."

She shifted, choosing to look out the window rather than at him. "I'm glad you've returned and will go through instruction, but I'm not sure how I feel about us."

"I get that. You need time. We need it. We've only known each other a little more than six weeks. But here's the thing.: I talked to my bishop and yours, and under the right circumstances I could move to Mirth, even go through instruction here, and that would give us time together."

"You've already talked to them?"

"Ya, but I'm not presuming your answer, and neither are they. I needed to make sure the spiritual heads were okay with what I hoped to do."

"I understand that."

"I was at your uncle's house, talking to him, when you called. And we both know that if I move here, our communities will talk as if we're already engaged. But all I'm asking is for us to date."

"Your efforts mean a lot, and I'm happy your head and heart are clear on who you are and what you want." She shook her head. "And

I'm sorry, Chris. I really am—for both of us. You tempt me to follow my emotions and throw caution to the wind, but I can't. Not even for you."

He'd known she wouldn't rush to accept him, but he'd hoped for a hint of her being open to his request.

They said nothing else. Soon he was driving into town, and he stopped in front of a hitching post. It was dark now, and most stores were closed. But the coffee shop at the end of the block had its lights on and the front door propped open, letting in fresh spring air.

She opened her door and hopped out when he did. He put out the flame of the lantern on the buggy, and they walked down the sidewalk of the quiet town and into the café, two Amish people side by side, one with a laptop. Once inside, they went to a table and he opened the laptop and connected to the internet.

The first message pinged with a date of February eighteenth. But it must have been sent later in the day after he'd connected to the internet at Doc Grant's clinic. The text messages were down-loading too fast for him to read any of them. He scooted the laptop to the side. "That's going to take a while. How about a drink and pastry?"

"Sure."

Once at the counter, Abigail ordered a decaf mocha latte, what-ever that was, and a blueberry scone. He got a regular decaf and a cinnamon roll. They returned to the table with a number to set on it so their order could be delivered shortly. In the meantime, the laptop was making soft pings every few seconds.

He had to push back against her answer. "When I stood there at the end of the fight, being told I could have a boxing career, I knew that life wasn't me at all. Insight clicked, and it changed me. I saw the hows and whys of needing to think differently, not just concerning Dan. I saw the importance of not giving in to anything outside my faith no matter how good it feels. I saw the importance of not trying to fix a problem someone else created. It's fine for you to be leery. Time will confirm the truth. But I'm all in, Abi, more so than if I'd never taken up boxing. I'd like to move to Mirth and prove it to you, even if it takes years. But my bishop won't approve that unless your uncle agrees to it, and your uncle says I'm only welcome to become a part of the Mirth Amish if you're okay with my moving here."

She lowered her eyes to the table, and the seconds slowly ticked by. "I'm sorry. I can't. Why would you be willing to do that to yourself? Why would I agree to it? Your moving here would only make it harder on us over time. It would make us long to be together and yet we know it wouldn't work."

He hadn't expected her to put down a boundary line that kept him from living in Mirth, but maybe he should have. "If I lived in Mirth, it would give us a chance. I had wanted us to have that chance, but at the same time, I kept stepping back because of my obligation to Dan and my confusion over enjoying boxing. Give us a chance, a real one."

"We did have a real chance."

"Did we? I know I didn't give us one." The words rushed out, and suddenly he felt like a high-pressure salesman. "But what about you, Abigail? What's the real reason you find something that raises a red flag about every man who is interested in you?"

Her eyes narrowed. "What are you saying, Chris?"

His words weren't coming out right. "I've said more than I should. Just do me a favor and think about what I said, okay?"

"I don't like what you're implying. Just because you see the futility of boxing and I'm not falling all over you for giving it up, suddenly I'm the one with a problem?"

"No. It's fair and reasonable that I show myself to be stable and reliable. I'd want the same of you if the tables were turned. But maybe I have a lot of trust to earn from long before we even met."

"Seriously?" Anger tinged her voice. "Just who broke trust with me that you're paying the price for?"

He couldn't retreat now. "Without telling me their names, think of five men you dated that you were the most attracted to. Men, for however briefly, you thought something along the lines of 'I could build a lifelong relationship with him.'"

"Okay, I have them in my mind."

"Think about the issue you had with each one."

A young man held out a large mug sitting on a plate. "A decaf mocha latte."

Abigail lifted it from him. "Thank you."

He set a regular decaf in front of Chris, and the two plates of pastry in the center. "Enjoy." Then he disappeared.

They sipped and ate in silence.

Her mug was half-empty when she plinked it onto the table. "Is your plan to discount my red flags and prove you need to be given a chance?"

Is that what he wanted to do? It took only a moment for him to know the truth. "Nee, Abi." He brushed away crumbs from his cinnamon pastry that had fallen onto the table. "I want you to see the wall that's formed around you. I can leave Mirth, and you can go on with your life. You should stay single forever if that's what you want, but don't deny love because you fear who a man is underneath or who he will become as time moves onward."

"I don't have a wall. I see things in men. I feel the earth cracking under them."

"Some of the time. Elam likes you. He's steady and kind. You knew his wife. Was he a good man?"

"Ya, and he's a great Daed."

"And so . . ."

Anger sparked in her eyes, a "how dare you" look. "Some men are just too nice."

"Too nice."

"I know where you're going with this, but being too nice indicates that he's a people pleaser. Do you know what it does to a spouse to be married to someone who wants to please the world?"

"Did his wife have that problem with him?"

"I didn't see it, but that doesn't mean it didn't exist between them. People pleasers will put their lives in danger for some stranger, not thinking what it could do to their spouses and their children if they die on the altar of *nice*."

"There were a lot of answers you could've given about Elam. That you feel nothing toward him. That the age difference feels like too much. That you aren't comfortable being a stepmom to his special-needs son. Those answers are about you and what you want.

Instead you say he's too nice, which makes him lacking. Do even the best of men come with a multitude of red flags?"

Her beautiful face became stiff as she raised an eyebrow. "You know, I would've expected you of all people to understand following one's gut instinct and trusting the red flags."

"Should your uncle's wife have seen the red flags? He's an addict who's turned their lives upside down to minister to other addicts. Is what they have not worth the work to get there? Is the relationship between Jemima and Roy not worth the hard work and pain they've been through?"

Her lips were pursed, and her stony expression conveyed her anger. "You think I've become spooked. Do you believe the red flags for each man were all made up in my mind?"

"Not all, no. But too many. If you've never cared enough about any man for it to break your heart that you're not with him"—he shrugged—"maybe there is a high and thick boundary wall around your heart."

"We can't say the same of you? It's been seven years since the relationship ended with your fiancée."

"Maybe. But only you truly caught me from the first second I saw you, and when an issue came between us, we got past it within one night of working side by side."

"You yourself said there were things that could derail us. You knew it, but now our going separate ways is because I have a thick wall around my heart."

Maybe he was off track, or maybe she wasn't ready to see it. "Okay, Abi. I hear you."

She scoffed and pointed at the computer. "The laptop has stopped pinging."

Chris took his cue and shifted the laptop. He ran a search for various words, skimming text messages and emails, but it was hard to concentrate. He could feel that Abigail's eyes were glued to him.

She tossed a wadded-up napkin onto the table. "If you were right about this and I realized it for the first time, maybe you just opened the door to my going back to one of the five other men and trying to make it work."

Chris steadied his racing heart. She was a boxer throwing punches to knock him off balance. "You could. That's true. But it's a very unkind thing to say to me. Ya?"

Her face flushed, and she seemed to be struggling with a myriad of emotions. He'd hit a nerve.

A bit of humor was needed. "But I won't call you out on being unkind or say anything about the fact that you can be a hard woman at times, Abigail Graber. Nope. I won't say those things to you."

She smiled, but her hands were trembling, and unshed tears brimmed. "Denki."

It rattled him to see her beginning to realize something she hadn't known about herself, and he wanted to wrap her in his arms. But now wasn't the time.

She clutched her hands together, probably to stop the trembling. "I remember"—she cleared her throat—"the first time I said to myself that I'd never let a man hurt me the way those women at the recovery center were hurt. I was twelve, and I've renewed that vow at least once weekly since then. As I talked to the women or listened to the men tell their stories of the stupid and mean things they had done while drunk, my heart was cut out time and again, and I determined never to go down that same path. How did I not see it until now?"

"I—"

"Of course you don't know." She pointed at the computer. "Get back to work."

Despite wanting to reach across the table and take her hand, he was unsure what to do with all she was feeling, so he returned his attention to the computer.

He soon uncovered texts from Tiffany about money, Heidi, and adoption with four different people. He leaned back in the chair, scrolling. The texts to the potential adoptive parents sounded sincere and stable, but the ones between her and her friends about those prospective parents told the real story. Tiffany intended to sell the baby to the highest-paying family.

Nausea rolled. "Abi, you'll want to see this for yourself."

Abi moved next to him on the bench seat and read what was on the screen. "I hurt for Roy. He was trying his best to do right by Tiffany while juggling work and family, and she spent her days calculating how best to manipulate him. Where is her conscience and humanity, not just toward herself but for her baby?"

"I don't know. Maybe she's so wounded and twisted she'll never get it."

"I'm beginning to understand how wounds shape people."

"I know they can change us and knock us completely off course. From what Roy's said, in Tiffany's case maybe because the wounds were more intentional to her as a child, they run deeper. I fear that one day when it's too late to fix what she's done, she'll see it for what it is."

Abigail moved back to her seat. "I'll text Roy and let him know that what we were looking for did download."

The swoosh of the text being sent was followed a moment later by her phone ringing. She answered and talked to her brother. When she ended the call, she asked, "Do we have what we need?"

"Not yet. We have to get to an office store before they close. We need a place that sells external hard drives so we can back up everything on this computer and put it away for safekeeping, and we need to print copies of some of this."

"There's a Staples less than two miles from here." Abigail stood.

Chris picked up the laptop, and they left the coffeehouse and walked toward the rig. They went to the store and spent more than an hour sorting through items and making copies. Outwardly they stayed focused on what they needed, but Abigail was eerily quiet. Her fingers trembled as they worked, and Chris knew she was deep in thought. They gathered the papers, paid for the items, and left the store.

They were halfway to his carriage when Abigail stopped. He followed suit.

She raised a brow. "There isn't another man I'd go back to."

Warmth ran through him. "Gut, Abi. The first time I saw you, I was awestruck, heard music, couldn't believe my eyes, and certainly couldn't speak." He smiled. "It's so cliché and corny that it's embarrassing to admit it."

"I don't think I've ever rendered a man speechless before, although I've been known to annoy a few so much they couldn't shut up."

"I can understand that," he teased.

She laughed and pushed his shoulder. A moment later she shrugged. "You're right about the wall inside me. I think I've known for years it was there, but I didn't realize I walled out all men, just the suspicious ones, which apparently is all men. And I don't think it's anywhere close to coming down."

"Ya. It might take some time."

"Maybe a lot of time."

"That's fine too."

She nodded and started walking again. She slid her hand into his. In that moment, all of life seemed to make sense. His mistakes and regrets. And hers.

She squeezed his hand. "You should live in Mirth."

He tugged on her hand, stopping her from walking.

She smiled and pulled him close. "You should," she whispered. Their lips met, and he knew this was where he was meant to be: beside Abigail Graber for the rest of his days.

Thirty-Two

With Roy and four of their five blessings out the door, Jemima picked up the stack of printouts. She knew enough without actually reading the messages since Abigail had given them an overview last night. Wasn't that plenty? Jemima had resisted the urge to read the documents last night and today.

She and Roy had gone to see their bishop last night to tell him the necessary information about what was going on. Much of the situation was private, meant to be kept between Roy, Jemima, Abigail, Chris, and Roy's parents. It was too easy for a personal story to be shared when it shouldn't be and get twisted and become idle gossip and speculation.

Heidi's cooing shifted into fussing, and Jemima peeked at the clock. Right on schedule. It was time for her to nurse and take a nap. Jemima set the stack of papers on the kitchen table and moved to the portable crib. "Hey, sweet girl." Heidi thrust her legs, and her little arms jerked about with excitement as she tried to make her voice work on demand. Her little lips formed a perfect O and she cooed.

"Ya." Jemima grinned. "Tell me all about it. I'm listening."

Heidi studied her and then smiled. Jemima picked her up. "Kumm on, little one." She cradled her in the crook of her arm and unfastened the nursing fold in the bodice of her dress. Before sitting, she grabbed the stack of documents.

Should she read them? Abigail said they were unnerving on multiple levels for more reasons than she could comprehend. She got Heidi attached and nursing, still wavering on whether to read them.

Jemima closed her eyes, praying, and in that moment, she knew she needed to read as many of the documents as she could before Tiffany arrived, which would be within the hour. She began reading, and her heart seemed to stop and to pound at the same time. Tiffany's manipulation of Roy was deliberate. Her actions cut Jemima's heart like a butcher's knife. The strangest part was that Tiffany had some deep-running feelings for Roy, but when he didn't return them, she turned mean and devious. This woman played him for a fool, using him for gain while he did his best to honor God.

But what tore at Jemima's emotions even more was what she— as his wife—had put him through. The angry words. The mistrust. The resentment over trivial things that happened at the start of their marriage, as if he didn't have any reason to have his own list of grievances. Shame pressed in on her as tears fell.

The back door opened. "Hey, the older four are settled in at Uncle Mervin's. Mamm and Daed were already there to help out, and they're praying for us."

Jemima nodded and pulled tissues from the hidden pocket of her apron.

"Jem?" Roy crouched beside her rocker.

"I have so much to make up to you."

He looked at the documents. "*We* have much to make up to each other, and I thank God we'll get the chance."

They had a second chance. Gratefulness flooded her as she thought about how Roy could have died the night Tiffany and her friends put a drug in his drink. "No matter how today goes, I don't want to hold on to anger with Tiffany. I want to forgive and be forgiven. Seems to me each one of us has fallen short in this mess, and I'm not interested in throwing stones or holding on to anger."

"I agree."

She caressed his cheek. "I love you, Roy Graber."

"I know." He lifted her hand to his lips and kissed it. "Your love was a huge part of what fueled your anger with me when you learned the truth, so I take solace in that."

"But it was so much more than that."

"Jem, it's okay. You'd sacrificed every dream for my dream, and for a season you thought it had turned out to be a nightmare." He smiled. "But we're going to work on fulfilling your dreams and Abigail's dreams too."

As much as she wanted that, and she *really* did, she also knew that it would require a sacrifice of juggling family needs around her work schedule. "It won't be easy."

"One of the things I've learned this past year is that whatever we choose to do sacrifices something else. Being dishonest to spare hurting you in the moment sacrificed trust later on. If we're going to give up something this next year, and we will, let's give up some of my work time with the horse farm so you can have one or maybe two days each week to run the food truck. When we're ready, we'll add days and be flexible and make it work."

She nodded. Being human was strange, really. Finding balance in life, not giving or taking too much, was a lot like making financial ends meet. It took constant effort and reevaluation and fresh starts.

Roy rose and kissed her forehead. "Chris is sitting on top of the picnic table, facing the driveway with the unloaded rifle lying across his lap."

Tiffany was likely to return with at least one thug, and they needed to make sure the guy stayed in his car. Chris wouldn't point the gun, but he would make himself known. They didn't like resorting to a show of force, but if the authorities had to get involved for any reason, Roy and Jemima would lose the power to make decisions for Heidi.

Roy moved the laptop from a high shelf to the kitchen table. "Abigail arrived from school about ten minutes ago, and she's sitting with Chris for now, talking."

"Those two talked half the night, I think." Jemima lifted the sleeping Heidi to her shoulder and burped her.

"I'm hopeful Chris is why Abigail never found the one."

"Ya, me too." Mulling over human nature, Jemima put Heidi in the infant car seat that was on the kitchen table. What had caused Tiffany to be so callous toward her baby?

The constant overwhelming temptation to be selfish and do whatever felt good began early in life. It was impulsive in desire and apathetic toward anything and anyone who stood in its way. But following those natural desires wounded the soul—the God-part of being human that thrived on being loving, kind, respectful, and loyal to everyone, starting with family and branching out from there. When people nurtured any desire that was in opposition to the God-part of being human, they began to lose the good, kind soul and strengthen the mean, selfish soul.

"I feel sorry for Tiffany. Everyone is born with positives or negatives working on their behalf—a good or bad family, prayers or meanness spoken over them. Seems to me that at least half of Tiffany's issues today are because she was born with a negative, probably a negative thirty. I was born with a positive thirty."

"Ya, I get it. I feel the same, but why she is the way she is isn't our responsibility. It's hers. Somewhere along the way, she knew she was making poor choices, and rather than getting help, she went with it."

"Ya." Jemima didn't want to talk about it anymore. She felt spacey and weird from the emotional inferno. But Tiffany would arrive soon, and Jemima had to pull herself together.

Abigail tapped on the door and walked inside. "There's a car coming up the driveway."

"Okay, denki." Jemima straightened the stack of printouts and traced her index finger down Heidi's face. "She's so beautiful that one would think she's ours."

"She's a cutie," Roy said. "But far more important, she has a calling, and we've been tasked with loving and protecting her."

"You?" Jemima mocked disbelief. "Tasked with loving and protecting? What was God thinking?"

Roy winked at her before he turned to Abigail. "You need to be on the stairs and out of sight."

Abigail hurried that way with her phone in hand in case she needed to call the police.

A minute later there was a rap on the door, and Roy opened it. "Tiffany." He gestured for her to come in.

"I want my laptop."

Jemima picked it up from the table and passed it to her. "We need to talk."

"I've said all I'm going to. Just hand over Heidi."

"Kumm." Jemima gestured.

Tiffany went toward the infant car seat, but when she saw Heidi, she stopped cold. "She's ready?"

"No," Jemima said softly. "Look at her. Isn't she beautiful? She loves being in her bouncer on the floor while the other children are playing around her. Carolyn, our five-year-old, is able to comfort her when no one else can, and she's begun smiling, and she makes a little throaty noise, as if she's on the verge of laughing."

Tiffany blinked a lot and scrunched her brows, seeming completely taken aback and confused.

"She has quite a grip when she's interested in something. When I'm nursing her and she manages to grab a string to my prayer Kapp, she smiles." Jemima chuckled. "Right then. Looks in my eyes and then goes back to nursing, quite pleased with herself."

"You nurse . . ." Tiffany clutched the laptop to her chest. "That was unnecessary." She grabbed the handle of the car seat.

From the other side of the table, Roy clutched the sides from behind the seat, pushing down on it so Tiffany couldn't budge it.

"Tiffany"—Jemima caressed Heidi's cheek—"look at your daughter. Isn't she worth more to you than a payday?"

"I don't know what you're talking about, and she's mine, so hand her over."

Jemima wiggled the printouts in her hand. "We'd like for this talk to be amicable. One day Heidi's going to ask about her real mom, and I want to be able to say that her mom chose to leave her with us, knowing we'd love her and take care of her in ways her mom couldn't. She needs to be told that you chose of your own free will what was best for her."

"I—"

"Before you say anything else, I need to tell you that we know everything." Jemima tapped the thick stack of papers. "Every single thing. All the new messages downloaded, and all the old ones you'd deleted were in a backup file in the library of your computer."

Tiffany's face drained of color.

"If you need money, earn it the old-fashioned way: go to work," Roy said.

"Roy." Jemima hardly spoke loud enough to be heard, but he looked her way and she shook her head.

He said nothing more.

Jemima turned back to Tiffany. "I want to be clear. You won't ever get your daughter back, not that you actually want her. But despite the evidence, you could possibly stir up enough trouble that we would lose the right to raise her. A judge could decide that it wasn't in Heidi's best interest to be raised Amish."

Heidi squirmed and poked out her bottom lip, and Jemima saw compassion flicker through Tiffany's eyes. Heidi opened her eyes, and when she saw Tiffany, her bottom lip quivered, probably because Tiffany was a stranger.

"It's okay, little one," Roy said.

Heidi arched her back, trying to see her Daed, who was behind her, and when she saw him, she bounced her hands and smiled.

"Fine." Tiffany tossed the papers onto the table. "What do you need?"

"For today we need you to make a video stating your desire to give up your parental rights and showing your driver's license. We need you to state your desire for us to raise her, and you'll sign a few papers. If you'll meet us at the lawyer's office to make it all official as necessary, at a date not yet set, then all evidence will disappear."

"We'd love to burn the paper, Tiffany," Roy said. "We don't want any record of your plots where Heidi could find them one day."

Tiffany stared at her daughter, clearly emotional as she faced the truth about herself. "How'd I get to this place?"

"You need help," Roy responded. "Who knows what any of us would be like if we'd been raised in your home. You were powerless then, but you're not anymore. If you'll get proper help over the next decade, you can come see Heidi and introduce yourself."

"You're a dreamer, Roy," Tiffany said. "I can't change. I've tried. I have, and how would I pay for the kind of help you're talking about?"

He held out the pen to her. "I think you'd be surprised what you could do for yourself if you put your energy into getting better rather than carrying out manipulative, deceitful plans."

She took the pen. "Not sure broken people work that way—able to pull themselves up by their bootstraps. But let's get this done. I want out of here."

The next twenty minutes went by quickly. Abigail recorded a video clip of Tiffany verbally giving up her rights as a parent as well as signing documents.

Tiffany clung to her laptop as she headed for the door.

Jemima followed her. "I'll text you a date, time, and address to meet us at the lawyer's."

She nodded and left.

Roy embraced Jemima. "We did it!"

Her head spun, and her legs wobbled like noodles.

Chris walked inside. "They're gone. How'd it go?"

Abigail grinned. "It went well. Let's call Uncle Mervin and let him and our parents know. Then we should order pizza, play games, and celebrate! The children are fine staying at Uncle Mervin's for a few hours while we enjoy this victory."

Roy grinned. "I like the way you think." He turned. "Jem?"

She felt rather detached from her body. "Sure, but I need a minute." She climbed the stairs, went into her bedroom, and closed the door. They'd won, but the task of raising a child to love and respect herself when her own mother didn't love her was daunting. Jemima whispered a prayer of gratefulness, and she felt God's peace surround her like a warm blanket.

She went to the bathroom sink to wash her face, which felt gritty from the salt in the many tears she'd shed while reading the print-outs. She stared into the mirror, determined to be a better person for Roy and her children. Life had already been merely a blink. In a few more she'd be old with grown children. "Show me how to live each day with wisdom and love."

"Jem?" Roy tapped on the bedroom door.

She came out of the bathroom. "Kumm."

He opened the door. "You okay?"

She moved to the side of the bed and sat. "Shaky, dizzy with relief, overwhelmed by the idea of how best to help Heidi once she's old enough to know she's not a biological Graber but a chosen one."

"We'll figure it out and stumble our way through, trusting God to fill in the holes we missed." He grinned. "Let's celebrate today, and we'll talk and make plans tomorrow."

She already felt better. Roy was very good at loving her, although neither one was close to perfect. They made mistakes regularly, and life doled out plenty of stress along with its joys and victories.

She patted the bed.

He smiled and sat down beside her. "Hi."

She ran her fingers down his cheek, turning his face toward hers. "Hi."

His lips were warm against hers.

Breathless, she put her forehead against his. "I think we should move Simeon and Heidi into the guest room, name it the nursery, and you move back in with your wife, who is very tired of missing you."

"But I've been right here."

"Have you?"

"Well, not right here"—he patted the bed—"but, you know, I've been close."

"I'm saying"—she kissed his neck—"that you should be closer. You want to argue with that?"

"No," he whispered. "Definitely not."

His lips found hers again and the kiss deepened.

"Roy? Jemima?" Abigail called. "Daed is on the phone in Uncle Mervin's phone shanty, and he'd like to talk to you."

"Our moment of solitude is up," Roy teased.

Jemima chuckled and kissed him again. "Meet me here tonight after the kids are tucked in bed."

Epilogue

Abigail twirled a badminton racket in her hand, catching it by the handle after each spin and feeling the squishy grip. Any moment now, Jemima or Carolyn would retrieve the birdie from the tall grass for the next serve, the one that would determine the winner.

A warm spring breeze stirred the air. Horses grazed and frolicked in the nearby pasture. The aroma of leftovers wafted from the picnic table: fried chicken, mashed potatoes, and homemade bread. It'd been a delicious meal with an abundance of chatter.

Giggles and squeals rose from the backyard, making her smile. Her parents were entertaining Nevin, Simeon, and Heidi by making giant bubbles from a family recipe. The little ones and grandparents were using an array of wands, ranging from the rings for mason jars to Hula-Hoops, to dip into a small blue plastic pool filled with the bubble solution. She had great parents, and she had high hopes that she and Chris would follow in their footsteps.

Laura was next to her Daed on the "court," badminton racket in hand, a grin on her face as Roy worked with her on her swing. She had been free of her crutches for some time now.

Chris moved closer to the net that separated them, stealing Abigail's full attention. His grin added to the multitude of things she was taking in and cataloging so she could draw strength from these memories during the harder days that life was sure to bring their way.

"You're twirling that racket like an expert. Have you been holding back on me?" he asked.

Abigail glared at him, trying not to smile. They both knew she'd hit air on the past three birdies that had been lobbed her way. "There seems to be a hole in the center of my racket." She held it up for her husband to inspect.

He ducked below the net and stopped mere inches in front of her, took the racket, and inspected it. "That's odd. It appears to be intact." His eyes met hers, and she recalled dozens of long nights and the silly banter between them. Love was so much fun and definitely worth the price. She pointed at the strings. "Maybe a hole opens as I swing at the birdie."

"Ya." He mocked seriousness. "That must be what happens"—he handed the racket back to her—"because that's the only way anyone can be that bad at hitting a birdie."

She stifled her laugh.

Chris kissed her forehead. "You can have my racket if you like. It doesn't have the magical power of the strings disappearing as the birdie comes toward it."

"I'm fine. But you just keep making fun of me. We both know I will have my revenge when we play horseshoes and volleyball." She looked at the racket. What was it about the birdie that made it so difficult to hit?

Chris put his hands on her hips and lowered his eyes to her belly. She and Chris had a secret. A new life had begun inside her. Everyone would be so excited, but she and Chris wanted to keep that news just to themselves for a while. But because they had been married for eighteen months, her pregnancy wouldn't be much of a surprise.

"Got it!" Jemima walked back from the tall grass, holding the birdie in question high in the air, and stepped into the play area. "Why haven't we cut that grass? It's not like we've been busy."

Abigail shook her head. That was untrue, and everyone knew it. What an amazing team her best friend and brother were these days in everything they did, whether it was running their business, raising their children, or even playing games. The storms in Jemima and Roy's marriage seemed to be in the past.

"My turn to serve!" Carolyn's English sounded perfect these days. She held out her hand, and her mother placed the well-worn birdie into it.

Roy smiled, nodding at Abigail. "Aim at your auntie. She looks distracted, and we need just one more point to win."

With a thwack, Carolyn sent the birdie flying, and it sailed toward Abigail. Could she get it? Maybe! She swung, and the birdie went right on by and landed a few feet behind her. She sighed.

Cheers went up from the winning side, but Chris simply smiled.

She joined in the cheering. "I'm the best asset your team had!" She chuckled and went toward the picnic table to set the racket on it.

Chris came up behind her and put his hands on her shoulders. "Care to go for a walk?" He kissed the back of her neck, making her shiver and smile.

She turned to look into his eyes. "Sure."

They ambled hand in hand, enjoying a rare afternoon of being completely off the job. Chris worked on the horse farm a few hours each day, and he helped with the food truck, sometimes cooking but generally keeping them well stocked so things ran smoothly. Most of his time, though, went to his true love: running a spectacular equine therapy clinic for the Amish and Englisch. Between supplements from the government and payments from those who had insurance, he made a good income. He'd turned the former poultry barn into a therapy classroom, using it in winter and inclement weather. He was fantastic with special-needs children and their parents, and sometimes he held weeklong camps that made lasting differences for all involved. She'd never imagined someone like Chris being so fulfilled. It altered how she viewed the men and their wives from the recovery house. The men needed to find something they loved, something that made them enjoy giving back into other people's lives.

They paused outside the split-rail fence near where Houdini was grazing.

She looked at Chris. "We'll blink and our little one will be here, making new memories with us."

Chris wrapped an arm around her shoulders. "I can't wait. We planned this well." He was right.

"I'm still surprised how much Daed enjoys working with me on the food truck." Maybe it shouldn't have been such a surprise. After all, he'd really enjoyed cooking at home with her.

His work with the food truck had begun naturally with her asking for his help here and there. He had really enjoyed it, and the next thing she knew, he was volunteering his time and was eager to learn how to cook on the truck's grill and stove tops. Now he knew how to prepare all the recipes, and they paid him for his time. With the three of them—Jemima, Daed, and Abigail—and their hired help, which was mostly young people who'd recently graduated from the Amish school, they managed to run a successful food truck business and still have time for their families and community.

How blessed she was to have a family that would step in and help her achieve her dreams. Joy flittered in her chest.

Chris pulled her closer. She turned around and snuggled against him.

Could the version of herself a few years ago possibly have imagined this moment? Doubtful. It took being vulnerable enough to let someone in, and it took hard work to juggle the many aspects of life, from spiritual to emotional to physical.

But here in his arms, she couldn't fathom a better life than the one that was before them, no matter what blessings or hardships were ahead.

Readers Guide

1. The book opens with Roy and Jemima still emotionally dealing with the trauma of the buggy accident that Roy and their eldest daughter were involved in one year prior. What could Roy and Jemima have done differently to help them heal emotionally from that trauma? If Jemima were your friend, what advice would you give her on how to deal with the long-term emotional baggage of that accident?

2. Did it surprise you that Roy (and many Amish businessmen) are allowed to have cell phones? What are some ways that technology has changed marriages today? In your opinion, what boundaries should couples put in place regarding cell phone use spilling over into family time?

3. Roy tells all sorts of lies—some small and some huge—to spare Jemima experiencing betrayal and unnecessary hurt. Was he right to try to protect her through lies? Lying can be helpful to the liar in the immediate situation (or else the person wouldn't choose to lie), but in the long run, does lying to a spouse ever make the situation better?

4. Was Chris in the right to take on the burden of his brother's debt? What about when it hurt his parents and forced him from his home?

5. Chris judges Abigail to be the type of person who loses her temper easily based on an interaction between her and Roy that Chris witnessed. Once he has more information about what is really going on, he apologizes. How could he have handled that situation better?

6. Abigail is increasingly bothered by the fact that Chris can be gentle and caring while enjoying the sport of fighting. Do you feel Chris was being a hypocrite to train in boxing while living with his Amish parents and attending his Amish church? He eventually sees the need to stop boxing, but he never really sees it as a sin or morally wrong the way the Amish see it. Does his lack of full-on remorse for training and boxing bother you? Was he worthy of being forgiven by the church?

7. Was Jemima justifiably angry with her husband? Should she have tried to excuse her husband's actions? Her rage began changing her, and even though she didn't like who she was becoming, she felt unable to stop those changes. Was it okay for her to go through that season of turmoil, or should she have forced herself to let go of her anger sooner? What are some steps the injured and tricked person can take to help forgive and let go of anger?

8. Roy and Jemima acknowledge the normal strain that having small children has had on their marriage, all the extenuating circumstances aside. What would've helped them more fully enjoy that wonderful, trying, and fleeting time of having little ones? What advice would you give to newlyweds who want children?

9. Even though the circumstances of Heidi's birth were chaotic and filled with scheming by her birth mother, they brought her to a better life with the Grabers. If you could talk to a teenage Heidi who knew the truth of her origin, what would you tell her to help her embrace her value, forgive her biological parents, and feel a true part of the Graber family?

10. Both couples—Roy and Jemima, Abigail and Chris—have to tear down walls, be vulnerable with each other, and forgive. Did you pick up on each one's need to forgive themselves? Even when they were fully innocent, they had something they needed to forgive themselves for, even if it was for being too trusting or naive. How important do you feel it is in every healing journey to forgive one's self?

Glossary

ach—oh

Aenti—aunt

Bischt—you

Bischt allrecht?—You all right?

Daed—father or dad (pronounced *Dat*)

denki—thank you

Englisch—non-Plain person, a term used by the Amish and Plain
   Mennonites

Es iss gut—It is good

Es iss Zeit esse—It is time to eat

geh—go

Geh langsam and schtamdhaft—Go slow and steady

Gern gschehne—You're welcome

Grossdaadi—grandfather

Guck—look

Guder Marye—Good morning

gut—good

hallo—hello

Ich bin gut—I am good.

**Ich bin gut at Bobbeli diapers. Daed saages es. Ich kann
   helfe.**—I am good at baby diapers. Dad says so. I can help.

Ich hab des—I have this

Kann Ich helfe?—Can I help?

Kann Ich kumm aa?—Can I come too?

Kapp—prayer cap or covering

Kumm—Come

Kumm guck. Zwee Bobbelis. Zwee!—Come look. Two babies.
   Two!

Kumm mol, Liewi. Loss uns geh.—Come on, dear. Let us go.

Lieb—love

Loss uns lieb meh—Let us love more.

Loss uns geh see Daed un Aenti Abi—Let us go see Dad and
   Aunt Abi

Mamm—mom or mother (pronounced *Mom* or *Mawm*)

Mei liewi—my dear

Mei lieb— my love

nee—no

Ordnung—order, set of rules

rumschpringe—running around

Un guck beim wege da gauls!—And look at all the horses!

Was iss letz?—What is wrong?

Wie—how

Wunderbaar gut—Wonderful good

ya—yes (pronounced *yah* or *jah,* also spelled *jah*)